WRETCHED AFTERMATH

E.G. MICHAELS

Wretched Aftermath

TITLES BY E.G. Michaels

THE WRETCHED SERIES

The Wretched

Wretched Culling

Operation Freedom (A Wretched Novella)

Wretched Retribution

Wretched Aftermath

KYLE SIMMONS SERIES

Before The Clock Strikes

The Countdown

On The Clock

Time's Up

Every Minute Counts

On Borrowed Time

COLE HUTCHINSON BOOKS

Gone Too Far

PROLOGUE

Night Two of the Reaper Outbreak
Location: Back streets of Rehoboth Beach

The little-traveled alleyway was dark and damp, but Silas Johnson didn't mind. It meant that there were very few people who would look for him there. The middle-aged man hunkered down between two trash cans. There was a roar of one of the monsters out on the street, and he huddled tighter inside his tattered coat. He had been renting a room in a shit-hole of a house nearby when those things had broken in last night. They may have gotten him if he hadn't shoved Mrs. Founders into the arms of one beast bearing down on him. Founders, the old fuddy-duddy who owned that place. She'd been on him about finding a job and paying the back rent he owed. Well, the joke was on her. She was dead now, and he wasn't. And there was no way in the world he was going to pay her anything now.

There was a noise in the alleyway, and his eyes immediately darted toward it. A lanky man started walking cautiously toward him. The man was holding a bat in one hand. There was a strange green band of cloth around his other arm.

"Hello. Are you hurt?" the man asked carefully.

"Who are you?" Silas croaked. He hadn't realized how dry his throat was.

"Name's Avery," the man said. "I'm with the Disciples. We are God's chosen ones."

"Chosen? Those things are chosen." Silas laughed bitterly. "We're just their food."

"Not true," Avery said. "Ezekiel and the Disciples have been chosen by God to be protected by those creatures."

"Yeah, right." Silas scoffed. "And what makes you different from the rest of us? That cloth?"

"It shows that I'm a chosen protector of God's flock. The creatures recognize that and stay out of our way." Avery took a small step forward and stared at Silas. "Are you okay?"

Silas smiled uncontrollably. So this nutjob's armband would keep him safe from those monsters. That was the best thing he'd heard in days. All he had to do was figure out a way to take it off this fool without drawing any unwanted attention. A plan began to form in his mind. He deliberately let out a low groan.

"Something wrong?" Avery asked.

"Sorry, I can't hear so well," Silas lied. "I lost my hearing aid somewhere."

The man came a little closer. "I said, are you injured?" he asked a bit louder.

"My leg," Silas said as he slipped his right hand into his coat pocket and wrapped his fingers around a serrated knife he had found somewhere.

"Have you been bitten, or are you—" The man gasped as Silas brought the knife up and slashed his neck. Avery dropped in a heap next to him, clutching his throat, as the crimson blood began to spill out. Silas watched with detached interest as rivulets of blood flowed freely from the dying Guardian's neck.

A voice suddenly called out. "Avery?"

Silas looked up and saw a man approaching from the end of the alleyway. Two more arm-banded men followed closely behind. Silas sprang into action. "He's hurt!" he yelled, clutching Avery's neck. He pushed the edges of the wound open more so it would bleed even faster. The bleeding Guardian vainly grabbed at his hands, trying to stop Silas's further actions.

"He was attacked. A pair of teenagers. They went that way." Silas pointed. "I don't know if I can stop the bleeding. Please, sirs. Please help me."

"Jonas, stay with him," the leader ordered. "Let's see if we can find those criminals." He took one of the other men and darted off in the direction that Silas had suggested. A third man, who must have been Jonas, stayed there to render aid.

Silas closed his eyes to think of a moment in his past. One of great sorrow and pain. He needed to sell this moment as convincingly as possible. There was one moment in his childhood. A time when he was forced to watch his father beat his dog to death in front of him. Despite his sobs and cries, his father hadn't relented once. Silas felt tears forming in his eyes.

"I don't know if I can stop the bleeding," Silas said as he watched as the life in the mortally wounded man's eyes begin to fade out. "I-I don't know."

"Slide over. Let me look," Jonas said. Jonas put fingers next to the side of Avery's neck and felt for a pulse. A moment later, Jonas stood up, shaking his head slowly. "He's gone."

"I tried," Silas said. "I-I really tried to help him."

"I know that," Jonas said warily. "Say, stranger. What's your name?"

Silas studied the man in front of him. The man was visibly on edge. He quickly weighed the odds and decided it was too dangerous for him to try to overpower this man and take his armband right now. It was even worse odds to lift one off the dead body. Even if he managed to kill Jonas, the other two Guardians could show up at any moment. He'd been able to lie to them about the guy he'd killed in the alleyway. But two sudden deaths? That wouldn't fool anyone at all. An alternate plan began to quickly form in his mind. These Disciples seemed to have a good thing going. Maybe it was time for him to take advantage of it.

"Silas," he said softly. "Your friend was trying to tell me about your group when he was attacked."

"Yes, that's right. We're part of a local group called the Disciples of the Divine."

"I want to learn more about your group," Silas lied. It was time to really go for the gusto. "Maybe this is a sign. A new calling. I feel like God wants me to learn more."

The man smiled broadly.

"Then you're in the right place," Jonas answered. "You'll definitely want to meet Ezekiel."

Silas smiled broadly. He didn't give a rat's ass whoever this guy Ezekiel was. He was having trouble remembering the name of the Guardian who was standing in front of him right now. But if it got him a chance to get off the streets, a safe place with some regular meals, some new clothes, and complete protection from those things, then he was game. He'd play along with their ridiculous cult beliefs. He'd play their little game until it no longer benefited him.

"Yes, I would like that," Silas answered with a practiced smile. "Heaven must have spared me so I could be discovered by your kindred souls."

CHAPTER ONE

Present Day
Location: Rehoboth Beach, Delaware

Malcolm Foster scooped another handful of cold water and splashed it onto his face. He felt a small portion of the exhaustion he was feeling shrink a little. He had managed to grab four hours of sleep, but it didn't seem to matter. In all his years of having been a Philadelphia police officer, he couldn't remember ever feeling this tired, even when pulling an extended shift.

Foster looked in the mirror and studied the visibly tired, crystal blue-eyed athletic-looking man looking back at him. He studied the image a bit closer. There was a time where he would have jokingly said he looked like shit warmed over. Now he would say he was simply surviving instead.

They had been attacked by the Reapers and the Disciples of the Divine at the marina. They had somehow survived the combined attack and managed to get away. Foster had managed his group to a new place safely. It was only a matter of time before someone checked the second floor of a locally-owned gun shop they had found. Then their new refuge would be gone, and they'd be on the run again.

Foster glanced over at the still-closed bathroom door. He knew that Nick Walker, along with a few others, were waiting outside for him.

Foster splashed one more handful of water on his face, then grabbed the towel next to the sink to dry himself off. He took a deep breath, steeled himself for the conversation about to come, and stepped into the common area.

As he cast his eyes upon the group in front of him, he saw a mixture of anxiety and exhaustion greeting him.

"Where are the kids?" Foster asked.

"Still sleeping," Lizzy Walker replied. Nick's wife was a nurse. Or had been, before the Reapers had shown up. Now she was part of a group fighting for survival every hour of the day. "Same with Amanda."

Foster nodded in approval. "Probably best that some of us do," he said. "It doesn't help if some of us are sleep-deprived."

"All of us need a lot more sleep," Lizzy pointed out. "And contrary to what my husband and you might believe, none of us are superhuman."

"Sounds like we both agree," Foster answered. "Best if we take shifts to grab some rest."

"Amanda wanted to stay up, but I overruled her," Lizzy continued. "She looked like she was ready to fall asleep on her feet."

"Good call," Foster said simply. His mind quickly diverted to thinking about the athletically built doctor. Amanda and he seemed to share a spark. They had even shared a kiss at one point, but with everything going on, would something more develop? It was hard to say. Right now, trying to stay alive needed to stay at the top of everybody's priority list. He turned his attention to a man who was busy loading bullets into an empty Glock magazine.

"Sams, how are we on ammo?"

Derrick Sams looked up from what he was doing and grimaced. The former Army Ranger was their resident smart-ass. Despite his regular verbal jabs about Foster's background as a cop, the two men had developed an unspeakable bond of respect and teamwork.

"Better than it's been in the past," Sams said. "But if we get in another firefight, then we're going to be throwing rocks instead of bullets pretty quickly."

"Two steps forward and two back," Nick Walker replied. "We lost a good amount of supplies when the boat blew up. We're back in the shitstorm again."

"In other words, we need food, ammo, and a safer place to hole up," Foster said. "We can't rule out anyone stumbling across us here."

"We're actually decent on food," Charles Powell said. The former priest absently scratched his chin before continuing. "We had managed to distribute it among everyone's packs, so we only lost part of what we had."

"Finally, something that resembles good news." Lizzy sighed. "We're so overdue for some."

"That may be," Charles continued, "but I don't think our current food supply will last more than a few days at most."

"Well, we've got about an hour until sunrise," Foster said. "At that point, I fully expect either the Reapers or their Disciple cronies will be looking for us."

"That's assuming they're not already," Sams pointed out. "We did put a serious hurt on both of them."

"Very true," Foster said. "Do we have any idea how many hostiles we might still have to deal with?"

"Are you thinking of taking the fight to them?" Walker asked. "I'm not sure that's a good idea."

"No, I'm not looking for a fight. Not if we can help it," Foster said. "My gut feeling is we're grossly outnumbered. But I'd feel a little better if I could confirm my hunch. Gregory, do you have any ideas on how many Disciples there might be?"

Charles's remaining son grimaced. His sister was one of the people who had died in the boat explosion only hours ago. And yet here he was, trying to keep the remains of his family still alive.

"Easily a couple hundred people," he answered. "I personally know about twenty people who joined the ranks when they were given the ultimatum."

Foster let out a low whistle.

Sams chuckled. "Disciples definitely had a hell of an ultimatum. Where else are you going to hear 'join up, or get eaten by the Reapers?'"

"Maybe their leader will run for president someday on that platform," Foster replied. "But right now, I'm more worried about getting all of us out of their territory and to someplace we can be safe from Reapers, too."

"Okay, let's review, Officer. They have hundreds of members," Sams said. "An unknown number of them actually know how to fight or fire a gun."

"You're on a roll," Foster said. "Keep talking."

"They're coming after the eight of us," Sam continued. "Which includes two kids, an old man, a nurse, and a doctor." He quickly added, "No offense to any of you."

"None taken," Lizzy said with a smirk. "Of course, you're welcome to head down to the shooting range with me sometime to see how this nurse handles her Glock."

Sams laughed. "That's a sucker's bet, if I ever heard one," he answered. "I know for a fact you and Nick used to go to the shooting range a couple of times a month. He probably taught you everything he knows about firing a gun."

"Not everything," Walker answered. "I'm still better on a rifle than my wife."

"Totally fine with me, dear," Lizzy said.

"Folks, we really don't have time for a dick-measuring contest," Foster scolded. "We need to stop wasting time and come up with a plan. Even if we were all bad-ass shooters—"

"We're not," Sams interrupted.

Foster shot him a withering look, and the former Army Ranger immediately shut up.

"As I was saying," Foster continued, "even if every one of us were excellent shooters, we're still grossly outnumbered between the Disciples and whatever Reapers may still be in the area. We know for a fact the Reapers can bring even larger numbers to this area, too."

"In other words," Walker interrupted, "we're deep behind enemy lines with limited resources. We need to come up with a plan to get the hell out of Rehoboth Beach. And then we need to find another way to get to Hope Island."

"Well, I think we can rule out leaving by boat," Gregory said. "Randy was the only one who knew his way around one."

"There's definitely plenty of ways we could get ourselves in trouble out on the open water," Walker admitted. "Like that Guardian guy said—"

"Walter?" Foster interrupted.

"Yeah, him," Walker agreed. "They didn't just booby-trap Randy's boat. They probably compromised every other boat in the marina."

"I'll be honest. At the time, I thought he was lying," Sams said. "But we found out the hard way that he wasn't. And I really don't want to have to hunt through every nook and cranny of a boat to find a hidden bomb before we can use it."

"With our luck," Foster added, "they could have a second device hidden somewhere else on the boat that they detonate as soon as we pull away from shore."

"Lot of work to booby-trap every boat in a marina," Walker thought aloud. "If it were me, I'd just have a few people trained to use an RPG. They could just blow any boat being stolen right out of the water."

"Leave it up to my military husband to offer an even nastier possibility," Lizzy snarked. "So it sounds like everyone thinks using a boat is out. And we definitely can't stay here for long. So what do we do?"

"We need to get out of Rehoboth somehow," Foster said. "Once we're clear, I can call Black and see if he can send somebody to come pick us up."

"By boat?" Sams asked.

"Maybe. Plane or maybe a helicopter might be possible, too," Foster said. "As long as it can get all of us to Hope Island safely, I really don't care what type of transportation we use right now."

"I am not riding a garbage truck," Lizzy said. "So don't get any ideas about hijacking one."

"Can't rule it out," Walker said. "They're built to take a pounding and could easily roll through any packs of Reapers we might encounter. If it rolls, then we can roll out of here."

"You might have a point, Nicholas." Lizzy sighed. "Right about now, I'd walk to Hope Island if I had to. I'm so tired of dealing with these Reapers. And now we got to deal with these knuckleheads who've pledged allegiance to them or joined forces with them."

"All of us want to get someplace safe again," Foster said. "I wish there was a way we could get even more people there."

"One step at a time, man," Walker said. "We need to get ourselves out of our current situation before we can worry about helping anyone else. Our current vehicles are burned. If they didn't recognize them before the marina, they certainly do now."

"Any chance we could buy new ones from anyone in town?" Foster asked.

"I doubt it," Gregory admitted. "If they're not already aligned with the Disciples, then they'd be scared to death of alienating them."

"It probably wouldn't hurt to get some additional supplies to replace what we lost in the boat," Sams added. "Bullets for sure, maybe food."

"It sounds like we need to do a couple things," Foster said. "Then we can focus on our escape."

"Such as?" Lizzy asked.

"Well, we need to do some recon and figure out where there could be a weak spot in the Disciples' security patrols. We need to find an area where we can get out of town with minimal conflict or opposition. We also need to get some new vehicles."

"That's something any of us could handle," Lizzy said. "Who do you suggest goes?"

"Not exactly. Anybody who goes out is definitely going to be at risk. If they're not spotted by the Reapers, they could be spotted by the Disciples."

"You mean someone who's ready for a fight, if they get in one."

"Yeah, I have some people in mind."

"None of us are getting any younger," Walker growled. "Quit stalling and lay it out already, Malcolm."

"Fine," Foster said. "I think our former Army Rangers, Nick and Derrick, are best suited for the recon mission."

"Sneak-and-peek mission," Sams said softly. "I'm down with that."

"Exactly," Foster answered. "You two take a look at what's going on outside this place. Find an exfil path for us. Just as important, don't get spotted, and don't draw any unwanted attention to our location. Any objections to those two guys handling that part of the mission?"

A series of shaking heads answered him.

"Good. To be honest, I wasn't sure anybody else would be as capable to pull it off," Foster said. "Okay, second mission. Like Nick mentioned, we're going to need some new vehicles."

"How many are we talking about?" Charles asked. "And we buying or stealing them?"

"At least two of them in order to fit everybody in," Foster said. "We'll focus on visibly abandoned trucks and SUVs." He heard a chorus of soft yeses sound out. No one in their group was interested in stealing someone's vehicle and leaving them in potential dire straits. Especially with so many Reapers prowling the area.

"Abandoned doesn't mean they're going to be easy to take," Sams pointed out. "Plenty of them are going to be locked up. And if you get into them, it doesn't mean you'll be able to start them without a key."

"I don't doubt it," Foster said. "The thing is, I'm a cop. I can't tell you how many times I've had to legally break into a car because their owner had locked themselves out. There's been a few times where I've had to hot-wire a car, too."

"It sounds like you're volunteering to handle finding us some new rides," Walker quipped.

"I guess I am," Foster admitted. "We need at least two SUVs, so I'd like to take another person with me to help bring the vehicles back."

"If you don't mind, I would like to go," Charles said. "I've worked with Malcolm before, and I feel comfortable working with him again on something like this. We have also posed as uncle and nephew in the past. If we run into any other people, we could certainly use the same story once more."

"All good points," Foster said, "but I'd like to take Gregory with me instead."

"What? Why?" Lizzy blurted out.

"Well, it would be really helpful to have a local guide. Someone who might know the best places in town to be able to grab an abandoned vehicle with the least amount of chance of running into Disciple or Reaper packs."

"So what are you going to have the rest of us do?" Lizzy demanded. "Dump babysitting duty on the women and grandpa again?"

"Honey, you know that's not how Malcolm feels," Walker said. "He's raised some really good points on why he's picked the people he did for each of these missions."

"I don't think calling it babysitting is fair to anyone," Foster said. "Sure, we need somebody to keep an eye on Emily and Henry. But we also need somebody to keep our base of operations secure. There's more than one entrance to the second floor. I think it's unrealistic to ask any one of us to do all of those things by themselves at once."

"The police officer raises several good points," Sams snarked. "I'm amazed he gave it that much thought in between donut runs."

Foster ignored the verbal jab and continued. "Lizzy. I value everything you do. Amanda, too. If it helps, I can leave the sat phone with you. You'll be able to keep trying to reach Sergeant Black. The sooner we can find out if it's possible to get a ride to Hope Island, the better."

"Uh-huh." Lizzy sulked. "Next time, you get to stay here and hang out with the kiddos while Amanda and I go exploring."

Foster lost his cool. "This isn't about playing favorites. This is about doing what is best for the entire group. And right now, all of us need to check our fucking egos and focus on getting shit done."

"Malcolm," Walker warned. "There's no need to curse."

"Hey, Nick. I'm not telling you anything that you don't already know," Foster continued. "Dammit, we need everybody to get on the same fucking page. Because the Disciples and Reapers aren't going to care who's doing a supply run or guarding our base. They'll gladly kill all of us if they get the chance."

"Okay, guys, this is starting to get a little much," Sams interrupted. "Chill out, everyone."

"No, Malcolm is right," Walker said quietly. "All of us can do a better job of keeping our eyes focused on the endgame. We need to work together to get all of us safely to Hope Island."

"Okay, well I think that settles things for now," Sams interrupted. He clapped his hands once with a fake flourish. "So unless anybody else has some objections, I say we get moving."

The room went silent for an uncomfortable moment.

"One more thing," Walker said. "Let Derrick and me do the recon and report in before you head out. We can let you know where the greatest areas of enemy activity are. That way, you guys don't stumble into a trap while you're looking for new wheels."

"Good point," Foster answered. "We'll wait to hear from you before heading out. It couldn't hurt to let some of the group grab some sleep while we're waiting, too."

"Uh-huh," Lizzy said. Her smile shifted into a playful smirk. "Since you'll be waiting for our local Army boys to come back, I'm sure we can find something for you to do in the meantime."

"Actually, if you and some of the other adults want to grab some sleep, I'll spend some time with Emily and Henry," Foster said. "It might be nice to get to know them a little better."

Lizzy did a double-take. "Really?"

"Yes."

"Thank you, Malcolm."

"You're welcome," Foster answered softly. "I'm happy to help. All you have to do is ask me nicely."

"You're right," Lizzy said. She released the hug and stepped back slowly. "We need to work better as a team."

"Okay, awesome. Hatchets have been buried, and not in anyone's skull," Sams said. "Now that that's out of the way, Nicholas and I are going to head out to see if we can figure out how to safely get the hell out of this town. We need everybody to play nice while we're gone."

"We'll be fine," Lizzy said. "If anybody gets out of line, Amanda or I will handle it."

"Game time, everyone," Walker added. "I don't expect us to have more than a day here before we get unwanted company. We need to be gone before that happens."

CHAPTER TWO

It's been said heavy is the head that wears the crown. As the unquestioned leader of the Reapers, Horatio Beeks was feeling the weight of leadership. He felt absolutely no shame in saying he was in the ultimate position of power. He could even argue that he was the most powerful being in the United States. And soon, his power would reign supreme over the rest of the world, too.

The U.S. military had attempted to defeat his warriors through a series of bombings, only to discover that the Reapers weren't killed by fire. It had been their strongest attack yet. Beeks had to grudgingly give credit for their effort, but it wasn't enough to topple his forces. And once he launched a counterattack, his forces crushed their opposition. Now, the shattered remains of the U.S. military had been forced to retreat in defeat.

But they weren't completely gone, and Beeks couldn't give up on the idea of killing every remaining military member. It was the only way to guarantee they couldn't attack his minions ever again. The problem was reaching them. Most of the human armed forces had retreated offshore. And much to his chagrin, his soldiers lacked the ability to swim.

He was arguably the most powerful being in the world. There were no rivals left to contest his place as the King of Kings. And Beeks was completely miserable. For starters, there wasn't anything for him to do. His soldiers kept telling him that it was too dangerous for him to go anywhere. Beeks couldn't see how that could be, but it was easier to humor them and just stay home. But staying home all the time meant he was bored as hell. He found his temper getting shorter and shorter all the time. Especially the minions who seemed to be dimwits. For all of their incredible physical abilities, some of them couldn't seem to remember to come in out of the rain, unless Haas or one of his Alphas told them to.

Haas. What was he going to do with him? It was obvious the soldier had great hatred for Beeks. He made the least amount of effort to try and hide it. Of course, Beeks couldn't really blame him. He had killed Haas' best friend in front of him. And before Giles' body had begun to cool, Beeks forced Haas to submit and swear fealty. Well, it didn't matter how much Haas might hate him. The King of Kings could do whatever the hell he wanted, and nobody could stop him. It was best for Haas to learn that now. Beeks had thought adding Haas as one of his Alphas would help. Except it hadn't. Haas was one of his elite warriors. Quite possibly the very best individual one under his command. But he spent most of his time sulking or doing the bare minimum to complete any assigned task. In short, Haas had become the latest pain in his ass. Maybe it would be good to give Haas something to do that would get him out of Beeks' hair for a while. Beeks glanced around his throne room, his eyes eventually settling on a guard who didn't appear to be paying attention.

"You there," Beeks said in a series of growls.

The creature went immediately ramrod at attention. "Yes, my Lord," the Reaper replied a bit too eagerly.

Beeks frowned.

"Go tell Haas and Achilles I want to see them."

"My Lord, couldn't you do that?" the soldier questioned. "I'm not supposed to leave my station."

"Are you questioning my orders?"

"No, sir," the young soldier stammered. He quickly backpedaled out of the throne room. He was barely out of sight, and his rapid footsteps could be heard almost instantly.

Beeks was pleased. It was good for these young bucks to remember who their master was. Especially important to quell any idea of ever challenging for his place in the pack. Things were going exceedingly well, and his pack now numbered in the millions.

Still, there was that one annoying human that somehow eluded his soldiers so far. *Foster.* He couldn't believe one human could be so damn lucky so many times in a row. Well, it was time to end this human's luck.

Beeks reached out to his messenger. "Tell them to hurry the hell up," Beeks commanded. "I do not like waiting."

"Yes, sir," he heard the soldier mentally answer. Beeks felt the creature's heart race even faster, and he couldn't help but smile. It might not be a perfect life, but it was still damn good to be the king.

CHAPTER THREE

Ezekiel Morgan checked his appearance in the mirror once more. The former conman turned self-anointed evangelist liked what he saw. He still looked calm and in charge, even if his stomach was churning out of control. It was that damn failed attack. *I should have told Giles it was a bad idea.* He shuddered at the thought. His former friend was now a Reaper. And with each day that passed, the former human seemed to be losing his grasp on his humanity and was becoming more short-tempered. Like a monster.

You're dealing with a dangerous animal that could turn on you at any time. When are you going to realize you can't control it? Ezekiel shuddered uncontrollably again. It was terrifying to think what Giles was capable of. Heck, Ezekiel had seen him tear apart nonbelievers at his signal, and that was just to scare others into joining his flock. Imagine what would happen if this non-human actually went rabid and started tearing people apart? There was no way Ezekiel could stop him, except to maybe plead with him to stop. Jesus, he needed a drink. Just a small one to help steady his nerves a bit more.

Ezekiel backtracked to his liquor cabinet. He pushed

aside several top-shelf bourbons and grabbed a half-empty bottle of Monkey Shoulder. He opened the corked bottle, poured himself a finger's worth of the blended Scotch, and then recapped the bottle. He slammed the liquor back and felt it burning as it worked down to his stomach. It would have been much better to sip the wonderful alcohol and let the elixir work its magic gradually. But he didn't have time to enjoy the drink. A rapid warming sensation began to spread through his body. He set the now-empty glass next to the bottle and started walking slowly toward the door.

He'd been drinking more often lately. It might be the pressure of keeping up appearances. Now, more than ever, his flock was expecting him to be their fearless leader. One who received guidance from God himself. A religious leader who the Divine had chosen to be able to communicate with these Reapers. Giles was right. He was pulling off the con of a lifetime. And now he needed Giles more than ever to keep the charade going.

This man, Foster, was dangerous. He'd been faced with overwhelming odds. And when the proverbial smoke cleared, there were bodies everywhere and Foster was still alive.

Worse, he hadn't heard from Giles. Was his friend hurt or dead?

Not dead.

Ezekiel hadn't heard of anyone killing a Reaper besides shooting them in the head. And Giles was too smart to put himself anywhere near a gunfight. Not when he had hundreds, maybe thousands, of foot soldiers to send in his place instead.

Ezekiel turned his attention to the door. It was time. He needed to speak to his congregation. He needed to inspire them to act. Despite their own doubts. Despite even his own doubts. Ezekiel took a long, calming breath and gave himself one last pep talk.

One more speech. Just a little one. Then I signal Giles that I want to talk. If I'm lucky, he won't see it until tomorrow, and I can just sit in my study and drink some more. Just enough to forget about things for a while.

———

There was a knock at the door, and President Mary Vickers looked up. "Come in, General," she said calmly.

The door slowly opened, and General Weindahl stepped into the room.

"How did you know it was me?" Weindahl asked. "Did your protective detail tell you that I was here?"

"No at all," Vickers answered. "You have a very distinctive walk."

"Really?"

"You have a tendency to drag your left foot a little bit."

"Just an old football injury that periodically flares up," Weindahl admitted. "It's been bothering me a little lately."

"Lately?"

"Just for a few days, ma'am."

"Then you should have the ship's doctor take a look at it."

"Perhaps I will," Weindahl said. "Once things calm down a bit." He stood still, waiting for the President's full attention.

Vickers internally groaned. Just once she'd like to make it through a day without some type of crisis or urgent matter that needed her attention. "Something on your mind, General?"

"Indeed," Weindahl said. "We've managed to locate a number of scientists and staff. I'm pleased to report we now have a research location set up in Hawaii."

"That's impressive. You managed to pull that together in a short amount of time."

"It was quite fortunate there was a location in Hawaii which met our specifications. We also had a bit of luck."

"How so?"

"There was a scientist who met our qualifications and happened to be in Hawaii."

"Vacation?"

"Honeymoon. In order to gain their cooperation, I thought it was best to skip some of the formalities and permit their new spouse to stay in Hawaii with them."

Vickers smirked. "Probably best under the circumstances. If this scientist is as good as you say they are, then we need them working with us, not against us."

"Indeed," Weindahl said. "We managed to secure several dead Reaper bodies for them to begin to study. Their early progress is good, Madam President."

"Any idea when we'll hear any of their discoveries?"

"I am being told that we could have an initial report as early as before the end of tomorrow."

"That's excellent. Was there anything else, General?"

"Yes. We managed to successfully draw back a number of our Tier-1 operators from overseas operations. We have currently situated them in Hawaii and several offshore locations."

"What kind of locations are we talking about?"

"Mostly ships, Madam President," Weindahl answered. "There is one island, a Hope Island, on the East Coast where a platoon of Rangers is already there. It's been brought to my attention from the base commander, a Lieutenant Abrahams, that he also has a partial SWAT team that they managed to retrieve from Philadelphia."

"Cops and Rangers," Vickers quipped. "Are those boys playing nice with each other?"

"It would appear so, under the circumstances."

"You know I was joking, right?"

"I'm afraid I must have missed your attempted humor, ma'am. My apologies."

"Geez, lighten up a little, Rasheed. This isn't a college exam."

"I shall keep that in mind, Madam President," Weindahl answered. "As for the Rangers and SWAT officers getting along, I would expect nothing less. Both groups have a well-earned reputation."

"Indeed. The lieutenant does report that the police officers are helping with island security and maintaining the peace."

"Has there been any trouble?"

"Only the kind that happens when you stick a bunch of people that don't know each other very well in a very small space."

"See if there's anything else he needs that we can get to them. I realize we're already stretched pretty thin, but we may need to call on them to help us at some point in the future."

"Already in the works. It appears the lieutenant may have a lead on some research which could help us."

"You're kidding?"

"I'm afraid this isn't something I would joke about, Madam President."

"Jesus, lighten up, General. It was a figure of speech. We're the only people in the room right now."

"Yes, ma'am. I'll make more effort to be lighter in our private talks," Weindahl said. He paused for a moment before continuing. "Apparently the SWAT Sergeant, a Sergeant Black, is a key player. He knows of another Philadelphia police officer who has a group of survivors somewhere on the East Coast. They have managed through trial and error to figure out ways to kill the Reapers quickly."

"You mean shooting them in the head, right?"

"Um, not exactly," Weindahl said. "From what Lieutenant Abrahams has reported, this Officer Foster claims to have discovered other lethal methods of killing the Reapers. They're awaiting their arrival at Hope Island."

"When?"

"Hopefully within the next couple of days."

"Let's hope they make it. Keep me up to date on that one, will you, Rasheed?"

"Of course," Weindahl said. "That's all I have for now."

"Thanks for the update. I appreciate it."

"Anytime, Madam President."

"Hey, Rasheed?"

"Yes, ma'am?"

"You need to go visit the doctor about your leg."

"I will. But I have a number of other pressing things that need my attention."

"You can have any urgent calls redirected to you at the med bay," Vickers pointed out. "Go get your leg looked at. Or do I need to order you to do so?"

"That won't be necessary, Madam President. I'll check in with the doctor now."

CHAPTER FOUR

Dwayne Haas moved cautiously into the throne room. His guard was up after receiving word that the leader of all Reapers, Horatio Beeks, wanted to see him. Haas wasn't going willingly. He was still bitter about having been conquered by Beeks and forced to submit. It seemed like every time he closed his eyes, the image of watching his best friend Giles die flashed through his mind again and again. Haas shook his head and pushed the image back with a low growl. It wasn't time to mourn. He needed to find out what the hell Beeks wanted with him. Right now it was best to keep a low profile, act like a loyal Reaper soldier, and wait for the right time to get his revenge. Haas moved into the throne room and saw that another Reaper was already kneeling in front of Beeks. He moved to the soldier's left and dropped to one knee as expected as well.

"Reporting as ordered, my Lord," Haas said slowly.

"Excellent," Beeks said smugly. "I have something for both of you."

"Yes, my Lord," the soldiers answered simultaneously.

Haas stole a glance to his right and saw the other soldier was Achilles. Haas quickly sized him up and decided if things ever got physical between the two of them, he would easily win. The fact that Haas was a former death row inmate just stacked the odds even more in his favor. He doubted Achilles had ever been involved in any prison yard fights where the loser could easily die at the hands of another inmate.

Haas turned his attention back to Beeks in time to see his boss pull out a red cape with a flourish. He walked over to the still half-kneeling Haas and began to drape it around his shoulders and neck.

"What are you doing?" Haas growled.

"Why, recognizing your rank, Dwayne," Beeks said, the glee barely contained in his voice. "As one of my army's elite commanders, you have earned the right for your status to be recognized. And you'll do so just like your predecessors, Nails and Malice, once did."

"They're dead, aren't they?"

"That's not important right now," Beeks answered. He took a step back and studied Haas. "Looks good," Beeks added with a smirk.

"I feel like a pretend magician," Haas complained.

"Well, get comfortable with it," Beeks said. "It's part of your role in my family."

"So I'm stuck with the cape?"

"Until I tell you otherwise."

"It's just going to get in the way."

"Enough talking, Dwayne," Beeks said. "I have new orders for you. We need to find the man named Foster. He is becoming a bigger problem for our family."

"Yes, my Lord," Achilles said.

Haas saw Beeks staring at him expectantly. He swallowed quickly and then blurted, "Yes, my Lord."

"I would like the two of you to take some fighters, spread out in the countryside, and hunt for him," Beeks said. "We do not know where he's currently hiding. But we will find him. And once we do, bring him to me alive."

"As you command, Master," Achilles said.

Haas looked toward the floor instead.

"Is there a problem with my order?" Beeks challenged.

"My Lord, if I may offer a different solution?" Haas offered.

"You have a better idea?" Beeks snickered. "Oh, this, I have to hear."

"I don't need your fighters," Haas said through gritted teeth, "Giles and I had our own pack of soldiers."

"Tell me something I don't know, Dwayne," Beeks mocked. "And make it quick, before I lose my patience."

"We had also a group of humans who pledged allegiance to us," Haas said carefully. He had to be careful not to give too much information away. The last thing he needed was for Beeks to decide he wasn't needed after all. Then he'd never get the chance to avenge his friend. "They had managed to track Foster and his group to one place in the town. I'm afraid with Giles' death I lost contact with those humans, but I know where to find them. With your permission, I could reconnect with those humans. I could direct them to find out Foster's last-known location. I might be able to use them to help us track Foster and his group down."

"Hmm," Beeks said. "Your idea has merit, and while I normally don't approve of others telling me what to do, I find myself agreeing with your line of reasoning. Very well. Haas, you are to reconnect with the human sheep and any of your soldiers still remaining. Begin your search for Foster in that area. I expect you to report in as soon as you get any information on his whereabouts."

"As you command, my Lord," Haas said. He stood up slowly and began to move away.

"Wait, where are you going?" Beeks asked.

"To begin my mission," Haas said. "Isn't that obvious?"

"I didn't dismiss you," Beeks snarled.

"Right, sorry," Haas said as he carefully knelt back in position.

"Achilles."

"Yes, my Lord."

"You are to head to the rest stop and work your way back toward Foster's last-known location at the farmhouse."

Haas snickered loudly.

"You dare to mock me?" Beeks demanded.

"Not mocking you. Just what you told him to go do," Haas answered between laughs. "You might as well tell him to chase his own tail."

"They could have retreated there," Beeks sputtered. "Or headed in that direction."

Haas laughed even louder. "And hidden someplace your soldiers found them before? There's no way Foster would do something that."

"Shut up, Dwayne," Beeks snarled. "I will not have you disrespect me in front of my warriors."

"I will go to the rest stop," Achilles said, his voice rising with each word. "I will obey your will, my Lord."

"Excellent," Beeks said. "Dwayne should learn to do the same."

Haas stared at the floor silently.

"Achilles," Beeks continued, "if you find any humans there who may have information on Foster's whereabouts, use whatever means necessary to compel them to answer."

"Your word is my command," Achilles said.

"Wonderful. That's what I like to hear," Beeks said. "You're both dismissed."

Haas saw Achilles stand up quickly, salute Beeks, and turn and leave the room. He couldn't help but think that the other soldier was a complete suck-up. For being an Alpha, Achilles seemed to lack a backbone of his own or the ability to question some of the ridiculous things that Beeks wanted them to do. Of course, it wasn't like Haas could actually disobey Beeks' orders, either.

Time. It's only a matter of time, Haas thought to himself. He needed to wait until an opportunity presented itself. And once it did, Haas would be ready to eliminate Beeks once and for all.

———

Achilles wasn't sure if he would actually find Foster, like his master had suggested. There was part of him that thought that this mission was highly unlikely to ever succeed. A phrase popped into his mind from the recesses of his brain.

A wild goose chase.

Yes. This had all the makings of one. Especially since the other Alpha had a better lead on Foster's whereabouts.

Even so, he couldn't disappoint his master. If it was important to his master, then Achilles would make it important to himself. He glanced back at Haas and tried not to smirk.

Haas had been wrong when he said that he looked like a magician. The other Alpha looked more like a show dog stuck doing a performance they didn't want to do. Achilles let out a low rumble of laughter.

"Something funny?" Haas challenged.

"No," Achilles said a bit too quickly. "It must be something I ate not agreeing with me."

"Huh," Haas said. "Perhaps you should stick with simpler foods." He strode away without a further word.

Achilles quickly looked away. It wouldn't please his master if he were to instigate a fight with Haas. Despite not liking the other Alpha, he would have to take care not to argue with his pack mate.

CHAPTER FIVE

After finishing their recon, Walker and Sams returned to the group's temporary base above the gun shop. Walker looked at the flurry of activity for a moment before letting loose a quick, sharp whistle. Everyone came to a stop and looked towards him unexpectedly.

"Good. Everybody here?" Walker asked. "No offense, but I don't want to have to repeat our findings twice."

"I think so." Foster grinned. "If not, I'll update any stragglers myself."

"That works." Walker grumbled.

"Any luck on finding an escape route?" Foster asked.

"Slim left town on the express train," Sams replied. "And he did it days ago."

"Huh?" Foster said.

"What our friend is trying to cleverly say and doing a terrible job of," Walker answered, "is that there's no good route for us to take out of here."

"Are you serious?" Foster said.

"Completely," Walker replied. "A number of streets have been blocked, barricaded, or blocked off using disabled cars or trucks. There are dedicated checkpoints on the major roadways that appear to be manned by the Guardians."

"Or they're setting up new ones," Sams said. "These guys have been busy beavers."

"Okay, hold on a minute," Foster said. "How do you know all of the vehicles are disabled?"

"Easy," Walker said. "Most of the ones we saw had their tires flattened."

"And the ones that didn't were missing their distributor cap or battery," Sams added. "Nobody is moving them without going through a lot of trouble."

"You think it was the Guardians?" Foster asked. "Or just some neighbors worried about someone stealing their SUV?"

"Not completely sure," Walker admitted. "The ones missing a battery could be the owner trying to prevent someone from stealing their ride. But my guess would be all of the vehicles have been disabled by the Guardians. Then nobody gets to go anywhere without their permission."

"Which goes hand-in-hand with their stranglehold on the marina," Foster said. "Damn, that's not good at all. Any idea what kind of weapons they're carrying?"

"Mostly rifles or handguns," Walker replied. "Several spots we've found are being patrolled by both Guardians and Reapers."

"A few others had just Reapers. And before you get excited, we're talking a few dozen Reapers doing guard duty," Sams pointed out. "Those freaky bastards don't seem to need to ever take a nap or a break with any regularity."

"This is not good," Foster said.

"Damn right. The best time to get out of town was days ago," Sams said. "Like it or not, we're looking at a battle to get out of this town."

"Dammit," Foster said, "I was hoping to avoid a firefight."

"Do you lack confidence in our group?" Charles asked. "All of us know how to handle a firearm."

"The numbers aren't in our favor," Foster said. "We don't know how many Guardians we're dealing with. And the Reapers? There's probably hundreds, maybe even thousands of them in Rehoboth. We honestly don't know."

"Yeah, it's not like you can ask them to line up to be counted," Sams pointed out. "And as soon the guns start firing, you can bet they'll have a shit ton of backup showing up to give them a hand."

"Maybe we don't have to engage in a firefight," Walker said softly.

"That would be great," Foster said. "You got something in mind?"

"Nicholas, do you want to tell him," Sams said in a badly faked British accent, "or shall I?"

A round of groans sounded in the room.

"Don't quit the day job, Derrick," Walker muttered. "Seriously."

"Fine." Sams sighed. "You tell them."

"We saw one lightly trafficked checkpoint," Walker said. "I think with a little planning, we might be able to sneak past the bad guys."

"I'm not sure I understand," Charles said. "Can you elaborate?"

"Uh-huh," Walker answered. "Right now, they're probably looking for our current vehicles. But with some different transportation, we should be able to act like some ordinary people trying to leave town and pass through their check-points without any trouble. As long as they don't recognize any of us, then it should work."

"Oh, it could definitely work," Sams said. "But not with our current vehicles. They'd probably recognize them on sight."

"Which means we still need other transportation," Foster said. "If we can find or repair two new SUVs, then we can definitely go with your plan."

"Sure, if it's something simple like swapping in a battery," Walker said. "Finding the right size tires to replace a bunch of flats could be a lot tougher."

"So we focus on grabbing two SUVs that already work or just need an easy fix," Foster said. "Worst case, we take our chances with our current vehicles and try to sneak out of town at night. Great intel work, guys."

"Thank you, thank you very much," Sams said in an equally bad Elvis impersonation.

"Seriously, man." Walker sighed. "You need to drop the impressions and stick with shooting bad guys instead."

———

The group dispersed, and Foster saw Walker standing in front of him.

"Something wrong?"

"Nope. Got a question."

"Sure, what's up?"

"Are you going to call Sergeant Black?" Walker asked.

"At some point," Foster said. "If we want to get to Hope Island, then we'll probably need his help."

"You think he'll understand?"

"Sure," Foster answered. "But it won't stop him from busting my balls."

"Comes with the territory of being a cop," Walker said. "Or a soldier."

"You know it," Foster said. "Especially when you're dealing with Black."

"Good luck, Foster-san." Walker quipped in a fake kung-fu master voice. "You will need it."

"Don't quit your day job."

Walker chuckled. "Wasn't planning to."

Foster watched as Walker stepped out of the room. Foster took one breath to calm his jangling nerves and began dialing the satellite phone. This wasn't going to be an easy favor to ask. He heard the call connect, ring three times, and then a gruff voice answered.

"Who the hell is this?"

"Foster. Don't you recognize the number?" Foster asked.

"Wasn't sure it was you," SWAT Sergeant Black answered. "For all I know, you got beat up by the prom queen and she took your phone."

"You can't make jokes like that anymore."

"Why? Because it's not politically correct?"

"That's one reason," Foster said. "But I was thinking there are a few former prom queens that are bad-ass martial artists. And they will gladly kick any guy's ass who disrespects them."

"You're not wrong. Listen, I've got some inquiring minds here that want to know when to expect you."

"We've had a setback," Foster said. He proceeded to tell Black what had happened and then about losing the boat.

"Dammit, Foster, that's more than a setback," Black growled. "That's a fucking steel chair shot to the nuts. What are you planning to do to get yourself out of that mess? Or are you calling to ask us to come get ya?"

"I don't think we need a ride, but I appreciate the suggestion. We might have a way to get out of here. But I'm unsure about using another boat."

"Why the hell not? Just grab another damn boat and go," Black said. "Anybody tries to stop you, then you shoot them."

"We only had two people in our group that knew how to operate a boat. Both of them died when our boat blew up. There's no guarantee that any other boats at the marina here aren't similarly booby-trapped."

"Well, that throws a fucking monkey wrench in things," Black said. "Maybe you need to evac from a different location."

"That's what we're thinking," Foster said. "But I'm still working on that part of the plan."

"Well, you might want to work a little faster. I'll explain to Abrahams what happened. Maybe he can make a few calls on your behalf."

"That would be nice. Especially since we have information on the Reapers that he wants."

"Uh-huh. Trust me, you're not going to sway him a lot with a big promise. Listen, if your nuts are truly in a vise, call me. I'll see what I can do to arrange for exfil for you and your group. But I gotta be honest, it won't be easy to make it happen."

"Why the hell not?"

"Because we only got one working Blackhawk," Black said. "And that copter is out on a mission right now. How many are in your group?"

"Nine, counting me."

"Should be able to fit all of you in the Blackhawk, then. Unless you've added a lot of weight since the last time I saw you."

"Black," Foster warned.

"I'm kidding. I'll talk to Abrahams about coming to collect all of you. But I'm guessing he would prefer to not risk losing his only helicopter doing a taxi run."

"I don't blame him. Give me some time to get my group to a less dangerous pickup zone. I'll call you and give you an update once I have one for you."

"There you go. Now you have a plan. That wasn't so hard, was it?"

"You really enjoy breaking my balls, don't you?"

"Of course," Black admitted. "Wouldn't you, if the roles

were reversed?"

"I guess."

"Stay frosty, Malcolm."

"You too, Black."

"Oh, and Foster?"

"Yeah?"

"If the prom queen comes looking for you, you might want to run the other direction."

Foster chuckled. "Or I'll just call for SWAT."

Black laughed. "Spoken like a true cop. All right. Got to run. Keep you and your people safe."

"You too, Black," Foster said before hanging up.

————

Foster was thirsty, so he headed into the impromptu kitchen to grab a bottle of water. It was really just an ordinary office, but whoever previously used it had installed a small dormitory-size refrigerator in there. As he stepped into the room, he spotted Gregory hunched over a plate of food.

"Just grabbing some quick lunch before we head out," the man mumbled.

"Good idea," Foster answered. He opened the mini fridge, eyeing the meager collection of food and beverages the group had managed to pull from their collective packs. He settled for grabbing a bottle of cold water and an energy bar. He closed the door and opened the beverage before asking, "Where's your dad?"

"In the other room. Said he wanted to pray a little."

Foster took a long pull from the bottle. The ice-cold water was a welcome treat. "Can you be ready to roll out in ten minutes?"

"Yeah, sure."

"Awesome sauce," Foster said. He left the room and headed to where he thought he'd find Charles.

As Foster stepped into the room, he saw the former priest was reading a Bible. He waited until Charles looked up and made eye contact. "You got a minute?" he asked.

"Of course," Charles said. "What do you need?"

"Actually, I'm not here for me."

"What do you mean?" Charles said guardedly.

"I'm wondering how you're holding up," Foster said. "You lost your wife, your daughter, and your son-in-law. And it happened in a matter of days."

"About as well as anyone could, I suppose," Charles said with a sigh. "Well, I feel like I'm on autopilot sometimes."

"I can't imagine how terrible you must feel," Foster said.

"It hasn't been easy," Charles said. "I keep wondering if this is all really worth it."

"It has to be. You still have other loved ones remaining."

"That's what I try to remind myself. Gregory and my grandchildren still need me. It's times like this that I reach out to God for comfort."

"Does he answer?" Foster asked.

"In his own way," Charles said with a forced smile. "Sometimes when it feels like we can't walk another step, that's when God seems to help us the most. I keep reminding myself he never puts a challenge in front of us that we're not capable of overcoming."

"Got a hell of a challenge with the Reapers."

"Of course," Charles said. "But from what Nicholas tells me, we've got several ways of dispatching them much quicker. If we can get the word out, then it goes from our small group of survivors to all of humankind fighting back."

"Yeah, still working on that."

"I understand," Charles said. "You've got a lot on your plate."

"So do you, padre. Listen, if you ever need to talk, don't hesitate to come to me, okay?"

"Of course," Charles said. "The same for you."

"Right," Foster said. "Okay, good talk. Listen, I've got to go get ready to go car shopping with your son."

"Good luck," Charles said. "Please keep my son safe. I'd ask you to order him to stay here, but I doubt he'd listen to me. Not when his own children need to get to Hope Island too."

"I'll do my best."

"That's all any of us can ever do."

CHAPTER SIX

It had been forty minutes since Foster and Gregory had left the group's base. The two men stuck to the shadows as much as possible as they moved through the neighborhoods. Time was of the essence, and with each passing hour, he felt like a proverbial noose was tightening around his neck. It wasn't a question of *if* but *when* they would cross paths with one of the groups currently hunting them. Foster heard someone clear their throat and turned toward them.

"What should we be looking for?" Gregory asked. "A car? Truck?"

"I'd prefer some type of SUV," Foster answered. "Something that is solidly built like the Suburban."

"Got you. Would a minivan work?"

"It wouldn't be my first choice," Foster answered. "Unless you're used to them, but I've found them awkward to drive. I'm also not sure how well they would hold up to any kind of Reaper attacks."

"Makes sense."

"In a perfect world, we'd find a couple Humvees sitting with the keys in the engine and a full tank of gas."

Gregory chuckled. "I think we're a long way away from a perfect world. Not much to choose from. I would have expected more abandoned vehicles here."

"Walker and Sams mentioned most of the vehicles they came across had been disabled. I wonder if the Disciples just confiscated vehicles from around here."

"Maybe. It's possible some folks managed to get out of town before things got bad."

"Do you know anybody who lives near this part of town?" Foster asked. "Someone who you already know that might have kept their SUV in a garage or carport to protect it from the weather?"

"You're thinking what we're looking for might have been missed by the Guardians?"

"Exactly. So, anyone come to mind?"

"I don't think so. Wait. Actually there might be. The Gallaghers. They were friends of my wife. I mean, former wife."

Foster had a feeling there was more to the story. "Go on," he said gently.

"They had a pair of Broncos. Red for him, blue for her. We used to joke that it was like his-and-her towels, except with vehicles."

"Got you. Any idea where the Gallaghers live?"

"I was only at their house once, which is why I didn't think of them before we left base."

"I understand."

"But if I remember correctly, I think it's about another block or so ahead."

"Any chance they're still alive?" Foster said.

"Hard to say," Gregory said. "If anybody would've joined the Disciples right away, it would've been them. They tended to be followers, if you get my drift. They wouldn't have felt comfortable striking out on their own."

Foster nodded his head silently. He could see how once the Reaper outbreak began, a group like the Disciples could take advantage. There would have been plenty of people who were terrified and looking for safety in numbers.

The two men quietly worked their way toward the next block. Foster saw a Chevy Suburban on the right-hand side. As he got closer, he saw that two tires were flattened on the driver's side and dismissed it as an option. The vehicle might have a suitable spare tire, but it would still leave him one good tire short. He slowly scanned his surroundings once more. This particular street appeared mostly abandoned, as if most of the residents were out of town or had fled when the Reaper outbreak began.

As they reached the middle of the block, Gregory muttered softly, "There. Third house up on the right."

Foster nodded once quickly and continued moving forward.

A few minutes later, they had reached the edge of the property.

"How do you want to do this?" Gregory asked.

"I doubt the garage door is going to be open," Foster said. "It's also in plain view."

"You don't want anyone to see us going into the place."

"Definitely not. Even if we get into the garage, we don't know if it connects to the house."

"I think it does."

"You think or know?"

"I-I'm not sure."

"Let's try the back door, then."

"Really?"

"Sure," Foster said. "That's what any criminal with a working brain would do."

"I'll take your word on it. You're a cop. I was raised by an ex-priest and a former nun."

"Good point," Foster said. "Follow me."

"How in the world did a cop get so good at breaking and entering?"

"You do this job long enough," Foster said, "you learn things on the street from observing criminals. Add that to what they teach you at the police academy, and you're left with a number of skills which can be extremely useful when you least expect it." He pulled out the lockpick set and went to work on the back door. In less than thirty seconds, he had the door unlocked.

Gregory started to reach for the doorknob, and Foster held his hand up.

"Wait. Door may have been locked, but it doesn't mean there might not be somebody home."

Foster gestured for Gregory to hug the side of the door. He reached over, rattled the doorknob once and mentally counted to five, then rattled it twice, and waited again. He heard no noises, and this time he opened the door. As he did, he saw the area was dimly lit, so he stepped in with his Glock in a ready position. He quickly swept the foyer, took two more steps forward, and motioned for Gregory to follow him.

Suddenly, there was a loud crash behind him and the room immediately went dark.

CHAPTER SEVEN

The sermon had been a massive success, and Ezekiel walked back to his private office on an emotional high. There had been times before in the past where he felt like he hadn't really reached his flock. But this time, he felt like he'd just experienced a new breakthrough. He could see far more people nodding and shouting in agreement. He would be sure to mention to Joseph a few parishioners who could be good candidates to become Guardians. The concept of avenging the loss of their Reaper protectors appealed to far more members than he would have ever guessed.

The cult leader stepped into his office, turned, and closed the door. It was dark in the room, which wasn't how he remembered leaving it. He leaned over and flipped the switch on the wall. As the room illuminated, there was a strange Reaper in the middle of the room. The creature was wearing some type of red cape.

"Who are you?" Ezekiel demanded. "And you're not supposed to—"

The monster moved like a blur across the room. Ezekiel

managed to emit a squeak of surprise a split second before he felt his body go airborne. A moment later, his back slammed into a nearby couch. The impact caused his body to ricochet off, and he landed in a heap in front of it.

"Who are you?" Ezekiel gasped.

Once more, the monster flashed across the room, grabbed the cult leader, and threw him in a different direction.

This time, Ezekiel felt his head and shoulders slam into his corner liquor cabinet. He heard some of the liquor bottles inside break from the impact, and his body crashed to the floor. Ezekiel felt his shoulder and head screaming in pain immediately. He scrambled backward until he felt his back touch the wall. "You can't touch me," he demanded. "I have a protector. One like you."

"You did," the Reaper growled. "Not anymore." He picked up Ezekiel effortlessly, pivoted, and tossed the man as if he weighed nothing.

Ezekiel saw his desk rushing up toward him and managed to get one hand up in time before his body smashed into the front of it. He landed awkwardly on the ground. A wave of panic coursed through his body, and he began half-crawling, half-scrambling to get away. "Stop. I'm begging you."

"Begging is a good start."

"Y-You can't do this," Ezekiel stammered. "I told you. I'm protected. You're going to have to answer to my friend Giles."

A low rumble came out of the monster's chest, sounding almost like laughter. "What does a worm like you know about friendship?"

"I've known him for years. You know, before he turned into..." Ezekiel let the sentence hang uncomfortably.

"Into a freak, like me?" the monster demanded. "Tell me, human. Do you want me to be your friend now?"

"What?" Ezekiel stammered.

The monster lifted him up and Ezekiel screamed. "Wait!" He felt his feet dangling in the air, and he lost control of his bladder. Ezekiel felt the warm liquid spreading down his leg as the creature brought him close enough that their noses were touching. Ezekiel had no choice but to stare into the monster's red eyes. This was a look of unrestrained hostility in the Reaper's eyes, and Ezekiel heard a whimper escape through his mouth.

"I'm only going to say this once. My name is Haas," the monster growled. "I am not your friend. I am your master. Do you understand me?"

"No. Giles is already my partner, and—"

Ezekiel felt his body launch backward through the air once more. He crash-landed into what felt like his desk chair, and the piece of furniture collapsed on impact.

"Giles is gone," Haas growled. "You are not my partner. You will never be my partner."

"W-what?"

"You are my bitch. Do you understand me?"

"Yes, I think so," Ezekiel stammered.

"Giles protected you. He kept you safe from harm," Haas continued. "And I will do the same—for a price."

"What?" Ezekiel whimpered. "You want money?"

"Not money," Haas growled. "Humans. And I don't want your rejects. I want the ones you find and add to your so-called flock."

"But, how?" Ezekiel pleaded. "We're already having trouble getting–"

Haas moved with frightening speed and Ezekiel felt himself being lifted off the floor again. A split second later, he felt his body flying across the room once more. Ezekiel slammed hip first into the corner of a wall and pinballed into another one. His body crashed hard onto the floor.

"Wait, please, no more," Ezekiel whimpered through bloodied lips. "Just tell me what you want."

"I want one hundred new humans every week."

"One hundred? That's impossible."

"If you fail," Haas continued, "if you do anything to disappoint me, I will kill you and find somebody else to replace you. Do I make myself clear?"

"Yes. But I don't know where I'm going to get one hundred volunteers for you."

"Volunteers." Haas chuckled. "That's a cute way to put it. I hate cute."

"I-I didn't know. I'm sorry."

"If you do not have one hundred healthy humans, then I take the rest from your little flock."

"Wait, you can't be serious."

"You cost me soldiers. Especially chasing after this human, Foster."

"No, no, no. That was Giles' idea," Ezekiel answered. "I had no idea who Foster was. Please be reasonable."

"You're blaming this on a dead man?" Haas roared. "How dare you."

"I'm telling you the truth," Ezekiel shrieked. "Please don't hurt me anymore."

"The time for reason is over," Haas said. "Find Foster and bring him to me. Bring me one hundred new volunteers each week. I will not tolerate excuses or failure."

"Okay. I-I will."

Haas began to head toward the door.

"Haas, wait," Ezekiel blurted out. "How do I contact you?"

The Reaper froze in mid-step and slowly turned around to face Ezekiel once more.

"You don't," Haas said. "Worms don't get to make requests. They only get to follow orders."

"O-Okay. No requests."

Haas let out a low growl before speaking. "One more thing. Worms don't get to call me Haas."

"W-what do I call you, then?"

"Master." There was a flash of red cloth, and then Haas was gone.

CHAPTER EIGHT

With a practiced motion, Foster spun toward the noise, pulling a penlight from his jacket with one hand. He shifted instinctively into a shooting position with the light held on top of his weapon. Foster actively scanned that part of the room, searching for any viable threat, but there was none.

Foster scanned the room once more, his eyes falling on a torchiere lamp lying on its side. In Gregory's rush to close the door, he must have knocked the lamp over. His eyes followed the lamp's cord until he saw its connection into a square electrical timer.

"Did I do that?" Gregory asked softly.

"You need to be more careful," Foster scolded. "No noise here on out. We take our time, go through each room, and make sure this house is completely empty."

"Right. Sorry," Gregory said. "It won't happen again."

"Let's clear the ground floor, then check the upstairs for any supplies we might be able to use."

"I doubt they left any food behind," Gregory said.

"I'm more concerned about medicine and medical

supplies. Once we leave town, those might be harder to find out there than food."

"True. I suppose we could always go fishing if we needed to."

"Exactly. Plenty of shellfish and fish in the bay," Foster said. "Stay close to me."

———

The two men cautiously proceeded through the ground floor. "Living room clear," Foster said softly. A moment later, "Kitchen clear. Let's backtrack."

"Should I open some blinds?" Gregory asked. "It might make it easier to see in here."

"No," Foster answered. "We don't want to tip off anyone outside that we're in here."

Gregory nodded silently in agreement. "Sorry," Gregory blurted. "I don't know why I didn't think of that."

"It's been a tough couple of days. Everyone is over-tired. Including probably you."

"I guess."

The two men worked their way to a staircase.

"Watch that door," Foster instructed to Gregory at the base of the staircase. "I'm going to go clear this top floor. Don't worry, I'll only be a few minutes."

"Got you."

"Anybody comes through there that's human, give a shout."

"And if they're a Reaper?"

"Shoot them between the eyes."

"Right," Gregory said nervously. "Makes sense."

Foster carefully took the stairs using his long legs to cover every other step. He stopped at the landing to visually sweep further up the stairs, saw nothing there, and proceeded up

cautiously once more. Once he reached the top of the landing, he saw the area in front of him was divided into an L
shape. Foster cleared the right wing carefully. The bedrooms
had obviously been emptied in a hurry. The larger bedroom
appeared to be a master bedroom, with its own bathroom.
There was a pile of random items scattered on the bed, with
several empty drawers lying on the floor. Foster took a
moment to look through the collection. Most of it wasn't
useful to his group's needs, and he quickly ignored it. But as
he moved several pieces of paper out of the way, he spotted
Gerber Gear.

"Nice," he muttered. He carefully examined the multi-
tool. It was in great condition and looked like its previous
owner had hardly ever used it.

Foster pocketed the multi-tool and quickly retraced his
steps. He moved back to the left wing, working his way to
another bathroom. He made note to come back and investigate both bathrooms more completely. But first, he wanted to
make sure the rest of the house was free of any potential
threats.

Foster worked his way downstairs to Gregory. "Anything?"
he asked.

"No, it's been quiet."

"I didn't see a basement here. Is there one?"

"I don't think so," Gregory said. "Some of the houses built
here don't have them."

"Cheap home builders?"

"More like the builders were worried about possible
floods from the ocean or the bay."

"Makes sense," Foster said. "Personally, I don't think I'd
want to own a house that didn't have a basement."

"Why?"

"Storage. You can put all your junk in the basement. Your
washer and dryer, too."

"Yeah, okay."

"Come on. This place have a garage?"

"Yeah, follow me," Gregory said as he grabbed the doorknob in front of them. As the man began to open the door, there was a loud click.

"Wait!" Foster shouted a split second before he heard a loud explosion and his body was propelled backward. Foster landed in a heap, his head cracking into something hard. A wave of pain rushed over him, and then everything went black.

———

The darkness began to fade away, being replaced by an incessant buzzing sound about him. Foster shook his head and tried to focus on his surroundings. As his senses began expanding, he realized the buzzing was actually a ringing sensation in his ears. He looked around and saw there was debris all around him. A small fire was burning about one hundred feet away, casting flickering light throughout the area.

"Fire. Can't stay here," Foster mumbled. He rolled on his side, coughing uncontrollably, and sat up. The back of his head began to immediately throb, and he reached back to touch it. He drew back his hand, and his fingers felt wet. He felt the area once more and found a lump in the center of the pain. Foster looked around him. As he did, his vision began to clear and become focused once more. There was a small blotch of blood on the corner of a wall. It looked like just as likely a place where his head might have hit.

Foster glanced at his arms and legs. He was covered in drywall dust and other debris. Parts of his body were starting to complain about the unexpected abuse they had received.

There had been an explosion of some kind. But where was Gregory?

"Hey, man," Foster croaked. "Where you at?"

He slowly looked around, taking in his surroundings. A narrow light was shining on the floor, and he scooted toward it. He pushed pieces of drywall, uncovering his penlight. Foster grabbed the light, grateful for the assistance at the moment. He began to slowly pan the light across the light. He spotted his Glock on the floor and quickly retrieved his weapon. He continued to survey his surroundings. It was partway through his second scan that he saw Gregory lying nearby. Foster slowly crept over to the motionless man. He gave Gregory a quick once-over and didn't notice any visible injuries. Foster grabbed the man's wrist and felt for a pulse. It was there. A little slow, but steady. Foster let out the breath he didn't realize he was holding.

"Gregory, come on. Talk to me, man. Are you okay?"

"W-what?" the man said groggily. "What happened?"

"Booby-trap," Foster said. "They rigged the fucking door to their garage."

"What?"

"Are you okay? Anything broken?"

"I don't think so," Gregory muttered. He began to try and sit up.

"Let me help," Foster said. He assisted the dazed man into a sitting position. The two men worked together to slowly scoot Gregory backward until his back was supported against the nearby wall.

Foster spotted Gregory's gun lying near the demolished doorway. He moved toward it, scooped it up, and returned. "Stay here," he said as he offered the weapon to the injured man. "Keep an eye out for any unwanted company. I'm going to check on our possible ride out of here."

"Okay."

Foster stepped into the garage with his penlight and Glock. He did a quick circle sweep. What looked to be a blue Ford Bronco was buried in rubble. One of the nearby walls was on fire, and he quickly backtracked inside the house. Foster glanced at the doorway. The door was history. It was only a matter of time until the unimpeded fire spread from the garage into the remainder of the house.

"Is the car there?" Gregory asked.

"Just the Blue Bronco, but it's under a pile of debris. Fire is in the garage, too. I'm going to go grab some stuff out of the bathroom. I'll be back in one minute. I need you ready to move then."

"I'm feeling a little..." Gregory slowly slumped over onto the floor.

"Dammit," Foster muttered. He grabbed the man and dragged him farther away from the garage. "I'll be back in one minute. Okay? Hang on, man."

Foster turned and bolted toward the stairs, taking them two at a time. He made a beeline for the bathroom in the master bedroom and began checking the cabinets. They were completely cleaned out. Foster retreated to the master bedroom and scanned the room. There was a pair of matching dressers with most of the drawers sitting open or on the floor.

Foster double-timed it to the other bathroom on the second floor. In it, he found a single half-empty bottle of aspirin. Foster grabbed the bottle, stuffed it in his jacket, and hauled ass back to Gregory's location. He glanced at the fire and swore under his breath. He'd been gone barely a minute, and the fire had grown even more menacing and dangerous.

. . .

"Gregory, we got to go right now," Foster said. He grabbed the wounded man around the arm and waist. "On three. One, two, three."

Gregory wobbled up onto his feet. There was a visible cut on the side of his forehead. Foster wasn't sure how he'd missed it when he looked the injured man over before. He made a mental note to take a closer look at it once they got out of the building.

Foster steered Gregory toward the front door. By the time they reached the entrance, the younger man had stabilized on his feet enough that he was able to walk mostly on his own. Foster opened the front door, stepped out, did a sweep, made sure there wasn't anybody waiting for them, reached back, and motioned for Gregory to follow. Gregory wobbled through the front door, not bothering to close it behind him. "Come on, let's go," Foster said. He grabbed Gregory by the arm with his left hand, steering him away from the house and back toward their vehicle.

"I can't believe they set a trap," Gregory mumbled.

"Me neither," Foster said. "Come on. It's not safe here. We need to get out of here before anybody else comes to investigate."

CHAPTER NINE

President Vickers waited impatiently in the conference room. She looked at General Weindahl, then at her watch and back to the only other person in the room. "Rasheed, would you consider it a good career move to be late for a meeting with the President of the United States?"

"I wouldn't recommend it," Weindahl replied. "My apologies, Madam President. I don't have an explanation for this. Doctor Compton was told about this meeting, and she promised to be here on time."

Doctor Amelia Compton was considered one of the United States' leading microbiologists. One of her friends, a professor at UCLA, had been concerned about her safety. She made an urgent phone call to her favorite uncle and told him about the type of viral research her friend regularly worked on. And once General Weindahl calmed his niece down, he put the military elements still in place into action. They caught a lucky break because the military had been able to track down the whereabouts of the missing researcher in a matter of hours.

It was an even bigger lucky break that she was on her

honeymoon in Hawaii when the Reaper invasion began. With the airport shut down, she and her new husband were left stranded in Honolulu.

Once someone explained what was happening with the rest of the United States, it hadn't taken much to convince the newlyweds to stay in Hawaii for the foreseeable future. Especially with a healthy promotion to head of a brand-new government program. The good doctor was more than qualified for the position. And it could be argued that she was their best shot at figuring out what made the Reapers tick and eliminating them before they wiped out the remnants of humanity.

The video conference line began to beep, and Vickers muttered "Finally," before smashing the answer button in front of her. The display lit up, and a frazzled-looking woman in her early forties appeared on screen.

"Doctor, you have kept the President of the United States waiting for almost ten minutes," General Weindahl scolded. "I hope you have an excellent explanation for being late."

"Sorry, General and Madam President," Compton said. "Things are pretty chaotic here right now."

"Anything for us to worry about?" Vickers asked.

"No, not at all. We're busy throwing stuff together. Just trying to get the labs and everything operational as soon as possible."

"Is there any actual work being done there at the facility?" Vickers asked.

"Well, I just told you we're getting things together," Compton said. Her tone of voice suggested she was addressing an easily distracted child and not the leader of the country.

"I meant in terms of the research," Vickers replied.

"Soon."

"Doctor, I'm going to need a more in-depth answer here."

"Right. Most of our programs are still being set up, and I hope they'll be ready to start in the coming days," Compton replied. "The only thing that has already been done are some impromptu autopsies. Somehow they had some Reaper corpses to examine."

"Somehow?" Vickers asked.

"It appears a small private chartered flight landed on the island. The pilot alerted the tower that several of the passengers were infected before making an emergency landing. The controller alerted the local military, and the plane was immediately isolated. The grunts apparently decided to shoot first and ask questions later, because they killed the three potential test subjects on sight."

"You'd prefer they would have attempted to capture them alive?" Vickers said incredulously. "Do you have any idea how dangerous those things are?"

"Everybody keeps telling me that," Compton replied. "In case you didn't know, I've been out of the loop. I was on my honeymoon. Well, until you all showed up and told me that I needed to get back to work."

"Doctor, the Reapers have killed or transformed millions of humans in a matter of days," Weindahl said with a practiced calm. "It's probably best if you stick to the research and not talking about your personal life."

"Okay, fine. It appears there are two distinctive types of the Reapers. Some of them have the hardening of the backs to their arms, legs, and along the posterior side of their body."

"Like a thicker skin?" Weindahl asked.

"Not exactly. It's more like a layer of protective armor plates, like body armor."

"Do all the Reapers have these?" Weindahl said. "It may impact what type of weapons our soldiers need to use."

"I don't think so," Compton said. "I'm working with a

limited number of test subjects, so I can't rule it out completely. But the early research suggests that some of them may have developed this armoring over time. This could make them resistant to melee weapon attacks, or damage from behind."

"Any distinctions on who gets it and who doesn't?" Weindahl asked.

"Like based on the Reaper's skin color?"

"No," Weindahl said. "I meant in terms of males or females being more likely to further evolve."

"As far as we know, there doesn't seem to be any differences between the Reapers."

"None?" Vickers challenged. "Not even by gender."

"Like I said, there doesn't appear to be any differences," Compton answered. "They all seem to look the same way after they've been transformed."

"I feel like you're tap dancing around the question," Vickers challenged. "So, I'm going to ask you one last time. Have you or your team found anything that can explain why some Reapers evolve more than others?"

"Not at this time," Compton admitted. "Our early research is still very incomplete. One of my assistants has theorized that Reapers may be developing these plate armoring over time. Like a gradual evolving or a development cycle. But it's just a theory."

"Let's hope they're wrong," Vickers said. "The last thing we need is our enemy getting harder to kill."

"Indeed," Weindahl said. "Do you have anything else to report at this time, Doctor?"

"Afraid not. Like I said, we're still very early in getting things set up. I could really use some additional help."

"What kind of help?" Vickers asked.

"You name it. We need it. But for starters, I could really use more research assistants and doctors."

"We are continuing to look," General Weindahl said. "The process has not been easy, because there's been a great loss of our population to either death or Reaper transformation. The universities appear to be equally hard hit."

"Honestly, I don't care if you've got to pull them out of some no-name lab in Greenland or Asia," Compton said. "We'll figure out how to communicate with each other. I just need people that understand *geek* to make the science work."

Vickers cleared her throat. "I'm not quite sure I follow."

"Right, you're not a scientist. Okay, let me try to explain this," Compton said. "There's a certain terminology that we biologists and virologists use. If we're all talking in that language, then translating it from Spanish to English or some other language becomes a lot easier."

"Really?"

"Sure," Compton snarked. "Ever heard of Google Translate?"

"You're assuming the Internet will continue working for the foreseeable future," General Weindahl said. "That's not a guarantee."

"Well, let's hope so," Compton said. "Otherwise, we won't be having meetings like this. Now, unless there's something else, I really need to get back to work."

"That's all for now," the President said. "Appreciate you taking the time to meet with us, Doctor."

"Uh-huh," the doctor said quickly before disconnecting the call.

Vickers turned to the general. "Charm school dropout?"

"It would appear so," Weindahl admitted. "But with our current situation, I'm afraid we don't have the luxury of being picky with who we work with."

"In other words, beggars can't be choosers?"

"I'm afraid so. Especially for microbiologists."

"Your niece alerted you about Dr. Compton?"

"Yes, that's right," Weindahl replied. "But she neglected to mention her lack of people skills."

"Your niece. Is she...?" Vickers let the question linger uncomfortably.

"She's safe. They managed to reach her husband's boat safely," Weindahl said. "They're anchored about ten miles from Southern California."

"Oh, thank goodness."

"Indeed."

"So while the good doctor and her team are working on figuring out the Reapers' weaknesses, do you have any other ideas for battling the Reapers?"

"We've got a couple of tentative plans in place, Madam President," Weindahl answered. "But nothing concrete. Operation Firestorm really set us back."

"Yes, I'm painfully aware," Vickers said bitterly. The recent military operation had been a complete bust. The failed firebombing hadn't killed any of the targeted Reapers. And from the drone footage, it looked like the bombing had just temporarily inconvenienced the monsters.

"One option is..."

"If you say nukes, Rasheed," Vickers warned, "So help me, I'll order you to clean every toilet on this ship."

"I understand your frustration, ma'am. I truly do. I just think that it's premature to rule it out as a possibility."

"Keep it parked on the back burner until I say otherwise," Vickers ordered. "What else do we have?"

"There are some options we haven't explored yet."

"Come on, Rasheed, talk to me," Vickers pleaded. "I just listened to a song and dance from Dr. Compton. I don't need one from you, too."

"With all due respect, Madam—"

"Our boys are getting killed out there, General. We need

something to knock these damn Reapers on their ass and start turning the odds in our favor."

"We're thinking some type of biological attack."

"Like anthrax?"

"No, more like some type of nerve agent, ma'am. They're living creatures. If they can't breathe, then they'll die."

Vickers sat up straighter in her chair. "Keep talking. Is there any way that we can just isolate the monsters and avoid any potential civilian fatalities?"

"Probably not at this time," Weindahl said. "It's difficult to determine what only kills the Reapers versus any humans in the area. I've been thinking it over. Instead of some type of nationwide multi-pronged attack, I'm thinking something smaller."

"Because we lack the personnel to hit more than one target at once? Or more of a test strike?"

"Both, actually," Weindahl admitted. "We're stretched really thin."

"So we don't know if this will work to kill the Reapers or not," Vickers thought aloud. "But if we tried a single attack at one location, then we'd know if it worked pretty quickly."

"Indeed, Madam President," Weindahl said. "If it works as well as we believe it will, we can roll out further attacks throughout the country."

Vickers steepled her fingers together. "I like it. Any particular area in mind?"

"It appears that Richmond, Kentucky, has a good number of Reapers."

"A good number?"

"Forgive me, ma'am. A wrong choice of words. Richmond is not a large city. At least not compared to many others in our country. Population in the area is also not as dense, so the risk of any potential collateral damage is further decreased. If we can identify a right location where there's a high concentration of Reapers, we could hit them with a tactical strike."

"I like it."

"Do I have your authorization for Operation Poison Arrow?"

"You're damn right you do," Vickers said. "It's time to hit these bastards and hit them hard."

CHAPTER TEN

Beeks strolled into the room like he owned the place. Which, being the King of all Reapers, he more or less did. The creature being kept in the room looked up at him with curious eyes. She had once been a human, and a part of Beeks' mind suggested that she had been an attractive one, too.

But in her current battered and bloodied state, she was anything but that. There was a patch on her shoulder that suggested she was a military pilot. He tried to recall her name. *Angel.* That was it. He wasn't sure he'd let her keep it. If he did, then it might trigger some of her past memories. But even in her current condition, Beeks found himself getting aroused by what he saw in front of him. A low growl of excitement exited his lips, and she looked away.

You, Beek said mentally toward her. *I command you to look at me.*

She slowly looked up at him. There was a look of defiance in her eyes. No fear there. Everyone else was afraid of him. Why wasn't this recently turned one, too?

"How are you feeling?" Beeks asked.

"Fine," she answered aloud.

"My soldiers tell me you refuse to eat."

"Not hungry."

"You will be soon," Beeks said. "You should eat something."

"No."

"There's nothing wrong with the meat. One of my best warriors personally killed the cow."

The female shook her head side to side vigorously. She wrapped her arms around her knees and drew them up tight to her body and began rocking back and forth slowly.

"I take care of all of my family, and you're one of my family now, too."

"I don't know if I want that."

"What?" Beek snarled. He lashed out mentally, and a small cry of pain came from his prisoner.

"What other choice do you think you have?"

"I-I'm not sure," she stammered.

"Sure about what?"

"My head. It hurts all the time."

Beeks reached to her and saw her pull away. He stopped and withdrew his hand.

"I don't know who I am," the female said as she continued to rock back and forth. "I don't know how I got here or what I'm supposed to be.'"

"You're with your family."

"Family? So how come I don't know anyone's name?" she shouted. "I don't even know my own fucking name."

"That language is unacceptable for a female in my family," Beeks scolded. "I won't warn you again."

She continued to rock in silence.

"Would you like me to give you a name?"

"I told you," she roared. "I can't remember my name."

Calm down, Angel, Beeks blurted out. He immediately regretted his mistake. Why did he share her previous name? He had named so many others in his family. It was an easy way to remind them that he was the one in control and not them. But Angel? The name did seem to fit the female in front of him.

"Angel?" she said softly.

Beeks let out a low grumble. "That's what you told me your name was before. If you want a different one, speak up now."

Angel immediately stopped rocking. "It's a good name," she said carefully. She tilted her head to the side and began studying Beeks. "Why am I here?"

"You're home. Here with your family," Beeks said. "Eat something, and rest. Soon we'll go out hunting."

"Really?"

"Yes. If you're not hungry, then at least get some rest before the big hunt."

He turned and strode out of the room. Stopping outside, he looked at the two guards standing outside the entranceway.

"If she tries to leave, stop her. But do not hurt her. She belongs to me."

"Of course, my Lord," one of the soldiers mumbled. The other appeared to be distracted.

Beeks felt his blood begin to boil. "Look at me," he growled. Both soldiers went ramrod straight. "If she dies, both of you will die."

Both soldiers immediately dropped to one knee and bowed their heads in front of him.

"Yes, Master," they both said together. "No harm will come to your female."

———

"You wanted to see me, sir?" Joseph said.

"Yes," Ezekiel said. He set his glass of bourbon down carefully on the only piece of still intact furniture in his office. The cult leader shifted uncomfortably on a folding chair. "We need to talk about the Guardians."

"Oh, my goodness," Joseph blurted. "What happened to your office?"

Ezekiel looked away. "I lost my temper. Took it out on some of the things in here. I'm better now."

"I see," Joseph answered with a measured tone. He wasn't about to ask his boss about the visible welts and bruises on his face. And Ezekiel didn't seem eager to volunteer the information, either. "What about the Guardians?"

"With the death of Walter, we need someone to lead them."

"It could be hard after that battle," Joseph confessed. "The people are a bit shaken."

"What are you talking about? I've never seen the congregation more committed to finding Foster and his group. They want to make them pay for what they did."

"But not the Guardians. They were the ones in the battle. They were the ones who bled and died. They saw how Foster and his group handled themselves. From what I've heard, his group is a bunch of trained killers."

"I don't want excuses. I want solutions," Ezekiel answered. "Find somebody among the Guardians who isn't scared. Bring them to me, and I will interview them personally."

"As you wish, Ezekiel."

"Joseph. One more thing."

"Yes, sir?"

"I'm growing tired of the condition of my office," Ezekiel said. "See if you can have someone bring in some new furniture."

"Of course. Do you have any particular requested pieces in mind?"

"Not at this time. Now that I've had time to reflect on my actions, I'm regretting my temper tantrum."

"I'll see what I can quickly collect and have delivered here."

"Thank you, Joseph," Ezekiel answered. "I don't know what I'd do without you."

"I'm just happy to be of service," Joseph said. "Now if there's nothing else, I'll see to finding some new furnishings for you."

"That will be all," Ezekiel said. "If you wouldn't mind showing yourself out, I would appreciate it." The cult leader reached for his glass of bourbon without waiting for an answer.

"Of course," Joseph answered quickly. "I'll be back when I have an update for you." He bowed quickly and retreated from the room.

CHAPTER ELEVEN

Their car hunting hadn't gone to plan, and now Foster was hoping that Gregory hadn't been hurt badly by the home explosion. Somehow the two men managed to get back to the gun shop without running into any more trouble. They were back on the second floor, and Foster was watching quietly as Amanda continued to examine Gregory thoroughly. Foster heard a noise and turned in time to see Lizzy entering the room.

"How did the vehicle shopping go?" Lizzy asked.

"A little rocky, but we survived," Foster answered.

"Wait," Lizzy said. "What happened?"

"They got a little banged up," Amanda said. She finished examining Gregory and gave him a quick, reassuring pat on the shoulder. "Especially Gregory. I'm surprised you didn't wind up with a concussion, considering you cracked your head."

"That's a relief," Gregory replied. "I guess I got lucky."

"My vote is hard head," Sams added as he walked into the room. "Probably got it from hanging out with Malcolm."

"Is anybody going to tell me what happened?" Lizzy demanded.

"Sure," Foster answered. He quickly explained about the booby-trapped house.

"That's crazy," Lizzy replied. "You could have been killed."

"Like Gregory said, we got lucky," Foster said. "At least the trip wasn't a total loss. I was able to find a black Chevy Tahoe on our way back here."

"You found one that wasn't disabled?" Walker asked. "I don't believe it. Derrick and I must have checked two dozen vehicles during our recon mission."

"Lucky break, I guess. It just needed a battery," Foster said. "I grabbed the one out of our old ride, and it started right up. The Tahoe might be tight quarters with all of us in it. But if we pack light, then we might be able to make it more bearable."

"Nice," Lizzy said. "As soon as we drain the fuel out of the Land Cruiser and put it in the new wheels, we should be ready to roll."

"Eh. My vote is to grab a second vehicle," Sams said. "More cargo capacity. What about painting one of our old vehicles again? That trick worked once before. It might work again."

"Already thought of it. The problem is we don't have any place to do the paint job here," Foster said. "Plus, we'd need to get the paint, too."

"A quick paint job might fool the Reapers, but it's not going to fool any human patrols," Walker said. "Don't forget we still need more supplies. Some of those Guardian armbands would be helpful, too."

"You really think they're going to work?" Sams asked. "I'm surprised they don't change the color on the bands every day."

"Why?" Walker countered. "It seems like they run this town. I doubt they have a problem with stolen armbands."

"Nick has a point," Foster said. "Most people here don't seem like they're willing to go up against the Disciples."

"Don't get me wrong. I still wouldn't mind having the armbands," Walker said carefully. "It's like having extra ammo. I'd rather have it than run out in the middle of a firefight."

"You're comparing bullets to armbands?" Sams challenged. "I'd expect something that weak from Foster, not you."

Foster decided to change the subject before things could become heated between the two former soldiers. "Speaking of ammo," he said, "we might as well pick some up while we're collecting food and medical supplies."

"Didn't we leave a bunch of stuff at Gregory's house?" Lizzy asked.

"No ammo, but we did leave some other supplies," Foster said. "It could save a lot of us some time to swing by there and collect it."

"Especially with the Guardians and Reapers actively patrolling the rest of town," Sams said. "Probably best to avoid a confrontation, if possible."

"I agree," Foster said. "All right, we need to swing by Gregory's house for supplies and getting the armbands. Am I forgetting anything?"

"Off the top of my head, we could use more food and medical supplies," Sams answered. "More coffee would be great. I'd love some alcohol, too. But not any of the cheap stuff."

"Call me crazy," Foster said, "but I didn't think you'd want to drink booze with some many hostiles breathing down our necks right now."

"It's for Hope Island. I doubt they have much alcohol there," Sams said. "And I plan on having several stiff drinks once I know we're safe from potential Reaper attacks. Ooh, just thought of something else. We gotta get some Tastykakes, too."

Several people in the room groaned at once.

"What?" Sams protested. "I haven't had them in ages. There's the chocolate cupcakes, the butterscotch krimpets—"

"Leave it up to Derrick to put in a junk food order," Walker quipped. "You eat too much of that stuff, and you won't fit in the Tahoe with the rest of us."

"Wait. Are you saying I'm getting fat? Because I could still outrun you—"

"Getting back to the business at hand," Foster interrupted. "I need somebody to go with me to pick up the supplies. Once we have them, I'll drop them and the supplies off here and then go after the armbands."

"Not a fucking chance," Sams said. "You're not Jack Bauer."

"Who?" Amanda asked.

"The do-everything hero from an old TV series," Walker answered. "Derrick has a good point. You don't have to do everything by yourself, Malcolm. There's a whole group of capable people in this room with you."

"At the risk of stating the obvious," Sams said carefully, "we do have two kids that somebody needs to keep an eye on. Plus we're almost black on ammo."

"No, Walker said we've got ammo," Foster said. "It just needs to be loaded into the magazines. Maybe whoever is here with the children can have them help with that task."

"Let me guess," Lizzy interrupted. "You want the little women to stay here, babysit, and hand load magazines while the big strong men go on the dangerous missions."

"Come on, Lizzy, be reasonable," Foster said. As soon as he said it, he immediately wished he hadn't.

"Be reasonable?" Lizzy shouted. "I'm sick and tired of

playing babysitter to kids that aren't mine. I've been on one mission so far. One. So when the hell do I get to go somewhere?"

"The same time the rest of us do," Walker answered. "Listen, babe—"

"Don't try and sweet-talk me, Nicholas," Lizzy Walker said with a warning tone to her voice. "You know I have a point."

"I wasn't trying to," Walker said carefully. "It's just that some of the boxes of supplies are quite heavy."

"Yeah right."

"I carried some of them into the attic myself," Walker pointed out. "Do you want to be the person lugging them out of an attic, down a flight of stairs, and to the trucks?"

"Not particularly," Lizzy said. "But I'd do it if I had to."

"Right. But there are other people here that are stronger and would have an easier time lifting heavy boxes."

"Uh-huh," Lizzy said. Her arms crossed in front of her body. "Keep digging, buster. You're neck deep right now. So what about the armband mission? Care to tell me why I can't go and get those?"

"Okay, let's talk about it," Walker said. He let out a low sigh before continuing. "The only place we think we can find them right now is off the dead Guardians by the marina."

"Well, it's not like I haven't seen dead bodies before," Lizzy said. "Or did my thickheaded husband forget that I was a nurse in a city hospital?"

"Please let me finish. And no, I didn't forget," Walker said. "Hon, what if they already removed the bodies? Or we cross paths with a Guardian patrol and get in a gunfight?"

"Or get attacked by Reapers," Sams pointed out.

Lizzy and Walker shot him a look, and the former Ranger immediately clammed up.

"There's a high likelihood that whoever is in an unplanned

firefight could be injured. So who do you suppose is going to patch us up afterwards?" Walker continued. "Do you think any of the men could deliver medical care as well as Amanda or you?"

"You could manage, if you had to."

"Hon," Walker said carefully. "If I've been shot and am slowly bleeding out, do you want Charles or Malcolm trying to administer aid because you're off on a different mission?"

"That's not fair, and you know it."

"This whole situation isn't fair. None of us asked for this mess. But all of us need to work together to stay alive and get through it."

"You made your point, Nicholas," Lizzy grumbled. "But don't think for a minute that I'm happy about it."

"Of course not, dear," Walker said. He paused for a moment before adding, "Thank you."

"For what?"

"For being a team player."

"Uh-huh," Lizzy said before turning her back to her husband, signaling the conversation was over for now.

"All right, two missions," Foster said, "Supply retrieval and armband collection. Anything else?"

"Three people would probably be the bare minimum for that retrieval mission," Walker said. "I'd post one person by the vehicle. They could guard your ride and still be able to keep an eye out for hostiles. The other two would retrieve the supplies and bring them back to the vehicle in the meantime."

"Well, how about if I take Charles and Gregory with me?" Foster suggested. "We'll head back to Gregory's house. With three of us, the box hauling should go quicker. If Gregory starts to feel light-headed—"

"I'm fine," Gregory protested.

"Well, that's right now. But if you need a break," Foster

continued, "your dad could help me while you guard our transport."

"That could work," Gregory answered. "But that leaves Derrick and Walker to go get the armbands by themselves. They're more likely to run into trouble than we will. Should they take Lizzy or Amanda?"

"Negative. That would leave only one adult to protect the children and our base of operations," Walker answered. "Don't worry. Derrick and I will be fine."

"Famous last words," Foster quipped.

"I think a pair of Rangers have better odds than a cop assisted by two civilians," Walker countered. "Besides, we're doing a snatch and grab. We run into trouble, we'll just shoot our way out."

"Wait, what?" Lizzy blurted. "Are you seriously looking to get into a gunfight?"

"Don't worry, I'll bring your husband back safe and sound," Sams interrupted. "I promise."

"I'm feeling so much better," Lizzy grumbled. "Two trigger-happy idiots going off unsupervised."

"Yeah, maybe we should get going, Nick." Sams chuckled. "Don't worry, we'll stay safe."

"All of us will," Walker added. "Come on, let's get going. It's not getting any earlier."

CHAPTER TWELVE

Ezekiel was struggling to get through the latest daily update. If he was being honest, it was the type of task that was far beyond anything the conman had ever had to do in his previous life. He wished he could dump the task onto Joseph, but the man was already overloaded with work and resistant to adding even more. And right now, there wasn't anyone else that Ezekiel felt like he could trust to read some critical and confidential information. He could feel a headache developing from reading over the boring material. Ezekiel tossed the stack of papers onto his desk and began to massage his forehead.

There was a knock at the door, and he called out, "Come in."

Joseph stepped into the room and gestured for someone else to follow.

"I don't believe we've met," Ezekiel said. He studied the man standing confidently next to Joseph. He looked to be about fifty years old and rough-looking. The man was wearing the appropriate Guardian arm bandage, which surprised

Ezekiel because he thought he had previously met all of the Guardian members.

"This is Silas," Joseph introduced. "He'd like to talk to you about leading the Guardians."

"I see. And what makes you believe that you are qualified to lead?"

"You want to talk in front of the pansy here?" Silas asked. "Or have a real heart-to-heart?"

Ezekiel's eyebrows shot up. "Joseph, perhaps you should wait out in the hall," he said slowly.

"Sir, I don't think—"

"I'll be fine," Ezekiel answered. "If I need you, I'll call you."

"As you wish, sir," Joseph replied. He turned and headed toward the door without pause.

Ezekiel waited until his trusted assistant stepped out of the room before he continued. "You seem to be a man who takes no issue with speaking his mind."

"Way I see it, when you and I talk, we can be honest with each other," Silas said. "Outside of this room, well, I'll tell them whatever you want me to say."

"Really?" Ezekiel said. "And why should I believe you?"

"You've got a good thing going here," Silas said. "Not sure how you keep those monsters in check. Don't really care, either. What I do know is that with Walter biting it, you need someone in charge of your Guardians. Someone like me."

"And why is that?"

"Because I ain't afraid to do whatever needs to be done." Silas stared intently at Ezekiel. "Anything."

"This man Foster and his group have become a serious headache for us," Ezekiel said carefully. "They've killed our protectors. They killed Guardians, too."

"So you want me to mess him up a bit? Or you want him dead?"

"I prefer you bring him to me alive."

"Huh. Well, might be a little harder, but okay, I can do that. What about the rest of his side flunkies?"

"They're yours to do whatever you want with," Ezekiel said. "Do we have a deal?"

"Oh, we have a deal," Silas said. "This is going to be fun."

————

Angel Vasquez awoke with a start. She looked around her and saw nothing but an unfamiliar environment. A dominant voice suddenly spoke up in her head, telling her that this was her home.

Not home.

Angel shook her head. This place felt wrong. It wasn't familiar to her. The voice spoke again, insisting that she was here with her family.

Angel quickly agreed. She didn't really believe what the voice was telling her. But it was the easiest way to get the annoying voice to shut the hell up.

She didn't know why, but she kept having this dream of falling out of the sky in some type of metal machine. She was holding something in her hands to guide this machine in the sky. A smaller voice quickly suggested she had been hunting the ones who claimed to be her family now.

Was she going crazy with all of these voices in her head? Or was it part of the truth? Angel just didn't know. She didn't have any clue where she was. Or why she was even here.

There was only one thing she knew: Every time she rebelled against that dominant voice in her head, she felt an overwhelming wave of pain and nausea. Maybe it was better for now to listen to that voice. She could quietly observe her surroundings and listen to what others had to say. That didn't cause her head to hurt.

Angel stood up and stretched her arms toward the ceiling. She walked carefully toward the open space in the wall. The small voice in her head called it a doorway, and she immediately felt that must be right. So far, the small voice hadn't lied to her. Maybe she'd try to listen to it more often. The trick was to do it without triggering the louder voice. Anything to avoid the pain that made her head feel like it was going to explode.

She inched her way to the edge of the doorway. There was a guard leaning against the wall with its head tilted back. The creature wasn't moving, and Angel inched forward cautiously. She crept toward it, stopping a few steps away. Angel watched its chest rise and fall, slowly. A low, rhythmic sound rumbled out of its body.

Snoring, she thought. *The guard is sleeping instead of watching me.*

Maybe it was time to do some exploring. A quick search of her surroundings to get some answers on her own. It wasn't disobeying the dominant voice. If anyone stopped her and asked, she'd say she was just looking around. Or maybe had gotten lost. It might be a tiny lie. But it was probably an easy one that wouldn't be questioned by most of these so-called family members. Angel glanced at the still-sleeping guard and then quietly headed down the hallway in the opposite direction.

CHAPTER THIRTEEN

It was late afternoon when the Tahoe pulled to a stop in front of Gregory's house. The front door was a splintered mess. The exterior of the house looked worse than Foster remembered. It was hard to imagine the damage was strictly due to the Reaper attack that forced his group to flee their previous base.

"Do you think the supplies are still there?" Charles asked.

"I sure hope so," Gregory said. "Otherwise, this is a wasted trip."

"They should be," Foster said. "Like Nick said, the attic is the last place that people will look when they're looting a house quickly or scavenging. Even so, keep your eyes and ears open. We don't know if there's any unwanted company in the house."

"How do you suggest we proceed?" Charles asked.

Foster studied the two men in front of him. Neither one was a trained fighter. Neither had any military or law enforcement background. While each was competent with a gun, he wasn't sure how well either one could handle themselves on their own.

"Pull up at the back of the house," Foster said. "We'll go through the back door and clear the ground floor together. Then I'll clear the basement and the upstairs before we proceed any further."

"What about the SUV?" Gregory asked.

"Make sure it's locked," Foster said. "We can't be in two places at once. I'd rather have the two of you watching each other's backs while we're in the house until we know it's completely secure."

"Are you saying that we can't protect ourselves?" Gregory demanded. "I'll have you know—"

"Relax, son," Charles said. "Malcolm would rather us be safe than sorry."

"What if one of you stumbles into a room with five Reapers in it?" Foster asked. "Do you feel like you could handle that on your own? Because I sure as shit couldn't."

"You think we shouldn't have come with you?"

"I didn't say that," Foster said. "Like your dad said, there's safety in numbers. And with more than one of us, we can make sure that nobody is sneaking into the house behind us."

"I guess," Gregory grumbled.

"That's why I suggested we clear the ground floor together," Foster said. "Then, I'll clear the basement while you two keep an eye on anyone or anything coming down the stairs from the second floor or the back door. Then we'll clear the top floor. Once we know the house is completely secure, we can start retrieving our supplies. I think we can grab the supplies and get back to base in time for dinner."

"Sounds good," Charles said. "We should get started while we still have plenty of daylight."

———

Foster was on his third trip to the attic when his comms came alive. "Malcolm, please answer. This is Charles."

"What's up?" Foster said.

"We've got company coming our way. About ten Reapers."

"Copy that. We're on our way back," Foster answered. He turned toward Gregory. "Head for the Tahoe. We need to back up your dad. Double time."

The two men began hustling down the stairs. Foster had reached the bottom of the stairs when his comms came alive once more.

"Malcolm, where are you guys? There's even more Reapers showing up. What do I do?"

"Get in the car," Foster said. "We're almost there."

As Foster reached the ground floor, he heard a door slam. He drew his weapon, anticipating an unknown number of hostile intruders. But as he rounded the corner, Foster saw only Charles. The back door was now closed behind the former priest, and he was gasping for air.

A moment later, there was a slam at the door.

"Dad, are you okay?" Gregory asked.

"Y-Yes."

Foster heard a second boom, and the door trembled from the blow. Then another slam happened a split second later. Foster looked at the door. There was no way in hell it was going to hold against the relentless Reaper assault.

"Out the front?" Gregory asked.

"No time," Foster said. "There's nothing to stop them from coming in that way. Fall back to the attic."

He brought up his rifle and took up a firing position as Charles and Gregory squeezed by him up the stairs.

"Come with us, Malcolm," the former priest pleaded.

"I'll be right behind you," Foster answered. "Don't worry."

There was a loud ripping sound, and a Reaper's head pushed through a hole in the rear door. Foster fired an immediate double-tap, scoring a direct hit in the monster's face. The Reaper's head disappeared from the opening, and a new one appeared in its place. Foster fired at the new enemy and watched it drop out of sight. The door started to crumble into the house, and Foster moved up two steps on the staircase. He set his feet and fired once more. Another Reaper dropped a split second before the rest of the door collapsed.

Foster opened fire, selecting targets as fast as he could acquire them. But the Reapers continued to pour through the doorway. He was hopelessly outnumbered. He continued to fire and felt the bolt on his rifle lock open. Foster let the rifle drop and felt the weapon's sling go taut as it broke the rifle's fall. He drew his Glock and continued to backpedal up the stairs to the second floor, working his way back toward the attic.

"Come on!" Gregory screamed.

Foster continued to back up until one of his feet bumped into the attic ladder. He risked a quick glance and saw he had bought himself a few seconds before the Reapers would reach his position. Foster holstered his weapon, grabbed one of the ladder rungs, and began climbing up. As he entered the enclosed space, a gun exploded near his head. The noise was deafening, and his ears immediately began to ring. Foster's instincts kicked in, and he spun where he was at on his belly to grab the rope for the attic ladder.

One Reaper was lying on the floor below, a pool of new blood forming by its head. Another one charged into view and leapt toward him. Foster flinched instinctively a moment before a gun went off near him once more. He saw several bullets strike the Reaper's body, and the creature tumbled off of the ladder.

"The ladder," he gasped between breaths. "Pull the ladder."

He felt his two friends moving around him and saw the

ladder begin retracting up into the attic. The attic door closed, and there was a loud crescendo of growls and roars underneath them.

"Too close," Foster said. He did a quick mental check. None of his body parts was reporting anything more serious. He'd have to check more thoroughly at some point. The ringing in his ear was starting to decrease, which was a good sign. At least the close-proximity gunfire hadn't blown out his eardrum. Another lucky break, and hopefully not the last one he'd ever get.

Foster turned toward where he thought Charles was and added, "Why the hell didn't you get in the Tahoe like I told you?"

"I'm sorry, Malcolm. T-There were just so many of them."

"Dammit," Foster said. "Does anybody have a light?"

A chorus of no's sounded out besides him.

"Great," Foster muttered. He began patting his pockets. The penlight that he usually kept in his pocket was missing. He must've dropped it in his hurry to get back to the attic. He reached down, felt for his rifle, and worked his way to the attached scope. He activated the light and then detached it from the rifle, shining it around the attic space.

"Do you think they'll go away on their own?" Charles asked.

"Let's hope so," Foster said. "Otherwise, we could be stuck here until someone comes looking for us."

CHAPTER FOURTEEN

Achilles came to a stop, his chest hitching from exertion. He looked to his left and then to his right. His soldiers had managed to stay close to him. It was admirable, because he had been running for several hours and had finally reached their destination. He stared at a sign. There were various symbols and letters on it. As he continued to study the sign, words began to form in his mind.

It said the Chauncey O. Simpson Memorial Rest Area, but he wasn't sure why he was able to understand the letters on the plaque. The more he thought about this unrealized skill, the more his head began to hurt. It was probably best not to try and use that ability again. Not unless he really had to. Achilles took in his surroundings. It was a quiet scene. There was nothing happening here. Achilles looked around slowly. From the looks of it, there hadn't been any activity at all in days.

There were a number of decaying bodies of Reapers killed at some point here. Of course, with the way things had played out, it wasn't like there was going to be anyone cleaning up after the gunfight anytime soon, either.

"Search," Achilles ordered. "Find any humans that are here and bring them to me."

"Yes, sir," the grunts answered as one.

He watched as a dozen of his soldiers spread out and began exploring. Achilles let out a low growl of frustration. It had been a complete waste of his time to come down here. Just like Haas had said it would be. And if he was being honest with himself, he had the same thought, too. A small voice in the back of his mind suggested it was a circle jerk. He wasn't sure what exactly it meant. Maybe it was getting sent to do something in a circle? Achilles dismissed the thought and began to walk slowly toward one of the buildings. He might as well help with the search. It might distract him from thinking about this fruitless journey.

A new voice in his head completely shattered his train of thought.

"Achilles, where are you?"

Achilles froze in mid-step. He felt his teeth clench and quickly forced his jaw to relax. *"Yes, my Lord,"* he replied in his mind.

"What's going on?" Beek asked. *"I want to know what you see."*

"We just arrived at the rest stop a few minutes ago," Achilles answered mentally. *"I have my warriors searching the grounds now. But it's very quiet. There doesn't appear to be any humans here."*

"Huh, maybe he retreated."

Achilles said nothing.

"Do you think you'll find anything?"

"We will do a complete search," Achilles said calmly.

"That's not what I asked you," Beeks said. *"What do you think you'll find?"*

"I don't believe we'll find any recent human activity here, my Lord," Achilles answered. He decided to take a small chance and hope his master would be agreeable. *"Shall we return back to the den?"*

"*No,*" Beeks answered. "*Do a complete search there, and make sure Foster and his group aren't hiding somewhere. After you're done, I want you to go back to the farm, where we encountered Foster before.*"

"*Are you sure, sir?*" Achilles asked hopefully. He really didn't want to do another long journey so soon. "*That's quite a distance away.*"

"*Do I sound like I'm not sure?*" Beeks challenged.

"*No, my Lord. It's just—*"

"*I didn't ask you to think, Achilles. I asked you to do.*"

"*Yes, my Lord,*" Achilles said. "*I'm sorry if I upset you.*"

"*Let me know the first sign of seeing Foster or any news you might have for me.*"

"*Of course, my Lord.*"

Achilles felt the connection break, and then Beeks was gone from his mind. A thought flashed into his mind, and he immediately dismissed it. He wasn't sure he could remember what a waste of time might be, but he had a feeling it was probably something like this.

Achilles looked down and saw his claws were digging into his hands. He forced himself to open his fists and watched as the cuts quickly healed up.

Backtracking to where Foster had been how many days before was likely another dead end. But it wasn't his place to argue with his master. And as long as he continued to follow orders and do what was expected of him, then Achilles was assured of staying in his master's good graces.

———

Beeks endlessly tapped his claws on the arm of his throne. He'd given out marching orders to several groups of fighters he recently sent out. He'd checked in with Achilles and was confident the Alpha would continue his needle-in-a-haystack search for Foster. Beeks' mind shifted to Angel. He needed to figure out what to do with her. He had mentioned going for a hunt, but she seemed strongly against the idea. Maybe she wasn't ready to spend time with him. Perhaps she needed to go with some of her pack mates instead.

That might work.

It could act like a form of shock therapy. Her primal instincts would kick in and take over, suppressing her old ways for good and introducing her to the preferred way of living as one of his flock. It was definitely worth a shot. Especially since he could dump the task onto his underlings to do.

"You," Beeks said, turning to one of his guards.

"Sir?" the guard said questioningly.

"I want you to bring me the new female."

The guard tilted his head to the side.

"Angel," Beeks growled. He made it a point to menacingly show his teeth. "Bring her here. Now."

The guard visibly gulped. "Of course, sir. Right away, Master." He spun around and scurried out of the room with his tail tucked between his legs.

Beeks waited until the minion had left the room to smile deeply. It was good to be the unquestioned master of his own domain.

————

Haas stalked toward the main street like a former human pissed off at the world. It was bad enough that he was on some fool's errand trying to find a group of humans. It was even worse that they had to move on foot to do it. A small, nagging voice in the back of his head kept telling him there was a form of transportation he could be using called an automobile.

But his instincts would override that voice each time,

telling him it wasn't the best way for him to pursue his prey. Of course, if he was being honest, he wasn't chasing after his own prey. He didn't know this Foster guy from any other human he might cross paths with. It was Beeks' prey. But like it or not, ever since he was forced to bend knee and submit, it meant that he was Beeks' personal bitch. And his new master's wishes had become his own.

Haas just couldn't understand why Horatio was so bent out of shape about a couple of humans. Beeks had millions of Reaper soldiers. What were a handful of humans in comparison?

A pack of his warriors were running toward him. They slowed to a stop, and two of his soldiers immediately dropped to one knee in front of him. The rest froze, unsure if they were required to bow to him like Beeks demanded.

Haas mentally dismissed the issue. He'd address it later. Right now he had more pressing matters than doing follow-up training with some of his warriors.

"Report," Haas said aloud. "And cut right to the chase."

"Sir, we don't understand."

"Of course you don't." Haas growled in displeasure. "Fine. Skip the formalities and tell me what I want to know."

"Oh, magnificent leader—"

"Where is this Foster?" Haas interrupted.

"We're not sure, sir," one of them stammered. "Fos-ter has eluded us."

"How?" Haas said. "Weren't you supposed to be looking for them?"

A soldier who had begun to speak whimpered in fear. A small yellow puddle began to form underneath them.

Haas felt a moment of disgust. "Get out of my face, you coward," he roared. "Do I have to do everything myself?"

"No, sir," another soldier answered. "Just tell me what you want us to do, and I'll make sure it happens."

Haas noticed the warrior was maintaining eye contact with him. Finally, one of his troops was showing a backbone. "Good," he said. "It's a couple of weakling humans. It shouldn't be too hard to find them in this flea ball town."

"We know where the other humans are."

"I don't care," Haas answered. He reached out mentally to his soldiers and projected an image into their heads. He watched several of his soldiers stiffen at his response. "This is what this Foster looks like. Find him. But do not attack. Tell me as soon as you see him or his people."

"Yes, sir," the soldiers answered together.

Haas flashed two more images in their minds. "These are the way they move about. They are called trucks."

"Rucks?"

"Close enough. You see them or Foster, tell me immediately."

The chorus of yips and growls sounded out.

"Dismissed," Haas said. "Don't disappoint me."

CHAPTER FIFTEEN

Beeks tapped impatiently on the arm of his throne. The guard still hadn't returned with Angel. He glanced at the nearby wall and realized there wasn't anything on there to signal how long he'd been waiting. He looked around his throne room. There wasn't a clock to be found on any of the walls. But then a clock was something that humans needed to worry about. And he was no longer one of them. He'd become something else. Something better.

Beeks let out a loud growl and heard a whimper from elsewhere in the room. He was tired of waiting. "Enough," he snarled. Beeks stood up and stormed out of his throne room.

He slowed his pace a little and walked carefully through his domain, watching quietly as his soldiers dropped to one knee and bowed in his presence. A few skittered away out of fear of facing their unquestioned leader. Beeks decided to let the lack of immediate respect being shown go for now. It was more important to him to check on the new addition to his family than discipline every minor infraction that may have happened along the way. With a growing family, he could spend every waking hour dealing with the petty crap and get absolutely nothing else done.

Beeks stopped outside a private dwelling. There wasn't any door there. None of the rooms in his domain had one for that matter. Something as simple as doorknobs had presented a puzzle that most of his minions had not been able to solve on their own. He'd discovered in talking with Haas that his soldiers had struggled with the same issue, too.

Haas. That was another one of his recent problems. He'd have to figure out how to get him to be more cooperative in a consistent manner. Beeks silently groaned. He was a mass murderer, not a manager. It wasn't that long ago people called him the Leola Butcher. He'd killed seven people before the police had finally caught him. Once in jail, he murdered four other inmates and hospitalized another seven others. Those men had been foolish enough to challenge his authority or had tried to kill him. But in this new world that he'd help create, he couldn't just kill everyone who didn't cooperate with him completely.

Beeks turned his attention back to the task at hand. He stepped into the room and saw Angel was sitting in the corner of the room. He immediately felt a wave of anger rush over him. He couldn't believe it. She was here in her room. So where the hell was the guard he sent to fetch her? The sheer incompetence was mind-boggling. When he caught up with the soldier he'd sent to retrieve Angel, that minion was going to wish he'd never been born.

He turned his attention back to the former pilot. Angel's back was toward the corner of the room and her legs were folded in front of her. Her arms were clasped around herself, as she rocked slowly to and fro.

A way of annoyance swept over him, and he fought to get it under control. "Angel, what's wrong?" Beeks said with what he hoped sounded like a caring voice.

"My head," she answered. "It won't stop hurting."

"You're hungry," Beeks said. "Have you tried any of the food that was offered?"

"I can't."

"Sure you can. It's meat."

"It doesn't taste right."

"If you don't want to eat what we are offering, then you need to hunt for your own prey."

"I-I'm not sure how."

"You need to feed," Beeks said gently. "Maybe you could go out with some others to go hunting."

"No," Vasquez growled. "Leave me alone."

Beeks did a double-take. How could this previously quiet creature show such a strong reaction?

"I could punish you, but I won't," Beeks said, choosing his words carefully, "because we're a family. I'm gonna give you some time to think about what you've said. And how you've been so disrespectful to your family and me. When I come back, I expect you to be ready to go."

He turned and left the room without waiting for her answer.

————

Angel waited for Beeks to leave the room. It had been a close call getting back before he arrived. Too damn close. It was pure luck that she'd overheard one of the guards asking another if they'd seen her, because they'd been ordered to retrieve her. That's all it took for her to realize that she couldn't risk being caught sneaking around right now. So she had carefully retraced her steps to her room. She'd made it with just a few minutes to spare before the leader of her so-called family showed up unannounced.

Angel silently scolded herself. She had to be more careful.

Because her gut feeling was things might go badly for her if she was caught wandering around without this Beeks character's blessing.

"General, do you have a report?" Vickers asked.

"Yes. Several Tier-1 operator reports have suggested that the armored Reapers—"

"You mean the more developed ones?"

"I suppose that's as good a way as any to describe them."

"Sorry I interrupted," Vickers said. "Please continue."

"Of course. The more developed Reapers will turn their bodies or curl up into a ball to absorb incoming damage."

"Using this armor like a shield?"

"Yes, that's right."

"That's not good."

"Indeed. Our men are reporting they are having a harder time killing these armored hostiles," Weindahl said. "There have been some reports of these Reapers rolling like a ball toward our troops before launching themselves airborne like a tiger pouncing on its waiting prey."

"Jesus. That thing would scare the shit out of me if I saw it coming my way."

"I'm sure most people would feel that way, Madam President," Weindahl said. "This development has definitely affected troop morale. But even so, it has created an opportunity for an effective counterattack."

"Really? Finally something that might pass as good news."

"If you say so, ma'am. They are still difficult to kill. But while the Reapers are rolling, they appear to be limited in their mobility. Several Tier-1 operators have been able to side-step the potential attack and execute a close-quarters counterstrike when the Reapers come to a stop and begin to return to a normal posture."

"Like a knife or sword strike?"

Weindahl chuckled lightly. "Perhaps on a TV show. Our operators are resorting to a simple shot to the head to eliminate the threat."

"What about their healing abilities for these things?"

"The normal Reapers? Or the more advanced ones? All types of Reapers do indeed have a highly-accelerated healing rate."

"Any difference between the two different types?"

"We're not sure," Weindahl admitted. "According to our preliminary research, the Reapers have an enhanced healing system. One that allows them to heal up to fifty times faster. A cut that takes two days to heal appears to heal in a matter of minutes. The same accelerated healing is also true for other types of wounds."

"Right," Vickers thought aloud. "If they heal that quickly, then it makes it even harder to kill them."

"Indeed. Which is why we've been forced to rely on head shots to kill them."

"What about the cop with the secret to killing these things?"

"Officer Foster?"

"Yeah, him. Anything new about him? Has he made it to Hope Island yet?"

Weindahl went ramrod stiff. "I believe it's still in the works."

"Uh-huh. I'm not sure I believe you."

"I'm not lying, Madam President."

"But you're not being completely honest, either," Vickers answered. "Rashced, what aren't you telling me?"

"Apparently, there was an issue with the boat they were going to use. They never got out of Rehoboth Beach."

"What the hell happened? And why am I just finding out?"

"Details have been admittedly slow in coming in."

"Well, that's the understatement of the day," Vickers said sarcastically. "Care to tell me how we found out there was a problem?"

"Apparently, SWAT Sergeant Black has a satellite phone."

"I'm surprised it wasn't confiscated by the Rangers when he landed on Hope Island."

"Indeed," Weindahl answered. "I suppose it's good that they didn't, because Officer Foster managed to call him on it and give him an update on their situation."

"And that update was?"

"It's challenging to say the least. They're dealing with a Reaper presence along with a group of humans who appear to be sympathetic to the monsters."

"You have got to be shitting me."

"I'm afraid I am not," Weindahl said. "Apparently these sympathizers have managed to convince the Reapers to protect them. The two groups have combined forces to take over almost the entire area surrounding Rehoboth Beach."

"So everywhere else the Reapers are killing humans left and right. And you're telling me that this one group of people have managed to tame them somehow. What the hell do they have? A magic bell that they ring?"

"We're not sure," Weindahl said. "We need to look into it."

"Perhaps it would be useful to capture some of those sympathizers and question them?"

"I'm afraid we have only the sketchiest intel on them."

"Does this Officer Foster have a plan?"

"Sergeant Black told Abrahams there's something in the works," Weindahl said, "but the lieutenant didn't provide any more details in his latest briefing."

"Well, he still is in our chain of command. So convince the good lieutenant to get us the full story. I'm tired of feeling like we're constantly operating in the dark."

"I'm afraid that's pretty much status quo these days in most parts of the country, Madam President," Weindahl said. "I will suggest to the lieutenant that he needs to determine if there's anything he can do to help Officer Foster out of his current predicament."

"Any update on Operation Poison Arrow?"

"It's still in the works."

"Care to elaborate?"

"We're moving needed assets into place. We're trying to identify some options to allow our soldiers to deploy the short-range missile strike safely. I believe I'll be able to provide a more detailed update in the near future."

"I look forward to hearing it, General," Vickers quipped. "Now, unless you have something else to discuss, I think we can wrap up this meeting."

"Nothing else at this time."

"Great, meeting is over," Vickers said. "Let me know if you have any new updates as soon as you get them."

CHAPTER SIXTEEN

The trip back to the marina had been surprisingly uneventful. Thanks to Walker's cautious driving, they didn't see a single Guardian patrol or Reaper pack along the way. It was almost as if both were looking busy looking elsewhere for them. Or maybe they were busy doing something normal instead of hunting around for used armbands. In either case, Walker was happy to take the break and avoid a battle while he could. He shifted the Land Cruiser into park and turned off the ignition.

"We should have taken the Tahoe," Sams spoke up. "This thing is burned."

"Thought about it," Walker answered. "But Foster and the other guys needed it for retrieving things from Gregory's house."

"Yeah, but we could have still lobbied for it."

"Nah. If we're lucky, we can swap this for something else we find. Besides, I feel better if we're the ones who have to deal with a Guardian checkpoint rather than the rest of the group."

"You say it like you're looking for trouble."

"More like expecting it and hoping to be proven wrong."

"This place is just creepy," Sams muttered. "I can't believe we're doing this."

Walker chuckled. "You volunteered. Remember?"

"No, I didn't. You volunteered both of us," Sams pointed out. "You're almost as bad as Foster with that volunteering shit."

"Really?"

"Almost as bad. There's still hope for you," Sams said. "The flatfoot is probably a lost cause."

"Uh-huh. We just need enough armbands to help us pass the patrols," Walker answered. "The way I see it, we got two choices. We can get them off the dead Guardians or go around robbing living ones."

"You're forgetting about the third choice."

"Oh, this ought to be good," Walker muttered.

"What's that?"

"I said, I'm sure it's quite good," Walker lied.

"Of course it's good," Sams replied. "I thought of it."

"You gonna share it or just brag about it?"

"Can't I do both?"

Walker shot him a look.

"You know, you can be a real killjoy sometimes."

"Can you get to the point before we're too old to remember it?"

"Fine. The third choice," Sams said. "We can just skip all this shit and sneak out of town in the middle of night instead."

"That's a good idea. One I might have fully endorsed in the past."

"But?"

"But we already looked for a clean exit path and couldn't find one."

"Except we looked during the day. It might be a lot easier at night. Especially if the Guardians are home sleeping."

"Uh-huh. What if they aren't?" Walker asked. "We don't know how many people they have in their group. It could be hundreds."

"It could be a handful, too. We did kill a good number of them at the marina."

"Even so, it might be nice to be able to talk our way past them without having to engage in another shootout."

"Yeah, maybe," Sams said. "Personally, I plan on keeping my rifle handy, just in case."

"Always," Walker said as he brought his rifle up into a ready position. "Come on, get this over with. This isn't exactly the highlight of my day or yours."

"If it is, then we need to start a new day, pronto," Sams said. He mirrored his friend's action and began scanning for potential hostiles. He said softly, "Moving out."

The two men slowly worked their way toward the marina. There had to be hundreds of dead Reapers and Guardians scattered everywhere with countless bullet casings mixed in between. Walker had taken care to park their vehicle far enough away that they could pull away without running over any debris on the road surface.

"Absolutely no cover here," Sams muttered softly. "I don't like this."

"Can't help it. At least it's just a snatch and grab," Walker replied. "We get in, grab what we need, and get out before anyone notices we're here."

"Speaking of grabbing, I don't see any rides worth taking. Most of these vehicles are smaller than your wallet."

"We have too many people and too many supplies to fit into an ordinary car," Walker said. "Besides, most of these vehicles are damaged. Nothing says stop and ask a bunch of questions to a security checkpoint than an SUV with bullet holes in it." He checked the area in front of him and moved forward carefully. The bodies, bullet casings, and random debris had created some very uneven terrain. With the way things had been going for them lately, he'd probably roll an ankle if he took a wrong step moving through this recent battlefield.

"See any armbands you like?" Sams said softly.

"Still looking. I'd prefer ones that aren't covered in blood," Walker answered in a low voice. "Less cleanup."

"I can't believe we didn't think to grab rubber gloves on any of our scavenging runs. I really do not like touching this stuff."

"I'll handle the bodies. You do overwatch."

"Are you sure?"

"Yeah. We've got some peroxide in the vehicle," Walker said. He pulled a white plastic kitchen trash bag out of his pants pocket and began to open it carefully. "I'll just use some of it to rinse my hands off afterwards."

"Copy that."

The two men shifted into a quiet rhythm. Walker worked his way through the dead Guardians, choosing the ones which appeared to have a clean armband still in place. He carefully removed each one and added them to the plastic trash bag.

———

Ten minutes later, Walker stood up slowly and stretched his back. "That should be enough armbands. Let's head back to the truck."

"Contact, ten o'clock," Sams said. "Six Reapers. I don't think they've seen us yet."

Walker quickly scanned the area around them. The nearest cover was the marina fence. The chain-link structure was partially collapsed and wouldn't offer any protection from Reaper eyesight.

"More incoming. Nine and twelve o'clock."

Walker risked a quick look. A midsize pack was closing onto their parked vehicle's location. There was no way he and Sams could reach it without a fight.

"Oh, shit. We've been spotted," Sams shouted. He immediately took two shots, shifted his aim, and fired twice more.

"How many?" Walker asked.

"Do you want me to count or shoot?"

"Good point," Walker admitted. He quickly scanned his field of fire. He was about to turn his attention elsewhere when three Reapers came bounding around the corner of a building. "Contact. Eleven o'clock," he announced.

Walker heard Sams begin to engage the incoming hostiles, and he turned his attention to his own looming threat. He sighted on the closest Reaper and fired. His aim was slightly off, and he saw the monster stumble as the shot struck it in the side of its shoulder. Walker exhaled quickly and adjusted his aim. He fired a double-tap and saw one of the shots slam the Reaper in the face. The creature staggered sideways, colliding with another pack member before it collapsed dead on the ground. Walker immediately fired another double-tap at the Reaper that was still trying to untangle itself from its now-dead brethren. He was rewarded for his quick thinking as both of his shots scored a direct hit to the monster's neck and jaw. He shifted his position and sighted on the lone remaining hostile. As he did, he saw five more Reapers bringing up the rear.

"Derrick," Walker said. "Got more incoming."

"Still busy," Sams yelled back. "Can you handle it, or do I need to shoot for you, too?"

"I got it," Walker answered back. "Just take care of your own hostiles."

"What the hell do you think I'm doing? Ordering a pizza?"

Walker turned his attention back to the Reapers charging in his direction. The five had increased to easily two dozen, and he began rapidly firing toward the closest ones.

"Reloading," Sams called out.

Walker shifted his aim toward Sams' side of the street, trying to buy his friend enough time to complete his ammo change. His eyes fell on a growing horde coming from that direction, and he unleashed a torrent of lead, cutting down the lead Reaper's legs. There was an immediate Reaper pileup as the still-charging monsters slammed into the back of the temporarily hobbled ones.

"Back online," Sams yelled.

Walker turned his attention back to his lane and continued firing. He wasn't sure how close he was to emptying his magazine, and he didn't want to run out of bullets at the wrong time. He decided to do a quick combat swap and keep track of his shots with the new magazine.

"Changing," Walker said. "Cover me." He began to execute a combat swap.

"What the hell?" Sams yelled. "You could have told me you had a shit ton of Reapers on your side."

Walker pulled the charging handle on his rifle and began firing again. "Back online," he said calmly.

"We're sitting ducks," Sams yelled. "We need to get out of here."

Walker risked a look to his right. *Bingo.* There was another street approximately three hundred yards away. A strip of retail stores lined the one side of the road.

"Two o'clock," Walker yelled back. "Group of stores. If we can get in one of them, we can use it as a bottleneck."

"And shoot them as they try to get through a door," Sams

said. "It'll be nice not having to worry about getting attacked from all sides."

"We get inside, scoot out the back of the building, and double back for the vehicle."

"That doesn't completely suck," Sams said. "As long as neither one of us runs out of ammo."

"Then move your ass already," Walker said. "And keep shooting."

The two men moved as one, moving and shooting as they worked their way toward the retail store strip. There were two different spots where new debris forced them to change direction and attempt to thread the proverbial needle between their attackers and getting cornered.

"Changing," Sams yelled.

"Covering," Walker answered.

"Back online. Last magazine left."

"I got three. Conserve your ammo, if you can."

There was an immediate decrease in firing as Sams shifted from firing three short bursts to selecting his targets. Walker scanned the battlefield in front of them as he continued to backtrack. He wasn't sure where the hell all of these Reapers were coming from. But it didn't matter. The two of them didn't have nearly enough bullets to kill all of the monsters.

CHAPTER SEVENTEEN

"This is unacceptable," Ezekiel said as he paced back and forth. "How hard can it be to find one man?"

He studied the group of men in front of him. Every single one of them was looking anywhere but at him. Well, except for Silas. The man was staring back at him with absolutely no sign of emotion registering. Ezekiel felt a chill run down his spine. The man was crazy. But his craziness was still useful to him. Even so, the Guardian leader staring that way at him was a bit unnerving. Ezekiel quickly looked away.

"But all I hear are excuses," Ezekiel continued. "You need to find Foster and his gang. These thugs are a danger to our community. A threat to our way of life. I don't care what you have to do to find them. I don't want to know what you do to end this threat, either."

"It's a lot of area to search," one of the Guardians stammered. "We need more people."

"Then find them," Ezekiel countered. "Ask for volunteers to join."

"It's not that easy," Silas said slowly. "It takes a certain kind of man to be a Guardian."

"What does that mean?"

"No cowards," Silas answered. "Knowing how to use a gun or weapon can be valuable, too."

"I'm sure you can find people who fit your needs. Start grassroots level."

Silas stared at him blankly.

"Ask your existing men to recommend someone," Ezekiel said. He tried to keep his voice from sounding as impatient as he felt. "Start with the candidates who are recommended the most and go from there."

"And if it's not enough?" Silas challenged. "What are you prepared to authorize? Maybe it's time to consider conscription."

"No, that's too drastic."

"If you say so."

"Yes, I do. I'll make an announcement at the next congregational address. But like you said, you don't just want people who can fog a mirror. They have to have a specific skill set."

"Okay, we'll do that for now." Silas nodded. "But you might want to start working on your 'it's time for a draft' speech in the meantime."

"That won't be a problem," Ezekiel said. "My words have never failed me. It's other people that have let me down again and again."

"Don't worry," Silas said. "We'll find Foster and drag his sorry ass back here."

"Good. I look forward to seeing him cowering in front of me," Ezekiel answered. "All of you are dismissed." He watched as the men moved as one toward the door, with Silas being the last one to leave. As the door closed, Ezekiel let out the breath he had been holding. He couldn't put his finger on it, but there was something creepy about Silas. But right now, Ezekiel needed him to run the Guardians. And that meant he needed to keep his worries to himself.

———

Silas waited until he closed the door behind him to speak.

"Boys, hold up a minute," he said. "I got something I wanna add to what the ol' preacher said."

The men stopped and looked at him expectedly.

"He's right. We need to find this guy Foster."

"We need more men," one of the Guardians mumbled. He quickly added, "Sir."

"Yeah, we do. And we'll get them. But we need something a bit more. Information. Put the word out. I'll give anyone who gives me a solid lead on Foster's whereabouts an extra day's worth of meals. Or a bottle of booze from his private stash." He motioned toward Ezekiel's still-closed office door.

"How are you going to get him to share his liquor?" one of the Guardians demanded. "He protects his stash like it's made out of gold."

"Let me worry about that," Silas said. "The sooner we find Foster, the better for all of us."

CHAPTER EIGHTEEN

Walker had lost all sense of time. When you were in the middle of a firefight, you had far more important things to worry about. Like not dying.

They had been shooting and retreating one step at a time. Dozens of Reapers lay dead or dying everywhere, but the monsters were still coming at them. It was getting darker, and soon they would lose what remained of the natural sunlight. Once that happened, the odds would shift dramatically in favor of the Reapers.

He heard Sams shouting, and that snapped him back to the present moment.

"What?" Walker asked.

"I said, I'm switching to pistol," Sams shouted. "Is this the store?"

"Yeah. Get that door open," Walker answered. "I'll cover you."

Sams took a step back and then slammed his foot against the door jamb. There was a loud crack as the wood gave way and the door slammed open.

"I'm in." Sams darted inside, scanning for any viable threats as he proceeded forward.

Walker followed his friend immediately, firing as he moved. A pair of Reapers leapt toward him, and he scrambled backwards to get out of their path. The monsters slammed into the door frame and landed hard into the doorway. Walker immediately fired a single shot into one Reaper's head and then shot the second creature in the ear before it could attempt to get back to its feet.

"Get the door," Sams yelled.

Walker grabbed the door and began pushing it shut. The door stopped short of latching, and a moment later there was something else pushing back.

"Derrick," he called out. "Hurry."

There was a loud crash behind him, and then he saw Sams was pushing a small desk toward him. He stole a glance and saw they were in some type of office furniture store. Walker waited until his friend had almost pushed the furniture into him before he moved out of the way. The desk slid against the door, and there was an immediate counter-push from the Reapers outside.

"Need something heavier," Walker said. He spotted a medium-size bookcase nearby. "Help me move that quickly."

The two men moved in tandem to grab and haul the furniture back toward the entrance and shoved it against the already moving desk.

Walker put his hands on the wooden furniture. "It's not heavy enough to hold," he said between breaths.

"Yeah, on it," Sams said. He rushed over to the next book-shelf, gave it an experimental shove. The half-empty unit moved a few inches. Sams moved to the side of the bookshelf and began pushing toward the door. Walker watched as his friend moved the furniture over to him before helping him shove it against the previous one.

"You're moving the next one," Sams gasped. "This sucker is heavy."

Walker sprang into action and grabbed several nearby reception area chairs. He tossed them onto the desk, building their barricade even higher.

"My turn," Sams ordered. "Watch the front."

Walker nodded once, grateful for the chance to grab a few heaving breaths. He turned his attention to their makeshift barricade.

A Reaper slammed its body into one of the storefront windows. There was a loud bang, and a hairline fracture in the glass began to form.

"We're out of time," Walker shouted. He grabbed one of his remaining rifle magazines and offered it to Sams. "Let's move out."

Sams grabbed the offered ammo and did a fast magazine swap. "I was afraid you were going to say that. I'll take point. You take care of any assholes that manage to get in."

"Done," Walker answered. "Find us a way out."

Walker watched as his friend moved toward the back of the store. He mentally counted to two and then followed. The light in the store quickly shifted into darkness, and Walker switched the light on his rifle. Sams was nowhere in sight.

"Derrick?" he called out softly.

There was a loud sound of glass breaking. Walker strained to pinpoint the direction of the noise. A loud growl sounded from the same direction. Then a second and a third.

"Possible breach," Walker hissed. "Where the hell are you?"

"Over here," a voice called softly. "Hurry."

Walker hustled toward the direction of the voice. *There.* A hallway with a sharp ninety-degree turn to the right. It would help to funnel their pursuers into an easy-to-defend firing lane. Walker hauled ass for the opening. As he rounded the corner, a door suddenly opened next to him. A pair of hands grabbed his backpack and yanked him off-balance. Walker felt himself stumble, and then someone yanked him into the darkness.

CHAPTER NINETEEN

"*Yes, what is it?*" Haas said. He set down the freshly killed bird he had been eating. The dead creature was small and somewhat pitiful looking. A little voice in the back of his head said it was just a snack, and he silently agreed.

"*My Lord, we have found him. The one you call Foster.*"

"*Are you sure?*" Haas asked. He didn't want to chase after a bad lead. Quite frankly, he'd gotten enough of them from Beeks to fill the quota for a lifetime.

"*Yes. The humans used the same motorized cart that you described.*"

"*Show me.*"

"*What? I-I'm not sure.*"

"*Your eyes,*" Haas said. "*Use them, and show me what you see.*"

"*How do I—*"

"*Hold still.*" Haas growled. He mentally grabbed the mind of the soldier reporting. He felt the creature's brain stiffen under his somewhat rough embrace. He eased back his pressure slightly. The soldier was of no use to him dead. He slowly searched the minion's memories, looking for what the loyal follower had seen.

"Dark truck. Excellent, I'm on my way. Do not let any of the humans leave the house until I get there."

"Yes, Master."

Haas released his hold on the creature's mind and began running. He had several blocks to cover in order to reach Foster's reported location. He picked up the pace and silently hoped the human didn't try to leave before Haas reached him.

———

Gerald hunkered down behind the SUV. He adjusted the armband on his left arm nervously and then pulled a walkie-talkie off his hip. He stared at it like it might come alive and try to eat his face. He'd become a Guardian for one reason. It was supposed to be an easier job than working any of the available blue-collar jobs. Except the job had completely changed lately. Now he had people shooting at him, which scared the absolute shit out of him. His old boss, Walter, had understood he wasn't much of a fighter. But Walter was dead now. And the new guy? Silas was certifiably nuts. It was only a matter of time before he got somebody killed. If he was lucky, he'd be able to avoid trouble with his new boss. And one way to do that was to be the guy who found Foster. That was sure to score points in his favor. Gerald had a hunch on where Foster's gang might be hiding out. He'd been on his way home last night and saw a light briefly on the second floor of a retail store. At the time, he hadn't thought it was anything. But the idea kept nagging him. So today he decided to park a block away and approach the stores on foot. Sure enough, there were some unfamiliar vehicles behind the buildings. Which struck him as odd because all those businesses had been closed by Ezekiel's order after they were deemed unessential for the church's needs.

As soon as Gerald saw the vehicles and people coming in and out of the buildings, he'd quietly retreated to his Guardian-issued truck. It had to be Foster and his gang. Nobody else would be crazy enough to move into an area that wasn't protected by the Guardians. That was just asking to be eaten by the Reapers.

Gerald shook uncontrollably. He really didn't want to report what he'd discovered. He'd heard Foster was dangerous. The guy had to be, having killed Walter and a bunch of other Guardians in the marina shootout. The scuttlebutt among the boys was that Foster had single-handedly slaughtered dozens of Reapers there, too. Gerald felt his heart race even faster. He definitely didn't want to cross swords with the guy. It seemed like an easy way to end up dead. It was near the end of his shift. Maybe he could just make his report and then go home, where it was quiet and safe.

"Guardian Central, please come in," the man said.

"This is Central. Who is this?"

"Gerald."

"You're supposed to use your call sign. Patrol Six. Remember?"

"Right. Sorry. It's just I was on my way home and spotted some people matching the description of our watch list."

"How sure?"

"Pretty sure. I saw a bunch of men and women go in. The men left, but the rest of their group didn't."

A new voice came across the walkie-talkie.

"This is Silas," the voice said. "What's your position?"

Gerald pressed the transmit button on his walkie-talkie and gave his location.

"I want you to stay there and watch the location," Silas ordered. "Report any more activity you see."

"For how long? I'm supposed to be on my way home."

"Do I sound like I care about your social life?"

"No, sir. Not at all."

"Stay where you are until I get there. If anyone else goes in or comes out, call it in. Got it?"

"Y-yes, sir."

Gerald released the transmit button on his walkie-talkie and slowly returned it to his hip. His hands were shaking uncontrollably, and he stuffed them in his pockets in an attempt to control them. Knowing that Silas was coming to his location scared him. Because he had a feeling that once his boss showed up, it wasn't going to be safe to be here.

CHAPTER TWENTY

Almost immediately, Walker began trying to regain his balance. He managed to get one foot planted, pivoted toward his attacker, and threw his shoulder toward them. The point of his shoulder struck home, driving the assailant into the nearby wall. Walker drew his knife, bringing the weapon up to strike. As he did, he saw he was holding a scrawny elderly woman against the wall and stopped short of driving his blade into her neck. He let his eyes run up and down her figure. There weren't any visible weapons on her body.

"Shhh," she whispered. "They'll hear."

"Who the hell are you?" Walker replied.

"A friend. Don't worry, I won't hurt you. Or the other one."

"You surprised me," Walker said as he slowly began to return the knife to its protective sheath. Who was this strange woman? And why was she here in this dark corridor with him?

"It's not safe to be here," the woman said, "Come with me. My husband and I have a safe place nearby."

"Nick," Sams' voice hissed from the hallway.

"Here," Walker said. He added in a low voice, "Got a new friendly."

Sams came around the corner, shining his light. The woman reflexively brought her hand up to cover her eyes.

"Walker, what the hell?"

"They're coming. They're coming," the woman said. "We need to hurry."

"She's got a place for us to hole up," Walker said. "At least till these things pass."

"Sure that's a good idea?" Sams asked.

"Sure it's not?" Walker countered.

"You think we should take a look and see what we got?"

"Bingo."

"Head on a swivel?"

"Uh-huh," Walker answered. "First sign of trouble, we eliminate the threat."

The two men began to follow the woman. She moved down the hallway back to the next intersection, stopped to look back at them, waiting for them to reach her, then headed to the left. The next intersection, she did the same thing, except this time moving to the right. She carefully moved a floor-to-ceiling curtain, revealing a set of stairs. She began moving down them, not waiting to see if the men were still following her.

Walker proceeded down the stairs carefully. As he reached the below ground level, he noticed there was debris everywhere in the new corridor. Walker carefully used the light on his rifle to light their way and avoid stepping on something that could cause him to turn an ankle. He followed the woman through three more turns before they reached a grate in the wall.

"In here. In here," the woman urged. "I'll close it behind you."

"How about you lead the way, and we'll close it behind

us?" Walker suggested. "That thing looks awfully heavy."

"Suit yourself," the woman snarled. "Just be careful of my Nelson, okay? He gets nervous around strangers."

"Gotcha," Walker said. He flashed a quick look at Sams and saw his friend give a quick nod. Both men were definitely keeping an eye out for two people now. One in plain sight and another one who might be hidden. Walker slowed his pace slightly and began actively scanning the area ahead. He'd be damned if he would let his guard down now and get jumped by surprise again. If someone was foolish enough to try attacking him, then Walker wouldn't hesitate this time. He'd be ready to act with overwhelming violence.

———

Walker stepped into the room, taking care to keep the strange woman in front of him. He began to slowly shine his rifle light around the room. As he did, he panned by one object in the corner and panned back. There was a visibly dead man propped up in a chair. From the blood splatter on the wall behind him and the revolver lying on the floor below his outstretched hand, Foster could only guess the elderly man had taken his life. He glanced at the body again. There was a bandage crudely wrapped around the man's forearm. A large amount of dried blood was visible on its exterior.

"Be a dear, and push those boxes back," she said. "It helps hide us from those things."

Walker looked at a stack of boxes near the doorway. The three boxes didn't look like they'd cover much of anything. They probably wouldn't stop much more than a toddler charging into the room, either. He decided to play along and keep the stranger on friendly terms. "Of course," he said quickly. He effortlessly slid the boxes in front of the entrance.

"Nelson, we've got company," the woman said. "What's

that? Nelson, don't be rude. They seem like very nice young men."

Sams looked at Walker with a knowing look. Walker nodded once, acknowledging that there was definitely something off about their host.

"How long have you and...?" Walker asked. He dragged the question out to avoid calling the dead man by the wrong name. If this woman was as emotionally unstable as Walker suspected, then he didn't want to risk triggering her anger and creating a new threat.

"Nelson. He's my husband. We've been married thirty-four years."

"I see. How long have you and Nelson been down here?"

"Not long. Not long. A week, maybe two."

"I see. Is Nelson okay?" Sams asked carefully. "He looks a little under the weather."

"He's fine. He's fine. Don't talk that way about my Nelson."

"Sorry, ma'am, my friend didn't mean anything by it," Walker said. "I think he saw the bandage on your husband's arm and was a bit concerned that he might be hurt."

"Nelson is fine. One of those things broke into our home. Managed to bite him. But my man's not a whiner. Didn't scream out or cry when it happened. Just shot that thing in the head."

Walker stole a quick glance at the dead body. The late Nelson might not have been a complainer, but he'd obviously realized he was infected and opted to end his life before he turned. "Fair enough," he said in what he hoped was a calming voice. "I'm sorry, ma'am, I didn't catch your name."

"It's Tina."

"Right. Okay, Tina," Sams said slowly. "You know, we probably should be heading back soon. The girls will be worried about us."

"Girls? There are others?"

"Not far from here," Walker said. "We help keep them safe. Like you do for your husband."

"Oh no, Nelson is the one who protects me," Tina said. "I feel so safe with him here. If any of those things got in here, I just know he would shoot them."

"I see," Walker said.

"It's not safe to go back right now. You need to wait."

"Gotcha."

"Tell you what," Sams said. "My friend and I are going to take up guard duty here by the door. Make sure that none of those things try to come in here, okay?"

"You wouldn't try and rob an old couple, would you?"

"Not at all," Sams said. "We're former military, ma'am."

"Uh-huh," the woman said suspiciously. "Where's your uniforms?"

"Former," Sams said. "We don't have to wear a uniform anymore."

"What's that?" Tina said. She cocked her head to the side, like she was listening to someone. "Nelson said there's a lot of people who claim to be in the army and are lying. 'Specially with what's going on out there."

"I'm afraid I don't have any identification with me, ma'am," Sams said. "I left it with my other belongings with my friends."

"Uh-huh," Tina said and crossed her arms in front of her. "If you say so."

"What my friend is trying to say is that we were both in the Army," Walker said. "Retired with honors and are now ordinary citizens. So we don't wear our Army unis anymore."

"Well, Nelson thinks we need to keep a close eye on you two," Tina replied. "You two just stay over there, all right? We'll wait for those things to go by, then we'll talk."

CHAPTER TWENTY-ONE

The sun was starting to rise as the Hummer pulled up to the shopping strip, drove past it, and stopped about a block away. The passenger door opened, and Silas slid out and began moving. He heard several car doors slam behind him and knew without looking back that the rest of his men were now following him.

Silas stalked toward his scout, who was partially hiding behind a parked vehicle. He watched as the visibly tired man froze in place with a terrified look on his face.

"I want an update," Silas demanded. "Has anyone left?"

"N-no," Gerald stammered.

"Are you sure?" Silas asked.

"Pretty sure," the guy said. "I ain't seen anybody leave..."

"You mean you haven't seen anybody leave?"

"Yes, that's right," the man stammered.

"Great," Silas said. "All right, you are coming with us."

"What? Why?"

"Because I said so," Silas sneered. "Or are you challenging my authority?"

"No, not at all, sir," the man stammered. "It's just I've been here all night watching the place. I really could use—"

"Suck it up, buttercup," Silas interrupted. "We had two vehicles being repaired last night, and I needed to let the rest of the boys get some sleep. Plus, we don't have any those fancy SEAL night thingies."

"Night-vision goggles?" Gerald offered.

"Yeah. None of those things," Silas answered. "How many people are up there?"

"Two women. I think they might have a few kids there, too."

"There you go again," Silas answered. "I don't want to hear what you think. I want to hear what you know."

"Four people," Gerald answered quickly. "No men."

"Good." Silas looked around. There were five soldiers with him now, counting the nervous scout. "This should be easy. Let's go collect these women and kids. They should know where this Foster guy is. We do this right, and he'll be able to get home to the old ball and chain." He pointed his thumb toward Gerald, and the man quickly looked at the ground. Silas felt a burst of glee, knowing he'd embarrassed the man. Served him right for being so pussy-whipped.

"Let's do this, boys," Silas said. "Gerald knows what these people look like, so he's going to lead the way."

"But sir, I'm not sure I should," Gerald protested. "I've been up all night. and—"

"Get a move on, buttercup," Silas said. "We don't got all day."

The man groaned in protest and began to move cautiously toward the strip mall with the rest of the Guardians following a few steps behind.

————

"Did you get any sleep last night?" Amanda asked. "You look exhausted."

"Not much," Lizzy admitted. "None of the guys made it home last night."

"Wait, what?"

"I haven't heard anything from them. I even tried calling Nick twice."

"And?"

"He didn't answer."

"There's probably a good explanation," Amanda replied. "Maybe they had to keep the radios quiet because of Reapers near them or something."

"Yeah, maybe."

"Don't worry," Amanda said. "They'll probably call when they're on their way back."

"I don't know. Something just doesn't feel right," Lizzy said as she paced back and forth. "We were supposed to get out of here already."

"You worry too much," Amanda said. "Look, we'll just leave once the rest of the group returns."

"I guess. I hope they're all right. Heck, I hope we're still safe here, too."

"Don't worry," Amanda said. "We set up the broken glass on the steps like your husband suggested. If anybody besides them comes up the stairs, we'll hear them. The kids are being quiet. You might as well take a load off your feet before you wear a hole in the floor pacing."

"I'm not wearing a hole in the floor. I'm—"

Suddenly, there was a loud crunch nearby.

"Did you hear that?" Lizzy hissed.

"Of course I heard it," Amanda whispered back. "It came from the stairs."

A male voice, heavy with a Southern twang, called out.

"That was clever, ladies. How about you come down here, and let's talk? Nobody needs to get hurt."

"Great," Lizzy whispered. "Now what do we do?"

"Emily!" Amanda shouted.

"What?" the teenager said, popping her head around the open doorway.

"Here, take this." Amanda shoved the walkie-talkie toward her. "I need you to get a hold of your uncle or Lizzy's husband. I don't care which one. Tell them we need their help. They need to get back here right away."

"OK. Got it."

"Oh, and Emily?"

"Yeah?" She popped her head back in the room.

"Close the door behind you and lock it. Keep Henry and you in there. Don't come out unless one of us tells you it's safe."

The teenager visibly went pale and nodded her head quickly before disappearing out of sight.

"The guys are going to need time to get here," Lizzy said.

"I know," Amanda said. "We need to stall."

"Do you want to do the talking or not?"

"I'll try to stall them. See if you can find a good spot to shoot from."

"Wait. Shoot from?" Lizzy asked. "Are you serious?"

"Right now, these guys think they've got a bunch of helpless women and children up here," Amanda said. "We might have to prove that they're wrong."

———

They had managed to get partway up when Gerald stepped on a bunch of broken glass and announced their presence.

That damn numbskull, Silas thought to himself. He had been tempted to shoot the man just out of a general principle. But the guy was more useful alive than dead right now, and that had stayed Silas's temper. Counting the numbskull, Silas had five shooters to overpower two women and a couple of kids. The odds were definitely in his favor.

Even so, Silas made sure he was safely behind solid cover before calling out, "That was clever, ladies. How about you come down here, and let's talk? Nobody needs to get hurt."

There was nothing but silence. Silas mentally counted to ten and then yelled, "Ladies. We've just come to talk. Why don't you bring the kids and come on down here?" he said. He glanced at the men. He said in a low voice, "Any sign of trouble, I want you guys to open fire. You hear me?"

"You want us to shoot women and kids?" Gerald protested. "Why?"

"Have you been paying attention, boy?" Silas said. He shifted into a deliberately mocking voice. "This is the apocalypse. A woman or child is just as likely to shoot you dead as a grown man."

Gerald looked down at his feet quietly and said nothing.

"Like I said, they start shooting," Silas continued, "I fully expect you boys to unload on their asses."

A mix of yesses and mumbled acknowledgements sounded out.

"Go away. We don't want no trouble," a female voice called out.

"Well, we don't want any trouble either, sugar," Silas said. "We just want to talk. That's all."

"So talk," a female voice said. "And don't call me sugar!"

"My apologies, ma'am," Silas said. He shook his head in disbelief. For someone who was only minutes from getting gunned down, this woman had some nerve. He took a slow, deep breath, plastered a fake smile on his face, and shouted, "Well, what shall I call you?"

"How about the woman that wants you to leave her and her friends alone?"

"See, I can't do that," Silas yelled. "It seems that some of your friends killed a bunch of my boss's friends. And now my boss would like to talk to them."

"I don't know what you're talking about," the woman's voice shouted back. "We didn't kill anybody."

"I don't believe you!"

"Believe what you want," the woman shouted back. "We're telling you the truth."

Silas turned to one of the other men and asked, "Any other way up there?"

"I-I think so..."

"Well, go find out," Silas growled. "I want you back here with an answer in three minutes."

"Y-yes, sir," the man stammered and then rushed out the door.

"Why don't you save us all of a bunch of trouble and come down here," Silas called out. "We just wanna talk."

"I don't think so. You stay where you're at, and we'll stay right here."

"I prefer talking face to face," Silas said. "I'll tell you what. I'll give you five minutes to think about it. And then I'll ask you what you wanna do."

Silas looked at his men and grinned. As soon as his man came back and told him there was another way upstairs, he was sending his Guardians to collect this mouthy little bitch and her friends. And once she was cowering in front of him, he'd find out where the rest of their group was hiding.

CHAPTER TWENTY-TWO

It had been a few hours since Walker last heard any sounds of nearby activity. He turned to Sams and said, "I think we're in the clear."

"Took long enough," Sams grumbled. "I feel like we've been here all night."

"I think we were."

"Great. The girls are going to be worried sick," Sams replied. "I promised your wife that I'd bring you back safe."

"You haven't failed yet."

"Uh-huh. So how do you want to handle breaking the news to Tina and her kind-of-dead husband?"

"As peacefully as possible."

"Fine with me," Sams said, "I'll follow your lead."

Walker carefully cleared his throat to draw Tina's attention. He waited until she turned to look at him before saying, "Ma'am. My friend and I are going to get going."

"Already?" Tina protested. "It's been so long since we had company."

"I understand, but I'm sure my wife is probably worried

sick about us," Walker said. "You know how your husband protects you? Well, I do the same for mine."

"Why don't you bring her back here? We can have a nice visit together."

"Perhaps we will."

"Couldn't you stay a little longer? It's been nice to have someone else here to talk to besides Nelson," Tina said. She leaned forward and whispered, "He's never been much of a talker."

"I'm not, either," Walker said gently. "Would you and Nelson like to come with us instead?'"

"No, no, no," Tina said. A look of panic came across her face. "It's not safe out there. Those things are wandering around out there. Nope. Nelson and I are staying right here, and there's nothing that nobody can say to change our minds."

"I understand," Walker said. "Thank you for your hospitality."

"What's that, Nelson?" the woman said. She cocked her head to the side as if she was listening intently. "He said, 'You're always welcome to come back.' I agree."

"Thank you," Walker answered. He paused for a moment, then reached into his backpack and pulled out a pair of armbands. "These are for you and Nelson."

"I don't understand," the woman said slowly as she accepted the gift. She looked toward her late husband and cocked her head sideways. "Nelson says he doesn't, either."

"The local church wears them. For some reason, those monsters won't attack anyone who is wearing them," Walker said carefully. "If the two of you put them on, they should keep you safe."

"What's that? Nelson says I should take them," Tina said. She snatched them out of Walker's offered hand and pulled them close to her chest. "T-thank you."

"You're welcome. If the two of you decide to leave here, just make sure you're wearing the armbands," Walker said. "And head to the Disciples of the Divine church. They have food and clean beds there."

"Nelson? Did you hear that? What's that? You want to think about it? Okay, if you say so."

"Would you like us to take you there?" Walker asked. "It's on our way."

"Nick, what are you talking about? That's the last place—" Sams blurted. A look of realization spread across his face, and he quickly added, "Unless we take that other route. Then we would be going right past the church. So yeah, like Nick said. It would be no trouble at all for us to escort you there."

"That's okay." Tina smiled. "We know where the church is. Maybe we'll go there."

"Okay, be safe," Walker said. "And thank you for your help."

"Okay, okay, okay. Nelson says good-bye, too." The woman turned her back to them, signaling she was done talking.

"I'll lead us out," Sams whispered.

"Right," Walker said. He saw Sams carefully move the boxes away from the entrance, step out, and turn on his light and begin sweeping in a forward pattern, looking for any potential hostiles.

Walker stepped through and pulled the boxes back in place behind him and hurried to catch up to his friend. He wasn't sure what had happened with the woman, but it was obvious that she was suffering from some psychotic break. He tried to reason with her to leave with them, but she had resisted his help. Walker said a quick, silent prayer that she would take their advice and head to the Disciples of the Divine church. The Disciples may be trying to hurt him and his friends, but his gut feeling was they weren't completely evil. If Tina arrived at their doorstep, he was

sure they would do the right thing and offer her a safe
haven.

CHAPTER TWENTY-THREE

Sams and Walker had managed to carefully work their way back to the Land Cruiser. To their surprise, no one had disturbed their ride, and the vehicle started up immediately without incident. With Walker behind the wheel, the two men made their way away from the marina.

"Where to?" Sams said. "Back to the hideout?"

"More or less," Walker said. "Let's take a different route. See if there's any suitable trucks or SUVs that we can grab."

"Needle in a haystack, buddy. The Guardians have confiscated lots of vehicles. The ones they've left behind were disabled. At least, that's what we've seen so far."

"I know," Walker said. "But I've got a feeling we'll get lucky."

"We might have used up the last of our luck. Need I remind you that we were just rescued by a lady who was not all there and her dead husband."

"That was a lucky break. It kept us from getting overrun by Reapers," Walker answered. "When you're neck deep in hay, you might as well keep looking for that golden needle."

"What the hell are you talking about?"

"I mean, we got nothing to lose by trying to find another ride. Foster got lucky. We might, too."

"Well, why didn't you just say that?" Sams said. "Just drop the woo-woo talk and get to the point already."

"Woo-woo?"

The walkie-talkie came alive. "Mr. Walker, Mr. Walker, are you there?" a young voice called out.

Walker looked at Sams and frowned. "Any idea who that is?" he asked.

"Charles's niece?" Sams answered. "Emily. Right?"

"Yeah. It can't be good if she's calling," Walker said. He picked up the walkie-talkie and said, "Go for Walker."

"I-I'm sorry. I'm trying to reach Lizzy's husband?" the female voice said.

"This is he," Walker said. "Who is this?"

"It's Emily. There are some men who just showed up. Amanda told me to call you and say that we need your help."

"We're ten to fifteen minutes out," Sam said. "We might not make it in time."

"We'll make it in five," Walker said. The engine immediately revved higher, and the Land Cruiser began accelerating. He cued the walkie-talkie and said, "Tell Amanda we're on our way. She needs to stall them as long as possible."

———

By his rough estimate, more than three minutes had passed, and Silas was getting pissed. They were still waiting at the bottom of the staircase, and Silas was no closer to knowing if there was another way they could attack Foster's group. There was a noise behind him, and Silas turned toward it. He watched as his scout came into view, stopping on the landing. The man immediately bent over, panting and out of breath.

"You're late," Silas blurted. "You better have a good reason."

"Sorry."

"Well?" Silas demanded. "What did you find?"

"The other way is barricaded," the man said between deep breaths. "No way to get through without making a whole lot of noise."

"You can't move it?"

"I tried. It's too much for me to move by myself. Sorry, boss."

"Damn it," Silas said. "All right, it looks like we're going up the stairs."

"Are you kidding?" Gerald protested.

"Do I sound like I am?" Silas challenged. "But since you can't keep your big mouth under control, you can go first."

"No way," Gerald said. "I ain't doing it."

"What?" Silas said.

"I can't just go shoot a bunch of women and children. That ain't right. And you better believe, when I get back, I'm gonna tell Ezekiel—"

Silas immediately drew his gun and fired. A hole suddenly appeared in the middle of Gerald's forehead, and the man dropped lifelessly to the floor.

"Anybody else have any doubts? Or wanna go tattle to Ezekiel?" Silas said, looking at the four remaining men. He looked at each one, daring them to make eye contact. Each man made a point of looking away. "That's what I thought. Now, if you boys can get your head out of your asses, we've got a mission to complete."

"What was that?" a woman's voice called out.

"None of your business," Silas hollered.

"It sounded like gunfire," the woman yelled back.

"Listen, sweet lips." Silas shot up the stairs. "I'm sick and tired of waiting for you to come down here. Now maybe you

don't want to bring those children with you. That's all right
with me. The brats will probably make so much noise, you
and I would have trouble talking. So how about you come
down here instead?"

"How about you go fuck yourself?" the woman answered.

Silas lost his cool. "Girl, I am done fooling with you. I'm
going to count to five, and then you're going to be sorry that
you back-talked me." Silas began counting down. When he
reached zero, he gestured for his men to charge up the stairs.

———

"You shouldn't have told him to go fuck himself," Lizzy
scolded. "That's just going to make him mad."

"I guess." Amanda sighed softly. "But the guy sounds like a
total asshole. I mean, 'sweet lips'? Who the hell talks that way
to a woman?"

"Shit, they're coming," Lizzy said. "Get ready!" She got
into a comfortable shooting position, hugging the doorframe.
After all the hours spent at the firing range with her husband,
the Glock felt completely comfortable in her hands. She
glanced across and saw Amanda had taken up a similar nearby
position. As the first man's head and shoulders appeared
above the stairs, Lizzy aimed her Glock, sighted on the man's
head, and shot once.

The gun reported loudly, and the man tumbled backward
down the stairs and out of sight. A loud grunt and the sound
of a collision further down the stairs. A second man appeared,
and Lizzy fired twice. The first shot missed, second one
tagging the man high in the shoulder, twisting his body to the
left. A second gun sounded out nearby, and Lizzy's ear began
to ring. She saw the bullet slam into the top of the man's
head, and his head snapped backward. He dropped face-first
onto the stairs. A barrage of bullets came flying back in

response, and Lizzy crouched down, trying to make herself as small as possible. She looked over at her friend Amanda and saw she was just as scared as Lizzy felt.

"Wait. Wait for them to reload, and fire!" Lizzy yelled back to Amanda. She saw her friend nod once and looked toward the stairs again. Lizzy heard more footsteps, waited. A hat began to appear and Lizzy eagerly fired, knocking the hat off. The man immediately dropped down the stairs, scooting backward.

Lizzy silently swore at herself. If Nick were here, he'd scold her for being too eager. She should have waited until the man presented himself more fully in her view. More bullets continued to fly, and she crouched down as low as she could. She could only hope that they could hold their position until Nick or Sams made it back to help them.

———

Beeks had been taking a nap on his throne when he heard a noise in the hallway. He sat up in time to see the guard he'd tasked to fetch Angel had finally returned. This time, he had brought two warriors with him. The three of them were forcibly dragging Angel into the throne room.

"Let me go," she screeched.

The guards dropped her unceremoniously in the middle of the room.

Beeks looked at the soldiers quizzically. "I asked you to bring her here. Care to explain why it took you so long to complete such a simple task?"

"Master, she wasn't in her room," the guard answered. "It took us a while to find out where she had run away to."

"I was walking around." Angel growled. "And these thugs grabbed me—"

"Shut up," Beeks interrupted.

"You have no right to talk to me that—"

"I said *shut up!*" Beeks roared. "When you are in my presence, you will show me the proper respect. Including knowing when you should speak. Now, kneel."

"No," Angel snarled back. "I kneel before no one."

"I said, kneel," Beeks growled. He reached out and grabbed her mind mentally, beginning to apply pressure. Beeks watched as her face slowly squinted in pain.

Angel reached out with one hand to her head, then the other, clutching her own skull. A low groan came out of her mouth, and she started to rock on her feet.

"I don't want to hurt you," Beeks warned. "Kneel before your master."

Two of the guards stepped forward, grabbing Angel by the shoulders and forcing her down onto one knee. She resisted at first, and then Beeks applied a little more pressure until he felt her mind begin to submit. The third guard pushed her head forward so that she was staring at the floor.

"Excellent," Beeks said. "You will learn. I am your King. You will do as I say, just like everyone in your family obeys. Do you understand me?"

Angel said nothing.

"I said, do you understand me?" Beeks roared.

"Yes," Angel said grudgingly.

"Good. I am sending you on a hunt."

"I don't want to go hunting."

"Fine. You'll go on a mission instead."

"A mission?" Angel's head popped up as she made eye contact with Beeks. Her head tilted instinctively to the side out of curiosity.

"Interesting," Beeks thought to himself. *"Her old memories recognize the word. Maybe I can use that to my advantage."*

"Yes, a mission," Beeks continued. "There is a group of hostiles who have taken up arms against our family."

"Go on," Angel said.

"They are nearby in a fortified structure," Beeks said. "I'm sending you with some of your pack mates to investigate."

"And do what?"

"Well, to talk with them, of course," Beeks said, with the most convincing smile he could muster. "If they won't listen to reason, then follow your pack mates' lead on how to best handle it. Do you understand what I ask of you?"

"Yes."

"Will you obey me?"

Angel said nothing and looked away.

Beeks reached out telepathically, grasped her mind, and squeezed it once forcibly. "I said, will you obey me?"

"All right," she yelped.

Beeks watched as Angel rubbed the sides of her skull. He paused a moment for dramatic effect before saying, "Excellent. Go with them, and make your family proud."

CHAPTER TWENTY-FOUR

Foster had moved away from the attic floor entrance, but it hadn't seemed to make much of a difference on the Reaper activity below them. The monsters had spent the entire night moving beneath them. At some point, the men had taken two-hour shifts of sleeping and keeping watch.

Even now, the Reapers were still making noise. But it had somehow escalated in the last fifteen minutes. Now it sounded like something was slamming into a wall. Based on how crazed he'd seen the monsters could get, he wouldn't put it past them that they were trying to knock down the fucking walls and bring the attic crashing down to the second floor.

The good news was the attic was mostly finished with wood flooring and drywall. The space seemed to be fairly well ventilated so they wouldn't need to worry about heat stroke while being trapped here. There was some natural lighting provided by a skylight that Gregory informed him had come with the house. The bad news was there didn't appear to be working electricity in the room. Foster wasn't sure if it was something as simple as a tripped circuit breaker. But he wasn't about to try going through an unknown number of Reapers below them to reach the basement and find out.

Despite the weak lighting, he had managed to reload both of his weapons and take some loose ammo he had in his vest to top off his magazines. He glanced over toward the opposite side of the attic. Gregory was there, frantically talking into the walkie-talkie. From the gestures he was making, Foster wasn't sure it was going well. He watched the man lower the walkie-talkie and come back slowly toward them.

"Problem?" Foster asked.

"You could say that," Gregory answered. "Gun shop's under attack."

"What?"

"Amanda and Lizzy are holding out. Nick and Sams are on their way back to assist."

"Reapers?" Charles asked.

"Guardians," Gregory said. "They must've found their location somehow."

"So we're on our own," Charles said softly. "There's nobody who can help us right now."

"Don't worry, we've been in worse situations," Foster answered. "Can I get my light back?"

"Sure," Gregory said. He handed the Eotech M914 vision monocular back.

Foster took the night-vision optic and began to slowly pan around the attic, taking a closer look than he had before. He was hoping he'd see something with the monocular that he'd overlooked before. As he scanned the room, Foster noticed most of the space had been renovated with wood flooring and drywall installed.

"You redo the attic yourself?" Foster asked.

"Previous owner," Gregory replied. "He was turning this space into a home office when he lost his job. It didn't take long for him to get behind on the mortgage. Eventually, he sold this place to my wife and me."

"I think you did him a kindness," Charles said. "You paid his asking price. He was able to avoid foreclosure. Perhaps even financial ruin."

"Yeah, I guess," Gregory said. "I always meant to finish this space, but never got around to it. There's always been more months than money to do things."

"That's true for most people," Foster admitted. His eyes stopped on the cedar chest once more. "What's in the chest?" he asked.

"Some old blankets. My wife stuck them up here when the kids grew tired of them. I probably should get rid of them. But it's one of those things. You get busy with other stuff and just getting through the daily grind. And those little minor things just get pushed off to the next day and then the next. And before you know it, you completely forget about doing that little chore."

"I think it's safe to say you've had bigger fish to fry until now," Foster quipped. As he slowly worked his way in a circle around the space, he passed one corner of the house with the light playing tricks with the shadows, then brought the light back. There was something in that corner, but he wasn't sure what. He took two careful steps toward it, trying to place his feet to make sure he didn't miss a step, then shined the light back in a corner.

"What's the black cord?" Foster asked as he pointed to a black cable in the corner.

"Oh, that's for the satellite dish. We got Direct TV in the house."

"Uh-huh," Foster said. "So where's the dish?"

"Well, on the roof, of course. Where else would you put it?"

Foster followed the black cord up the wall until his eyes stopped on where the cord exited the roof next to the large skylight in the middle of the ceiling. A plan began to quickly form in his mind. "Maybe we're not stuck here after all," he said slowly. "I think I've got a way to get us out of here."

———

Thirty minutes later, Foster had a clear plan formed. He'd already gone over it twice with Gregory and Charles. Even so, he was a little nervous that both men would remember and execute their parts correctly.

"Okay, I think we're ready," Foster said. "Are you both clear on what you need to do?"

"Of course," Gregory answered. "When we hear things go boom and the Reapers run out to check it, we head right for the truck and don't stop for anything."

"Good," Foster answered. "Who's driving?"

"My dad," Gregory said. "I'll cover him."

"Good, protect each other. A few minutes from now, we should all be in the Tahoe."

"I guess," Gregory answered. "I still think we could all go out the skylight."

"I thought of that," Foster said. "The problem is getting all of us off the roof without drawing attention. Don't worry. My plan will work."

"I think it will," Charles said. He nervously clenched and unclenched his hands.

"I'm ready," Foster answered. "Just take your time."

"Don't worry," Gregory answered. "I'll help my dad to the exit and then come back to help you."

Foster watched the two men move into position by the attic's folding steps. The Reaper activity had calmed down somewhat below them, but it was obvious the monsters were still in the vicinity.

Foster glanced back at the desk they had positioned directly under the skylight. They had stacked two chairs and the cedar chest on top of it, forming an impromptu pyramid that Foster had already climbed up. There was still a little bit of glass from breaking out the skylight. Gregory had initially objected to the idea of busting up a perfectly good skylight in his own home. But once Foster pointed out that they hadn't been able to raise anyone to help them on the radio all night and why he needed to get up onto the roof, the man had reluctantly agreed.

Hopefully he didn't get cut when he climbed through onto the roof. He patted his pocket to make sure the Gerber Gear was still there. It had been a great find in his recent scavenging efforts. He'd need it for the next step of his plan.

Gregory handed him a folded blanket. Foster accepted it and draped it across the frame of the broken skylight. He carefully pulled himself up and onto the roof, feeling his body armor brush against the blanket. Foster climbed onto the roof and did a quick check of his body. There was a new tear in his sleeve, but that was it. He said a silent prayer of thanks that he hadn't gotten cut by any glass shards.

"You all right?" Gregory called from below.

"Yeah. Toss the rope, please."

Foster saw the handmade rope sail up through the opening and grabbed it before it could fall back down.

"Got it," he answered.

Foster glanced at the rope. It was composed of several blankets they had found in the cedar chest. Hopefully, it would be strong enough for what he had planned.

Foster took a quick look around him. The Reapers were still gathered by the back door and a few by the car. He worked his way over to the satellite dish. It was time for stage two of his plan.

———

"Are you guys in position?" Foster asked over the comms. He carefully pushed the screwdriver back into his Gerber Gear and put it back in his pocket. Once again, the multi-tool had been a difference maker. The satellite dish was now lying by his feet with its base still attached to the roof. He had tied one end of the homemade rope to the dish's base. The metal structure appeared to be bolted securely to the roof.

"Yes," Gregory answered. "Just waiting for your signal."

"Got it," Foster said. "Starting now." He picked up the detached satellite dish. The pure metal dish was large, but still lightweight. He picked it up and turned in the opposite direction from where Charles and Gregory were going to need to exit. Foster reared back and threw the dish like a frisbee off the house. He watched as the metal disc spun through the air. The metal object sailed downward until it impacted a nearby parked car with a loud bang. Almost immediately, the car's alarm began sounding off. Foster watched as the Reapers began to move toward the noise. One Reaper rushed toward it. Then two more appeared. Then five. And suddenly there were two dozen monsters surrounding the vehicle, trying to get into it. Foster grabbed the homemade rope and gave it a final tug. It still felt secure. He hustled toward the edge of the roof. He was counting on the other men getting to the truck safely. It would do him no good to get off the roof and not have the vehicle to get into. Foster dropped the rope over the side of the house and began descending. Something groaned above him, and he moved down a bit quicker. It was a gamble that the blankets would hold his weight without tearing. But from the sound of things, the satellite's base might come out of the roof first. As he worked his way downward, the rope didn't reach completely to the ground. He slowly climbed down to the end of the blanket rope and let his body hang as far as he could, and then released his grip. As his feet hit the ground, Foster bent his knees and immediately tucked and rolled to help break his fall.

He came up looking around him. There was a sound of gunfire nearby, and he drew his rifle and rushed toward it. There were a handful of Reapers still around the truck, and he saw his friends were in the midst of battle with them.

Foster sighted on a Reaper. The monster hadn't seen him yet, and Foster seized the opportunity. He fired once, striking the monster in the back of the head. There was an immediate exit of brain matter from the front of its head, and the Reaper immediately dropped face-first onto the ground. He adjusted his aim, sighting on another monster that still didn't realize its peer was dead. Foster fired once more, scoring another kill shot.

A third Reaper, hearing the new gunfire, turned toward, him. The creature let out a growl and Foster fired a double-tap, striking the monster in the neck and in the cheek. The Reaper did a pirouette of death before collapsing onto the ground, lifeless.

"Get in the truck!" Foster shouted. He continued to fire, working his way there. He saw Gregory climb into the back of the Tahoe and worked his way to the passenger door. Two Reapers were left in the immediate vicinity, and Foster fired quickly, killing one and wounding the other. A loud roar sounded out nearby, and a dozen Reapers came rushing back around the corner. Foster opened the door to the Tahoe, jumped in, and slammed the door behind him, immediately engaging the door locks. "Drive, drive, drive!" he shouted. He felt the Tahoe surge forward. A moment later, two Reapers slammed into the back of the SUV, and the vehicle shook on its frame momentarily before gaining speed and beginning to distance itself from the oncoming horde of monsters.

"Damn, that was close," Gregory said.

"Too close," Charles said. "Back to the gun shop?"

"Absolutely," Foster said. "Now, let's go make sure the girls and kids are okay."

CHAPTER TWENTY-FIVE

For nearly two decades, Haas had lifted heavy weights. Especially in prison, where being bigger and stronger than most men granted you additional respect. At his previous best, he had been stronger than an ox, but couldn't run more than a few blocks before needing to stop for a breather. Like many hardcore weightlifters, he had always despised doing any form of cardio, too.

But all of that changed with his transformation. It was amazing the things he could ask of his body now. He had just run from one end of town to the other, a long distance that his mind or his mindset called miles, and he hardly felt winded. He pulled up to a stop in front of a trio of Reapers. And as he did, each one chose to look down or away instead of making eye contact with him. "What's wrong?" he asked.

"Sir, I'm sorry to report the human Foster and his friends managed to elude us."

"What? Was my order not clear?" Haas growled. "I told you not to let them leave."

"They were, sir. It's just the humans—"

"Yes?" Haas interrupted.

"They were armed. We lost many of our pack mates trying to stop them."

"This is unacceptable," Haas said as his voice gradually rose in volume. "You had several dozen pack mates, and you failed to stop two humans."

"I-it was actually three of them."

"I don't care." Haas snarled.

A series of low whimpers sounded from the soldiers.

"You disappoint me," Haas said. He reached out and mentally touched all of their minds. He gave a small squeeze to each one of them. The minions grabbed their heads as one and dropped to the ground in pain. He immediately released the hold. He wanted them motivated, not dead. Dead soldiers were of no use to him right now. Not when he still needed to find this damn human and his friends.

"Get up," he hissed. "Find the humans, or next time I will not be so forgiving."

"Yes, sir." The soldiers scrambled to their feet and scattered in different directions.

Haas sighed. He didn't know which way Foster and his group went. He doubted his soldiers did, either. They were damn near back at square one. Hopefully, he'd find a new lead before Beeks contacted him again. Because the last thing he wanted to do was give that overbearing asshole any more bad news.

———

Silas was furious. These women were quickly becoming a serious pain in his ass. Two of his men had been gunned down trying to charge up the stairs. A third one lay at the base of the stairs, bleeding from a light scalp wound where a bullet likely grazed him. The bullet wound in the man's leg was much more serious. The poor schmuck caught a bullet ricocheting in the firefight. Of course, it didn't really matter to Silas how the man got shot. Based on the growing pool of blood underneath the man, Silas doubted the guy was going to live. He watched unemotionally as his lone uninjured shooter was trying to stanch the blood flow of his injured squad mate.

"Leave him," Silas said. "He's only going to slow us down. It's time for us to leave."

"But—"

Silas raised his gun and pointed it at the protesting man's face. "I just gave you an order. You can leave with me or die where you stand. Your choice."

The protesting man glared back at him. He released his hold on the injured Guardian and stepped away from them.

"Good choice. Head to the truck now," Silas said. "Keys are above the driver's visor. I'll be right behind you."

Silas watched the man move past him. He waited until the Guardian stepped out the door before moving in the same direction. If anyone was going to get shot by Foster's gang, it would be the man in front of him. It was better that way. In his mind, the men were replaceable, and Silas wasn't.

———

Walker brought the Land Cruiser to a screeching halt behind the retail center. He cut the engine and leapt out of the SUV.

"Wait for me," Sams called out.

Walker didn't pause one bit and charged into the building. He spotted a downed hostile clutching a bloody leg. The man moaned softly, and Walker came to a sudden stop. He brought his rifle up to finish the injured Guardian. As he did, he heard Sams shouting behind him.

"I got him," Sams yelled. "He's unarmed. Go check on the rest of the group."

Walker moved around the wounded man and then took the steps two at a time, racing up toward the second floor.

"Lizzy!" Walker shouted as he moved up them.

"We're okay," his wife called back.

Walker charged into the room and grabbed his wife, lifting her up into a strong embrace.

"Oof. It's okay, Nick," she murmured. "We're all okay."

"Amanda," Sams called out. "I got an injured hostile. I could use your help."

"Why don't you just, you know, end him?" Emily asked.

"Information," Sams answered. "I want to know how these assholes found us. And anything else they can tell us." He turned his attention to the man lying on the floor. *"Comprende, amigo?"*

"Yeah," the man answered with gritted teeth. "I understand."

"Amanda?" Sams called out. "I need your help."

"I'm on my way," the doctor said as she began to descend the staircase. She took one look at the downed man and added, "I'm going to need everybody except Lizzy to give me space to look at this guy."

"You got him, Derrick?" Walker said.

"Oh, yeah," Sams answered. "Me and wounded doggy here have an understanding. Our doctor is coming down to look at your leg. You even look at her cross-eyed, and I'll shoot you between your eyes. Nod your head if you understand me."

The injured man nodded his head very slowly. "I'll cooperate."

Sams heard someone coming down the stairs and stole a quick glance. Walker and Amanda were heading in his direction. "Good," he said. "Glad to hear that, *amigo*. You wouldn't lie to me, would you?"

"I'm not lying," the man said. He laid his head back down on the floor. "No reason to."

Sams slid over a step to let Walker pass by him. The former Ranger stopped and stared at the injured Guardian.

"Uh-huh. You act up, and I'll turn you over to this guy," Sams said. He gestured toward Walker with his head. "His wife was one of the people you were busy shooting at."

The man glanced toward Walker, saw the visibly pissed-off former Ranger, and gulped deeply. "No tricks. I swear."

Amanda glanced at Sams, hovering near the downed man. There were about six inches of open space for her to work in. "Guys, I need some room to be able to look at his leg," she said softly.

"Walker," Sams answered. "You want me to stay with our new friend or set up a perimeter guard?"

"He's not our friend," Walker said. "I'll take perimeter." He bent over, scooping up the injured man's gun before stepping back outside.

———

Amanda quickly scanned the Guardian lying on the floor in front of her. There was a growing pool of blood under the wounded man. She moved to stanch the blood slowly leaking out of his leg.

"Are you hurt anywhere else?" Amanda asked.

"Just my leg," the man answered. "I can move over if you need more room."

"No. Stay put," Amanda said. "I need to see how bad you're hurt."

"I'll try," he answered. He stiffened in pain as the doctor began poking inside the bullet wound. "Sorry," he mumbled.

Amanda began to examine the man's leg. "No exit wound. The bullet is probably still in your leg," she said. "I think it nicked an artery."

"Can you save him?" Lizzy asked.

"I don't know," Amanda muttered through clenched teeth. "He's lost a lot of blood already."

The man moaned aloud and jerked at Amanda's touch.

"Emily," Lizzy called out. "See if you can find a blanket or some towels."

"Okay, will do," the teenager answered back.

"Hold still," Amanda scolded. "I'm trying to save your life."

"Why did you attack us?" Lizzy demanded.

"Not now, Lizzy," Amanda said. "I need him to stay calm."

"I-it's okay," the man said in a low tone. "I don't mind."

Lizzy flashed a knowing look at her friend before turning her attention back to the wounded man. "I'm Lizzy. This woman trying to save your life is Amanda."

"Larry," the man said softly. "Sorry we had to meet like this."

"Larry, why did you attack us?" Lizzy asked. "We have children upstairs."

"I-I didn't know. Silas. He made us. Said you were dangerous. That you were with some guy named Foster, who had killed a bunch of our people."

"Silas?"

"He's new. In charge of the Guardians. Not like the old leader."

"How so?"

"Walter was reasonable. Tough, but fair."

"And Silas?"

"He's no Walter."

"Can he be reasoned with?" Lizzy asked. "We have supplies we could trade. We're just asking that they let us leave the city."

Larry let out a low chuckle and immediately winced in pain. "That was a mistake. Hurts too much to laugh."

"Sorry. I'll try not to do that again," Lizzy said. "You were telling me about Silas."

"Yeah. He's fucking nuts. Dangerous. The rest of the guys are afraid of him. When you started shooting at us, one of the other guys got scared and tried to run away. Silas gunned him down like he was a rabid dog. Told the rest of us he'd kill anybody else who tried to leave."

Lizzy glanced at her friend. From the look on the doctor's face, she was feeling the same thing. This Silas person was definitely a threat to their group.

"I'm cold," Larry said.

"Dammit. He's bleeding internally," Amanda muttered. "Larry, stay with me."

"Don't lie to me, Doc," the man said softly. "I'm not going to make it, am I?"

"I'm not giving up on you," Amanda answered. "Come on, stay with me, Larry."

"We found you...because of your truck," Larry said. His voice was almost in a whisper now. "Silas won't stop. He'll be back. You need to get those kids and get out of here."

Emily returned with a ratty-looking blanket. "That's all I could find."

"Thanks," Lizzy said. "Can you check on Henry and make sure he's okay?"

Emily glanced at the still bleeding man on the floor, nodded once, and retreated from the room.

Lizzy waited until the teenager was out of sight before she took the blanket. She carefully draped it across the wounded man's torso and side, avoiding the area where Amanda was still working feverishly. Lizzy glanced at Larry's face. The man was deathly pale and his breathing was extremely shallow.

"I mean it," Larry said. "You need to get those kids out of Rehoboth. Silas won't hesitate to kill any of you."

"We're working on it," Lizzy said. "We need a vehicle."

Larry gave a weak smile. "I can help."

"Come on, Larry, stay with me," Amanda said. "Can somebody get me some more bandages?"

"Keys in my left front pocket. They're for my brother's place. It's the only yellow house on Fieldcrest Drive. I was house-sitting for him while he was on vacation. He's got a Suburban. Silas doesn't know about it. None of them do. It was my backup plan in case things really went to shit."

"Larry, you don't have to—"

"It's the least I can do. You all have been good to me, even though you have every reason not to. Just get them kids and you out of here. Okay?"

"Okay, Larry, we'll do that," Amanda said. "Just hold on. I'm losing him."

The man nodded once quietly. His chest hitched twice, and then he went still.

"He's gone," Amanda said softly. She stood up slowly and stepped away from the dead man.

Lizzy shifted the blanket to cover his face and torso.

Walker stepped back into the building.

"Foster, Charles, and Gregory are a few minutes out," Walker said. He glanced at the covered body and then turned his attention to the rest of the group. "Why don't the rest of you head upstairs, and I'll let you know when they get here?" He turned and stepped back outside before anyone else could answer. There was nothing he could do for the dead Guardian. He had nothing else to do but wait for the remainder of his group to arrive. And make sure no one else got another chance to harm his friends.

CHAPTER TWENTY-SIX

Despite the recent firefight, Foster gathered the group above the gun shop once more.

"This is a really bad idea," Sams said. "We need to get our shit and get out of here. This guy, Silas, sounds crazy."

"We're only staying here temporarily. Let me see if I have this straight," Foster said. "One of Silas's men told you about a vehicle that the Guardians didn't know about."

"Yes," Amanda said. "We have a key ring here," Amanda said, holding up a fob with a car key and what looked to be a house key attached on the ring.

"Do we know where it is?"

"Larry, that's the Guardian who gave us the tip, said it was the yellow house on Fieldcrest Drive."

"This is crazy," Sams answered. "This guy was shooting at us and then had a sudden change of heart? I don't buy it. For all we know, he could be sending us to Silas's headquarters."

"I don't think so," Amanda answered. "He sounded like he was trying to make amends before he died."

"Well, he was busy dying," Sams pointed out. "It might

have been hard for him to gather his last thoughts together. Or maybe his brain wasn't working right, and he told us the wrong place by mistake."

"Even if he did, we still need to check this lead out," Foster answered. "Otherwise we're looking at having to use the Chevy Tahoe I found and our old Land Cruiser."

"Which is a hell of a risk. The Guardians already know about the Land Cruiser," Walker pointed out. "They'll be on the lookout for it if we try to leave town. Derrick and I took a chance using it to go retrieve the armbands. But there's no guarantee we'll get lucky and avoid detection again."

"So do we stay or go?" Amanda asked. "Because I'm not feeling safe here anymore."

"Sams is right. It's not safe here," Walker said. "It's only a matter of time until Silas brings even more men back to storm this place."

"We're not ready," Foster said. "And we're not sure this other place is secure, either."

"Secure? Hell, we don't know a thing about this new place at all," Sams pointed out. "It could be a trap."

"You really think Larry would have set us up?" Amanda demanded. "The man was dying."

"You don't?" Sams countered. "It would be the perfect screw-over."

"Okay, settle down," Foster interrupted. He made a calming gesture with his hands. "Fighting with each other isn't going to solve the problem."

Sams looked away, and Amanda glared at him in response.

"Look, I got an idea." Foster grabbed the piece of paper, looked at the keys, and wrote the address down. "This is the address. Everybody memorize it or write it down. I'll go check it out and see if the place is secure and if the Suburban is there. Once I can confirm the coast is clear, I'll call it in and everybody will move to that location. We'll use it as our temporary base until we're ready to leave."

"The idea doesn't totally suck," Sams admitted.

Foster took a deep breath and then continued. "I can go on my own, but I'd probably go faster to clear the place and check the vehicles for possible booby traps if someone else comes with me."

"No offense, Malcolm," Walker said, "but with what shit just happened, there is no way in hell I'm leaving my wife here alone."

"I'll do it," Sams said. "And before any of you ladies object, I had basic munitions training in the Army. I know what to look for in terms of possible booby traps."

"Oh, so now you're a bomb expert too?" Lizzy quipped. "Why am I not surprised?"

"Nope," Sams answered quickly. "Never claimed to be. But I suspect I know more about rigging tripwires and booby traps than most of the people in this room. Just like you know more about medicine than I ever will."

"Good point," Lizzy said. "Sorry, Derrick. I'm still a little rattled by the Guardian attack here."

Sams nodded in acknowledgment and turned his attention to giving his rifle a once-over.

"All right, that works," Foster said. "In the event the location isn't secure, we might still be able to collect supplies. What do we still need?"

"It's only a matter of time before somebody else shows up," Walker said. "I say we take what we got and get the hell out of town as soon as it's dark."

"Except we don't have a clear way out of town," Sams reminded them. "Short of shooting our way out. Or creating some kind of distraction like an explosion."

"Any idea where we might get some explosives?" Foster

asked. "Because I don't think the Guardians are going to let us into a sporting goods store to grab any Tannerite."

"Probably not," Sams said. "Seeing that we snuck into one and killed a bunch of Reapers last time, I doubt we'll get a chance to do it again."

"There was some construction happening not far from here," Gregory blurted out.

"Really?" Walker asked. "What can you tell us about it?"

"Not much, really," Gregory admitted. "They're supposed to do some demolition soon. Well, they were, before all this happened. I bet we could sneak in there, grab some explosives, and get out."

Walker's eyebrows shot up. "You know how to handle explosives?"

"Not really," Gregory answered. "But as long as there's no detonator connected to it, we should be in the clear. Am I right?"

"Depends on the type of explosive," Walker said. "No offense, man, but I don't think it's a good idea to ask a bunch of civilians who've never handled explosives before to go scavenge them."

"What about some type of homemade device?" Charles asked. "Is it possible to use some household products to create something?"

"We could probably scavenge what we need," Sams said carefully, "but we'd need to take the time to find the right materials and to make an explosive device."

"And time is the one thing we don't have a lot of right now," Foster said. "Let's table the distraction idea for now. Where are we at in terms of supplies?"

"Need more silver bullets and food," Sams said.

"You guys haven't turned up much in the way of medical supplies," Amanda pointed out. "We really need more bandages, antibiotics, and pain meds."

"I might have a lead on that for us," Gregory said. "There's a veterinary clinic not far from here. I doubt there's anybody in there."

"You mean besides a bunch of hungry, starving animals?" Sams answered. "I hate to say it but if they're not dead, then it's only a matter of time before a pack of Reapers goes in there to feed on them."

"Maybe not," Gregory said. "This place wasn't very busy. The owner was planning to retire before the end of this year."

"So he may not have had many animals in there," Lizzy said excitedly. "But I'm sure he still has the basic medical supplies. Like bandages. They might have antibiotics, too."

"I bet they do," Foster said. "They use antibiotics like erythromycin and tetracycline for animals, too."

"I'll need somebody to go with me," Gregory said. "Any volunteers?"

"I'd like to go," Charles said. "We don't need to clean the place out. We just need to find enough to take with us. If we happen to run into one of the staff there, perhaps I can barter with them."

"That could work," Foster admitted. "Which vehicle do you want to take?"

Gregory scratched his head as he thought for a moment. "I heard what you said about the Land Cruiser being known. But I think my dad and I could be all right to use it. The clinic is a few blocks from here. If we get stopped by a Guardian patrol, we can always play dumb and say we found it."

"Are you sure?" Foster asked. "Derrick and I are better prepared for a potential confrontation if one comes up."

"The ladies said the Guardians are looking for you," Gregory pointed out. "If you get stopped in a vehicle they know to look for, then there's going to be trouble."

"The kid has a point," Sams said. "Like it or not, Foster is top of their most wanted list."

Charles smiled. "Don't worry, Malcolm, we'll be fine."

"Let me see you out," Foster said. He walked the two men out to the car. "Are you sure you two will be okay?" he said. "I'll go with you or I could send Sams with you, if you want."

"We'll be fine," Charles said with a smile. "We can always use the bartering idea if we need it."

"Fair enough. If you have any trouble, you don't hesitate to call," Foster said. "You got me?"

"Of course," Charles said. "Don't worry, we'll be fine. We should be back in an hour or two."

The two men got into the Land Cruiser. Charles turned the ignition, and the vehicle started right up. He gave a quick wave to Foster, put the vehicle on drive, and pulled away from the retail strip.

———

The Reaper moved cautiously behind a row of bushes. His master had told him it was important not to be seen by any humans, and he took care to stay hidden. He looked cautiously and saw three humans standing near a vehicle. He saw two of them get into it, and a moment later there was a loud noise which made him flinch. As the motorized cart pulled away, he saw one man standing alone. The human then turned and went back into the building.

"Sir, I think I have found them," he said mentally to his commander.

"Who?" Haas said.

"The one they call Fos-ter. He was meeting with two other humans who have left. I believe he's alone now. Shall I attack him?"

"No. I want you to follow the other humans."

"But, sir, I thought we were supposed to find Fos-ter."

"You did," Haas said mentally. *"You've told me where he is. But I doubt he is alone."*

"I don't understand. I saw Fos-ter. He was alone after the others left in the loud machine."

"There could be more inside the building that you can't see. Forget about Foster for now. I want to know where the other ones are going."

"Of course, sir."

"I will send other warriors to your current location to watch Foster and keep an eye on him," Haas answered. *"But I want you to find out where the other humans are going."*

"I must hurry, then. They're near the end of the road."

"Do it," Haas ordered. *"Report to me when they have stopped and gotten out of the vehicle."*

"I follow and obey your command, sir."

————

A few blocks later, the Land Cruiser pulled to a stop, and Charles put it in park before turning off the engine. The parking lot for the veterinarian's office looked completely abandoned, and despite no one being there for several days, there were a large amount of leaves and trash scattered throughout the parking lot.

"This place could use a serious cleaning," Gregory complained.

"This is good," Charles said. "It means most have probably ignored this place."

"Good point, Dad." Gregory said. "Let's go in and get what we need."

The two men disembarked from the vehicle and walked towards the building. Gregory tested the front door and found the knob locked.

"Let's try the back, shall we?" Charles suggested.

The two men worked their way around the back of the building. The door lay on the ground, facedown and broken.

"Looks like we won't need to break in," Gregory quipped. "Someone else already did it for us."

"Yes," Charles said. "But we should still be cautious going inside."

The two men worked their way into the building. All the animal cages were opened, and nothing was in sight. It appeared that someone had released any animals that were in the veterinarian's care. When, at some point, Charles had no idea. He softly said, "This place is so quiet."

"Feels weird," Gregory said. "A little spooky, even."

"I was thinking something along the same lines," Charles said. "At least we don't have to worry about any animals having starved to death in the office. Any ideas where they would keep the medication or the bandages?"

"There would be some bandages in each treatment room. But there's probably some type of central pharmacy for the medications."

"Amanda said medicine is a top priority," Charles said. "Let's start looking for those first."

The two men worked their way through the building till they reached an area that looked like what they were looking for. Some of the cabinets had been broken open, and there were pills and debris scattered everywhere. Whoever had looted this place had shown no regard for anyone who might follow after them.

"What a mess," Gregory mumbled.

"I agree," Charles answered. "Let's put anything we want to take with us over on that counter. Make it easier to pack up when we're done. Anything that ends in a -cine is probably an antibiotic."

"Like tetracycline?"

"Yes, that's right. If you see anything that says antibiotics or pain reliever on the packaging, then we should take those, too. We can let the ladies tell us what they are once we get back to base."

"Seems kind of wasteful."

"Perhaps."

There was a loud crunch of glass being stepped on nearby.

"Wait," Gregory hissed. "Did you hear that?"

"Shhh," Charles whispered. He moved and closed the door they had come through, then retreated to the center of the room.

————

The Reaper stood panting heavily. He'd had to run very fast to catch up with the humans in their loud machine. Fortunately, they hadn't noticed him before they entered the building that he was currently watching. He had moved over to a large viewing portal and seen them moving around inside. He retreated before they saw him and reached out mentally to his master. As he stepped back, there was a loud crunch under his foot. He felt a small pain and paused long enough to remove some sharp material sticking out of the bottom of his foot. It had taken longer to remove the offending item than for his appendage to self-heal.

He retreated behind a nearby row of bushes. It was time to make his report. He was surprised when his leader answered immediately.

"Yes?" Haas answered.

"*Sir, I have news for you. The humans have stopped and gone inside a structure.*"

"*Show me,*" Haas ordered.

The soldier stood still and stared toward the building in front of him.

"*I know this place,*" Haas said. "*It is near us. Wait there. Observe, but do not engage.*"

"*As you command, Master. But sir, what should I do then?*"

"*Wait for us to arrive and join you. If they leave, I want you to follow them without being seen.*"

"*Yes, sir,*" the soldier replied simply, turning his attention back to watching the building. He felt a brief burst of pleasure, knowing he had pleased his master.

CHAPTER TWENTY-SEVEN

"Malcolm, you got a minute?" Lizzy asked.

"What's on your mind?" Foster said.

Lizzy cleared her throat before continuing. "Are you sure we're going to get to Hope Island?"

"You don't think we can get out of town?"

"No, not that."

"So you're worried Black won't come through?"

"You have to admit it's a possibility," Lizzy answered. "We're counting on him being able to convince the powers that be to send a plane or helicopter to come get us."

"I'm confident that Black will come through."

"And if he doesn't?"

"We're just going to have to wing it and hope for the best."

"You're kidding," Lizzy exclaimed. "That's your plan?"

"I'm not sure what other realistic options we have right now," Foster admitted. "We're in a beach resort town. The ocean is to our east. Without a boat and someone who knows how to navigate the open waters, that's not a good option. If we head south, we're going to head deeper into Disciple territory and move farther away from our intended destination. If we head north toward Philly, there's a good chance we could run into a lot more Reapers."

"What about to the west?"

"Already considered it," Foster said. "Nick said that's where there's a heavy amount of Guardian and Reaper patrols."

"All right, I'll admit, those options don't sound very promising," Lizzy answered. "But what would help improve the chances of the military sending a plane or helicopter to us?"

"Besides what we've already promised to share with them?" Foster asked. "I'm not sure."

"Well, what if we made it a safer pickup? There's a few airports in Delaware. Maybe they could pick us up from one of them. If we pick one that is far enough away from Rehoboth Beach, then the Disciples won't be an issue."

"It's possible. But to be honest, the larger airports have probably been run over by the Reapers."

"Really?"

"Sure. Take Dover Air Force Base," Foster said. "It's a military installation. It wouldn't surprise me in the least if they got attacked by the Reapers at some point."

Lizzy chuckled. "Sounds like a death wish. We have the largest military in the world."

"I'm not sure how much that might matter against these things. No disrespect to any of our armed forces, but the Reapers aren't easy to kill."

"Unless you have silver bullets."

"Right. But I don't think they know about the Reapers' weakness," Foster replied. "To be honest, I'm using the information to get us sanctuary on Hope Island."

"You need to tell them."

"I will."

"And what happens if something happens to you?"

"Then someone else in the group will tell them."

"Malcolm, I don't think you're listening to me. If this information were to die with us, then what happens to the rest of the human race?"

"And if I don't use that information to get all of us someplace safe, then where are we?" Foster countered. "I don't think it's the kind of thing they'll just accept me telling them over a sat phone, either."

"Meaning?"

"I think I'm going to have to prove to them that it works," Foster said. "I might have to show them proof."

"Are you serious?"

Foster said nothing.

"You are, aren't you?" Lizzy demanded. "How in the world do you walk through doorways with that inflated head of yours?"

Foster saw red. "Take a look around you. Everyone looks to me for the answers." His voice grew gradually louder. "It's not ego. It's doing whatever the fuck it takes to keep everyone in this group safe. And I do it without asking for any pats on the back or praise."

"You're shouting at me."

"Sorry." Foster took a deep breath to calm his nerves. He lowered his voice, then continued. "I do it because I don't want anything bad to happen to any of you."

"I know," Lizzy said as she looked toward her feet. "You're just trying to keep all of us safe. Including me."

There was an uncomfortable moment of silence as neither one of them seemed ready to speak up again. The seconds seemed to stretch out to minutes.

"Malcolm?"

"Yeah?"

"I just thought of another place that might work," Lizzy

said carefully. "I mean, it could pass as an airport."

"What do you mean, *pass?*"

Lizzy proceeded to explain, and as she did, a smile began to form on Foster's face.

"That's brilliant," Foster said excitedly. "Especially since a lot of people aren't likely to know about it."

"You really think so?"

"Absolutely. Great thinking, Lizzy," Foster said. "Let's gather the group, and we'll share the news with them."

"I'll do that."

"Actually, give me a few minutes. I need to make a call."

"Black?"

"Yes."

"You got it, Malcolm."

Foster waited till Lizzy left the room and pulled out a satellite phone and dialed it. It rang once, and then he heard a male voice answer.

"Black here."

"It's Foster."

"Uh-huh."

"We might have a possible exfil location. Is that copter back yet?"

"Negative. Why?"

Foster began to tell him about the possible location.

"Are you there yet?" Black asked

"No, we haven't left yet."

"Kind of pointless to set up a pickup without knowing if you can land a chopper there."

"I'm confident the place is secure. From what my source is telling me, we should be able to exfil from there."

"Uh-huh. Lemme talk with Abrahams and see what we can do."

"Any idea how long would it take the copter to get here?"

"Damned if I know. I'm not a pilot."

"Best guess, Sergeant."

"Once it's in the air," Black said, "I think the Blackhawk could probably get there within an hour."

"Great. I'll call you back once we get there."

"Tell you what," Black said. "Why don't I call you back once I make sure that Abrahams is willing to send the chopper. Otherwise, you could be standing there holding your dick and waiting for a ride that is never coming."

"Point taken," Foster said. "We'll lay low and wait for your return call."

"Copy that. Keep those people safe, Foster." Black said. "I'll be in touch once I have an update."

"Okay, will do. Stay frosty, Sarg."

"Always do," Black answered before disconnecting the call.

Foster chuckled softly. Things were still unpredictable and chaotic. But he always knew what Black's reaction and behavior would be. He fully expected the SWAT Sergeant to lean on Abrahams as hard as it took to get them the copter they needed.

There was a knock on the door.

"Come in," Foster answered.

The door swung open, and Amanda appeared in the doorway.

"Got a few minutes to talk?" Amanda asked.

"Sure."

"Good. I asked the rest of the gang to give us some privacy."

Foster's eyebrows slowly went up.

"Easy, boy," Amanda teased. "I wanted to be able to talk with you without anyone else interrupting."

"All right," Foster said quickly. "So what's on your mind, Doctor?"

"Are you worried about it?" Amanda asked.

"About what?" Foster said. "Reapers?"

"That goes without saying. We have to always be worried about them. But that's not what I meant."

"Okay," Foster said. "So what's on your mind?"

"Hope Island. Is it really as good as Sergeant Black says?"

"Why would he lie about it?"

"He doesn't have a reason to, does he?"

"I don't think so," Foster answered. "I mean, unless Abrahams is forcing him to."

"Do you really think they could?"

"Short of holding his men hostage, I doubt it."

"I can't wait to get there, to Hope Island, I mean. Just something resembling a normal life again."

"Yeah, I guess," Foster said. "I mean, it could be better than any of the places we've already been."

"How couldn't it be better? There's no Reapers. We can continue to go back to the kind of life we used to have before all of this madness began."

"I hope you're right."

"You know I am," Amanda took both of Foster's hands in hers. She leaned forward and gave him a quick kiss on the lips.

"What was that for?" Foster asked.

"For being patient," Amanda said with a smile. "For being willing to wait for us through all this craziness."

"That hasn't been easy sometimes."

"I know."

There was a tap on the door. Sams called through the door, "Excuse me, I hope you lovebirds are fully dressed. I really don't want to see Malcolm's night stick."

"Derrick, give it a rest," Amanda snapped. "Nothing is happening."

"Right, sorry," Sams said before stepping into the room. He glanced at both of them before continuing. "Oh, good, you're already dressed. I mean, still dressed. Listen, the day's wasting away, Malcolm. We need to go check out the new potential base."

"Right, be there in a minute," Foster said. He made a shooing motion to Sams.

The former Ranger nodded knowingly, tapped his wrist as if it had a watch on it, and retreated from the room.

Foster sighed. Derrick was reading far more into where things were between Amanda and him. He'd have to figure out a way to bring it up to his friend and set the record straight. He turned his attention back to Amanda.

"Can we pick this up later?" he asked. "We do need to check out the alternate site."

"Yeah, go on. Keep Derrick and you safe. I'll see you soon."

"You can count on it." Foster flashed a boyish grin before ducking out of the room.

CHAPTER TWENTY-EIGHT

The Tahoe pulled to a stop in front of the only yellow house on Fieldcrest Drive. Foster shifted it into park and turned the engine off. He paused for a minute, listening for any sounds of incoming vehicles or Reapers.

The neighborhood continued to be extremely quiet, and Sams let out a low, appreciative whistle. "Cute little place. Just screams suburban homeowner."

Foster glanced at the property. It was a light-yellow colonial home with a tan roof. There were two full picturesque windows to the left of the entrance and one to the right. A white picket fence enclosed the front yard. A detached two-car garage sat farther back from the house.

"Could be," Foster answered. "Let's check it out."

The two men quietly climbed out of the Tahoe, taking care to close the doors as quietly as possible. They proceeded to work their way toward the house, carrying their rifles in a low-ready position.

"Go in through the front or the back?" Foster asked.

"You're asking me?" Sams said.

"I'm asking you in terms of likely booby traps."

"Hmm. Good point. I can try and look through the window, see if I see anything," Sams said. "Otherwise, we would be taking our chances."

"Let's go to the back then," Foster answered. "Less likely that anybody sees us going into the house."

"Good point."

The two men worked their way to the back of the house and then stopped next to an eight-foot privacy fence that contained the property's backyard.

"Larry's brother really likes fences," Sams quipped. "I thought they could only be six feet high, though."

"Depends on the township," Foster said. "I'm guessing he got some type of exemption to make his taller. Someone that worried about their privacy might have rigged their fence gate to stop possible intruders while they were gone."

"Yeah, hold on," Sams said. He pulled out a fiber optic camera and slid it under the fence, angling it and looking.

"Nice toy," Foster quipped. "I didn't realize you had it."

"Yeah, something I found when I was out scavenging," Sams said. "Didn't see an immediate need for it, so I put it in my backpack. I figured it was better to have and not need it than the other way around."

"Good point."

"Can't get the right angle. Dammit," Sams muttered. He carefully retracted the cable and gathered it back up. "I wanna see what's on the other side of the fence. Give me a boost, will you?"

"Up and over?"

"Up for now. Wanna see if I missed anything with the camera, like a sleeping dog."

"Good point," Foster said. "On three?"

"Yeah, sure."

Foster bent down and cupped his two hands together, forming a bridge. Sams lifted his right foot up, put it in

Foster's hands, grabbed the top of the fence, and pushed up. Foster lifted him higher so that Sams could see clearly above the fence.

"Looks clear," Sams said, stepping back down.

"You might wanna take a step back, just in case," Foster said as he moved to the side of the fence door. He held his rifle in a low-ready position and waited for Sams to open the door. He watched as Sams took a nervous breath, exhaled, grabbed the handle, and opened the fence's door slowly. The gate swung silently open, and the former Ranger stepped into the yard, bringing his weapon up into play.

Foster followed behind, doing a circle sweep to cover the left half of the yard, with Sams covering the right. He reached back, closing the fence door behind them.

"Glass doors," Sams said. "If they're like my folks, they never lock them."

"Really?" Foster said. "Why the hell not?"

"They got a privacy fence and three Rottweilers," Sams said. "If you're dumb enough to hop over the fence, you got the Rotties to deal with. But if they accidentally lock themselves out, then it's just a matter of going through their own privacy fence and sliding the door open to get back in the house."

"Makes sense," Foster said. "Let's keep moving. The rest of the group is waiting to hear from us."

Sams examined the sliding glass door, looking through the glass from several angles. "No visible traps," he said. He grabbed the door handle, testing it with a gentle tug. He adjusted his feet, ready to jump back at the first sign of trouble. Sams grabbed the handle and yanked it. The door slid quietly open. Sams stepped into the house, bringing his rifle up into a shooting position.

Foster followed him, closing the sliding door behind them. "All right, let's clear this place, then check out the garage," he said. "Just to warn you, last house I went in with Gregory, the garage door was booby-trapped."

"Good to know." Sams said. He brought the fiber optic camera out of his backpack once more. "Let me check before we try and proceed."

———————

Ten minutes later, they had cleared the house from top to bottom and were standing on the side of the detached garage. Sams slid a telescoping mirror under the door and examined the door frame thoroughly. "No wires, no booby traps that I can see."

"Are you sure?"

"As sure as I can be. If it makes you feel better, you can move over there to avoid getting blown up."

"That's not funny," Foster scolded. "I already told you, the last place we checked was booby-trapped."

"Yeah, I remember. I also told you, I think we're clear."

"Where do you want me?"

"Over there," Sams said. He pointed to a position approximately forty-five degrees from the doorway. "Cover me while I open the door."

The two men moved into position. Sams grabbed the door handle and gave it a quick yank. The door swung open harmlessly, revealing a well-kept two-car garage. A white Suburban sat quietly in one of the bays.

"Is it possible we found the only house in Rehoboth that doesn't have dead bodies, Reapers, or booby traps?" Sams said aloud. "Maybe our luck is finally improving."

"Don't jinx us," Foster said. "Come on, let's clear the garage. If it's like the rest of the house and checks out fine, then we need to call the others. Because right now, it's looking like we have a new secure location."

CHAPTER TWENTY-NINE

Sergeant Black knocked on the closed door in front of him. He waited patiently until the voice behind the door told him it was okay to enter. As he opened the door, he saw Lieutenant Tom Abrahams sitting behind a desk. There was a large stack of papers on his left side and an equally large pile on the right.

"You got a minute?" Black asked.

"If it gives me an excuse to avoid all of this paperwork, I've got as many of them as you need," Abrahams said with a smile. "You would think in the middle of a shit storm where enemy combatants are busy killing humans that I'd have more important things to deal with."

"I'm guessing that's not the case?"

Abrahams laughed bitterly. "I'm afraid not. I'm used to being on the front lines with my men. But with all this shit going on, I'm riding a desk and leading this base. At least, until someone higher up shows up to relieve me. But you didn't come here to listen to me complain. What's on your mind, Sergeant Black?"

"Just spoke with Officer Foster in the mainland. They've run into a few snags."

"Like what?"

"Well, for starters, the boat they were going to use was booby-trapped. It killed two of their party. The rest barely managed to escape."

"Shit. Was Foster one of them?"

"No. Fortunately, he and some of his other key personnel are fine. The problem is the marina is controlled by the Disciples of the Divine, a cult in that area."

"A cult?"

"Apparently, this cult has some kind of control over the Reapers in that area."

"Wait, what? There's a way to control the Reapers?"

"Between you and me, I think it's a load of horse shit," Black answered. "But a lot of people in that area seem to buy into it. Damned if any of us know why. Anyways, Foster says these Disciples control the marina with the help of the Reapers."

"Can't they just commandeer another boat?"

"Yeah, I asked him that. The problem is, it's the same marina their boat was located in. If their boat was booby-trapped, there's a good chance other ones in the same area are, too. They don't have any way to safely determine that while avoiding Reaper and Guardian patrols."

"Guardians?"

"Right. That's the armed enforcers for the cult."

"I can see where that would create a problem. I'm guessing they're trying to avoid a firefight?"

"Right," Black answered. "Foster's group is extremely outnumbered right now. And unfortunately for them, the group members killed were the only ones who knew how to navigate a boat."

"So what do they plan to do?" Abrahams demanded. "We're on an island. They can't exactly walk here."

"Foster said he's working on it. He might have a way to get his group out of Rehoboth and away from this cult. If he can find a suitable place for an exfil, then he was wondering if you'd send a helicopter to pick them up."

"How many people in his group?"

"Nine, including Foster," Black said. "I explained to him that you only have one working helicopter right now, and it was currently out on a mission."

"I don't know if we can send it."

"What are you talking about? He's got intel that you need."

"No, he's telling me he has intel," Abrahams corrected. "It's unverified."

"You gotta be kidding me."

"No, I'm not. Do you really want me to risk our only way to get anybody on or off of this island on an unverified hunch?"

"It's not a hunch. Foster has the proof to support his findings," Black said. "Are you telling me we don't have any boats on this island?"

"That's correct. All of us were brought in by the helicopter. It was one of the reasons why I agreed to take Foster's group in."

"They were bringing a boat," Black said. "It would have given you another way to run missions."

"That's right. Especially any kind of scavenging or salvage ones."

"Couldn't we just grab some nearby boats?"

"It's possible," Abrahams said. "But we'd have to improvise a bit."

"I'm not following."

"Unless someone on your team is secretly a skipper, we currently lack any experienced boat hands."

"I'm guessing we're going to have to figure it out sooner or later."

"Of course," Abrahams said. "We need more supplies and food. Especially food."

"What about fishing?"

"Do you really think we're gonna be able to catch enough fish with homemade fishing poles to feed everybody on this island every day?"

"To be honest, I hadn't given it much thought," Black admitted. "I've been busy with other things."

"Well, feel free to take a look around. There's no crops or greenhouse in place," Abrahams said. "And in case you hadn't noticed, we're in the wrong time of the year to start planting a garden. Which really ties my hands to make sure we keep everybody here properly fed. It's only a matter of time before we run out of what supplies are already here."

"In other words, as soon as Foster lost the boat and people who knew how to take care of it, he lost his usefulness."

"I didn't say that."

"What are you saying, Lieutenant? That Foster is on his own?"

"I don't know," Abrahams said, throwing his hands up in the air. "I hope not. Look, I'll see what I can do, okay?"

"Uh-huh."

"I'm serious. Let me make some calls. Maybe there's another military division that can do an exfil. You say he's in Delaware?"

"Yeah, Rehoboth."

"If he can get to somewhere away from this cult, it'll make it easier to arrange for a pickup."

"Understood."

"Anything else?"

"No, not at this time."

"Then if you don't mind seeing yourself out, I need to get back to tackling this paperwork."

"Right." Black turned and started to walk away.

"Sergeant."

Black paused in the doorway.

"Yeah?"

"This guy Foster," Abrahams asked. "How well do you know him?"

"Pretty well. Why?"

"Can we count on him?"

"When my team got cornered coming out of the Philadelphia airport, Foster led a group of his people into the fight to help us out," Black answered. "He's a cop. When the shit starts hitting the fan, he doesn't run away. He runs toward the trouble and does whatever he can to help. If Foster says he's got information that's a game changer, then I'm willing to bet that's exactly what he's got."

"Thank you, Sergeant. I appreciate your honest opinion. I'll let you know as soon as I have any news to give."

"Uh-huh. Okay."

"Hey, Black."

"Yeah."

"I meant what I said. I'll do what I can. I hate the idea of leaving any of the good guys or gals in a bind. Especially with the Reapers. I wish I had more than one copter to send out, but I don't right now. Let me see what I can do on my end to make it happen, okay?"

"You got it, LT," Black said. "Thanks."

CHAPTER THIRTY

There was a loud banging on the door, and Gregory looked at Charles with a look of panic in his eyes.

"We need to block the door," Charles said. "Grab as much stuff as you can."

"And if that doesn't work?"

"Then pray they go away," Charles said. "Come on and help me."

The two men sprang into action and grabbed a desk stationed halfway between the door and window. The duo worked in tandem to shove the bulky furniture in front of the door.

"Chairs," Charles said between breaths. "Stack them on the desk."

"What about the window?" Gregory asked.

"Bookcase," Charles pointed. The faux wood furniture was filled with a mix of pamphlets and different stacks of paper. The two shoved the bookcase in front of the window, darkening the room considerably.

"There," Charles whispered as he pointed to where he

wanted Gregory to move. "Behind the chair." He took position behind a matching one catty-corner to his son.

The tension in the room was almost unbearable. The
looming threat suddenly became very real in Charles' mind.
There was a very real chance he and his son could be slaughtered by the Reapers in this enclosed space and nobody else
would be able to help them. Charles felt a wave of panic rush
over him, and his body began shaking uncontrollably. He
forced himself to take several calming breaths and locked his
eyes on the barricaded door.

There was a loud bang, and the door rocked within its
frame. Two more thuds sounded, and the door suddenly flew
open. Two Reapers appeared in the doorway. One of the creatures roared and slammed its hairy fist against its chest
before taking a step into the room. The Reaper immediately
stumbled over the top of the stacked chairs and landed hard
on the floor. As it began to rise, the second monster tripped
over the same chairs and landed on its ally's back, knocking
both of them onto the floor together.

Charles heard Gregory fire twice and saw one of the
Reapers take a direct head shot. There was a third shot, and
the former preacher saw the shot strike the remaining
monster in the arm. The creature yelped in pain. It snarled
and turned its attention toward the trapped men. It let out an
angry roar and began to advance on Charles' position.

There was an even louder crash. Charles stole a look
toward the noise and saw the desk splinter as five more
Reapers charged through it.

Charles brought his shotgun up into a shooting position
and opened fire. He saw the closest Reaper go down for good.
He shifted his aim on the next creature and fired once again.

"Dad, behind you!" Gregory shouted.

Charles turned and looked just in time to see the bookcase toppling over. A moment later, two new Reapers crashed through the window and landed in a heap inside the room.

Charles aimed at the closest one and fired. As he turned toward the second one, he saw a blurred motion swing upward. There was a tremendous blow as a Reaper's hand struck his weapon and knocked the shotgun out of his hands. The monster moved with inhuman speed and struck him again. The blow to his chest sent Charles reeling, and he landed hard on his back. As he struggled to sit up, he froze in terror. The monster was holding Gregory by the neck in front of him. The shotgun lay harmlessly on the ground behind them.

Charles scrambled to pull the gun in his holster and aimed it shakily at the monster. He noticed for the first time that the Reaper was wearing a red cape.

"Drop the gun, or I will kill him," the monster announced. "Now."

"If I do," Charles answered, "you'll kill us both."

"Do you really want to take the chance?"

"Please, there's no need for violence," Charles said in as soothing of a voice as he could muster. "We'll leave peacefully."

A low rumble came out of the monster's chest. "Peace, you say. Such a quaint old idea. You know Foster."

"W-What?"

"Don't deny it," the Reaper continued. "We've seen you with him. Bring Foster here, and I will release this man."

"How do I know you won't harm him as soon as I leave the room?"

"I give you my word, human," the red-caped creature said. "Tell Foster I wish to meet under the terms of a cease fire."

"What?" Charles said. "I-I don't understand."

"Tell him to come alone."

"Dad," Gregory said between clenched teeth. "I-I'll be okay."

"I'll be back as soon as I can," Charles said. "If you hurt him, so help me, I'll—"

"You'll do nothing, old man, and you know it," The Reaper chuckled. "Go on, before I change my mind and kill both of you."

Charles ran from the room. Before he knew it, he had reached their vehicle. He tried to unlock the door and immediately dropped the keys. Charles bent down and picked them back up. He put his finger on the fob instinctively and immediately froze. The Reaper had told him to go get Foster. But what if there were others in the area who hadn't gotten that message? Or Guardians. They'd already tried to kill all of them once. If he alerted them and was killed before he could reach Foster, then his son might die at the hands of the red-caped monster.

Charles slowly removed his thumb from the fob and shifted his aim. He attempted to insert the key into the driver's side lock and missed badly. The former preacher glanced at his hand and saw it was shaking uncontrollably. Charles brought his left hand up and grasped the key with both hands. This time, he succeeded in getting the key in the door. He carefully turned it and was rewarded with the sound of the door unlocking. Charles climbed into the SUV and pulled the door closed behind him. He grabbed the walkie-talkie he had left under the driver's seat and keyed the transmit button.

"Malcolm, it's Charles, come in," he pleaded. "Come in, please."

There was an immediate response, and Charles felt a wave of relief rush through him.

"What's wrong?" Foster asked.

"They... They took Gregory."

"Who?"

"One of the Reapers. He had a red cape," Charles said. "He wants to meet you, Malcolm. He says he wants to talk to you. Something about a truce. No, wait. He said cease fire."

"What else did he say?"

"He's holding Gregory hostage until you show up."

"We'll get him back," Foster answered. "Give me your address and I'll be there."

Charles looked at the front of the door and read out the address. He repeated it a second time.

"Got it. All right, I'm leaving now," Foster said. "Don't leave."

"Just hurry Malcolm. Please. M-my son-"

"I'll be there as soon as I can."

———

Foster lowered the walkie-talkie and looked at Sams.

"Yeah, I heard the whole thing," Sams muttered. "You want me to come with and back you up?"

"Normally, I'd say yes."

"But?"

"Someone needs to keep this place secure until the others get here," Foster answered. "Otherwise, they have to go through clearing the whole property again."

"You still need backup. This whole lone wolf gimmick could get you killed. Especially if you're dealing with a bunch of Reapers."

"I don't disagree," Foster answered. "But I will have Charles and Gregory there, too."

"Who could be compromised."

"Got any paper?" Foster asked.

"Yeah, why?"

"Because I'm going to give you the address. As soon as the others get here, you can shift into standby. If I need you as backup, I'll call you and you can be there in a matter of minutes."

"Like a quick reaction force. A QRF."

"Exactly."

"One war, one Spartan."

"You're a former Ranger," Foster pointed out. "Not a spear and shield-carrying Greek."

"Same concept, better weapons."

"Uh-huh. So as soon as the rest of the group gets here, you're my QRF," Foster said. He began checking the magazines in his vest to confirm they were all fully loaded. He double-checked the silver dagger was still secured on his hip. "I think we should regroup and spend the night here. It'll give us time to go through all of the supplies and inventory them. Make sure we aren't missing anything critical we need for the trip."

"Sounds like a plan. I'm sure all of us could use a solid night of sleep. Seeing that we were in a firefight and holed up underground all night, Nick and I definitely could use some quality shut-eye. We can leave at first light and get the hell out of this town."

"Gregory, Charles, and I were stuck in an attic with a bunch of Reapers banging on the walls the whole time. So we're functioning on willpower and caffeine, too."

"The girls started their morning with a gunfight. So I'm sure they would appreciate a night of uninterrupted peace, too."

"Yeah, probably," Foster answered. "Hopefully this Reaper really just wants to talk."

"Hopefully. These things do some crazy shit sometimes."

"You mean, like raising its paws in the air in surrender?"

"Yeah, I had some strange dreams about that one afterward. You think you can talk this Reaper down?"

"Let's hope so. I'm not sure if Charles could handle losing his son, too."

CHAPTER THIRTY-ONE

Foster brought the Tahoe to a stop behind Charles' parked vehicle and cut the engine. He opened the driver's side door and took care to close it quietly. A moment later, Charles emerged from his Land Cruiser.

"Are you okay?" Foster said.

"I'm fine," Charles answered. "Thank you for getting here so quickly."

"Let's go get your son back."

Foster followed the former priest into the building, his nerves jangling like crazy every step of the way. There was a wild range of possible outcomes, and not all of them were good. He was ready for the worst and hoping for the best one. If this was the end of the road for him, then he was fully prepared to take as many Reapers as he could with him.

———

The two men made their way carefully through the building. Foster kept his eyes constantly moving, looking for any potential ambushes or traps. But there was nothing waiting to attack them, and they reached a closed door in a matter of minutes.

"In there?" Foster asked.

"Yes," Charles said. "They were at the opposite end of the room when I was told to leave."

"Anything you remember about the space?"

"There's a window on the side. Some different furniture we tried to use to barricade the door and window. Not that it worked."

"Okay, good to know," Foster said. He took position at the doorframe and motioned for Charles to take position behind him. "I'll count to three, and then we're going in. I want you to cover me."

Foster silently counted down, grabbed the doorknob, and yanked the door open. He charged into the room, bringing his rifle up, sighting on targets.

"That's far enough, human," a voice called out.

Foster turned his attention toward the sound. There was a large Reaper standing at the opposite end of the room. A trio of creatures were spread out in front of it. His eyes quickly shifted back to the group's leader. The monster wore a long, flowing red cape and easily towered over the trembling Gregory. The Reaper had one hand on the man's shoulder and the other braced against his neck.

"Are you all right?" Foster called out.

"I'm touched that you're worried about me, human," the Reaper answered.

"I wasn't talking to you," Foster answered. "Gregory, are you okay?"

"Y-Yes," the man stammered.

"All right, I'm here," Foster said. "What do you want?"

"Are you Foster?" the Reaper asked.

"Yes. What do you want?"

"Did the other human not tell you?"

"Look, I'm here," Foster said. "There's no reason for you to keep him any longer."

"Drop your weapons, and we'll talk."

"No can do," Foster said. "Last time I checked, those claws of yours were considered a weapon."

The Reaper let out a low growl. "I ain't asking you again."

"I need a sign of good faith. You let him go, and I'll remove my weapons."

"Okay." The monster chuckled. "Drop the knife and the gun. Then I let the pup go."

Pup? Oh, he must mean Gregory, Foster thought.

"I meant what I said, Foster," the Reaper continued. "I want to talk. Don't try me, or I may change my mind."

"All right, take it easy," Foster answered. "I'm gonna put my weapons over on that table, okay? I'm moving slowly. Don't hurt him."

"Slowly," the Reaper commanded. "No sudden moves."

Foster took his rifle and set it down on the table. He repeated the process with his Glock and then made a show of removing the dagger and putting it on the table, too. He took three steps back from the table and looked toward the Reaper to see if it was going to release Gregory as promised. Foster was still close enough to his weapons that, if he needed to, he could make a play for it. Worst-case scenario, he still had his backup gun in his ankle holster. It wasn't loaded with silver bullets, but it could deliver the needed headshots to kill all three Reapers in the room.

The Reaper released Gregory and took a half-step backward. The creature had positioned himself in front of a closed door.

Smart, Foster thought. *If this deal goes to hell, he's ready to bolt out the door. Don't underestimate this one, Malcolm.*

"Leave us, pup," the creature said. "And take the old man with you."

Gregory looked at Foster for reassurance.

Foster nodded slowly. He gestured with his head toward the exit. He turned his attention back to the red-caped Reaper. "Is it okay to talk in front of your sidekicks?"

"Leave us," the monster rumbled. The two minions retreated through the door behind their master. The creature waited until it was just Foster and it in the room before adding, "Don't worry, human. I'm fine with just the two of us in here."

"You got others watching this place?"

The Reaper's chest puffed up noticeably. "My soldiers. They're loyal to me."

"What should I call you?" Foster asked.

"Haas," the red-caped monster answered. "Fos-ter, I wish to make a trade."

"What kind?"

"Information."

"You want me to give you information?"

Haas chuckled softly. "No."

"I see," Foster said. "You have information you think I might want."

"Yes."

"And what do you want in return?"

"My freedom."

"Last time I checked, you can walk out the door any time you want."

A low growl came out of Haas' chest. "It's not you keeping me here."

"I don't understand."

Haas gestured toward his own body. "My friend and I were transformed into this."

"Who turned you?"

"That's not important," Haas said. "We were minding our own business. Trying to exist on our own here. At first, we focused on the old and the weak to feed. A few we used to create new soldiers to protect ourselves. Then someone else discovered us."

"What's their name?"

Haas growled. "I won't tell it to you right now."

"Why?"

"Too risky. I don't know who else might hear it and tell him that I'm talking. He is the true Alpha. All others must kneel before him."

"Including you?"

Haas growled.

"Sorry, I meant no offense," Foster said quickly. "I'm trying to understand what happened."

"I had no choice." Haas snarled. "He killed my friend in front of me, and I couldn't stop him. Then he gave me a choice: Submit or die. Dying wouldn't bring my friend back. So I swallowed my pride and submitted."

"Why don't you kill him yourself?" Foster asked. "I mean, you'd have an easy time getting close to him, right?"

"He doesn't let his guard down around any of his soldiers. And if there was an attempt on his life, I would be the first one he suspected to be behind it."

"Why are you telling me this?"

"Simple. With a little help, perhaps you will get lucky and get rid of our mutual problem."

"The enemy of my enemy is my friend?"

"Yes," Haas said.

"And if I fail, then you're still in the clear with your boss."

"Of course. But I think both of us would prefer to see you succeed."

"And if I do this, what do you get out of it?"

"Freedom," Haas rumbled. "And I will no longer be forced to cater to his every whim."

"If he's dead, where will you go?"

"I haven't decided yet," Haas admitted. "Some place far away from humans. Preferably quiet, remote, and with some local wildlife that I can hunt."

"In other words, you won't be a problem for anyone once this boss is gone?"

"That's right."

"All right. So where is this King of Kings?"

"Not here," Haas answered. "He has a place where he rules from."

"Like a kingdom or a lair?"

"Yes."

"Hmm. I'm interested. But..."

"But what?"

"We need a way out of this place," Foster said. "Between the Reapers and the Guardians around here, it seems like every way out of town will result in a big fight."

"You can't leave on your own? Like you said before, I'm not holding a weapon on you."

"That's true," Foster said. "But if we have to kill some of your soldiers in order to make an escape path, then you are okay with that?"

Haas growled softly. "You made your point, human. Let me see what I can do to create an escape route for you."

"Great. One more thing," Foster said carefully. "I need to talk to the rest of my group first."

"What?" Haas snarled.

"Relax, big fellow," Foster said. "Before I put their lives on the line, I need to make sure they're willing to take the mission, too. Otherwise, I'm looking to take out the leader of a huge army by myself."

Haas grumbled. "I've said too much."

"Your secret is safe with me," Foster said. "You'll need to trust me on this. We both win if this head honcho is removed."

"How long until you've made a decision?"

"Give me two days."

"No. I can't wait that long for your answer."

"All right," Foster said. "By sunset tomorrow."

"Fine."

"How do I get a hold of you?"

"You won't," Haas answered. "But you'll hear from me by then." The Reaper turned and then bolted out the door behind him.

CHAPTER THIRTY-TWO

After the impromptu meeting with the red-caped Reaper, Foster sprang into action. He made a quick call to Sams and let him know that everything was okay. He took a few minutes and helped Charles and Gregory load some medical supplies into the Tahoe. The Land Cruiser was on the Guardians' radar, so they left it with the keys on the dashboard at the vet's office. From there, he brought Charles and Gregory back to the new base. The two men stayed long enough to retrieve the Suburban and then took both vehicles back to the gun shop. About an hour later, the entire group was reunited in their new base of operations. Of course, if they stuck to their current game plan, they wouldn't be staying here or in Rehoboth Beach much longer.

Foster and Sams were in the kitchen, enjoying some actual coffee that they had found in the house. And always the two men had found a topic worthy of debate.

"Come on, man, admit it," Sams said. "Football is the most physically demanding sport."

"The international sport?" Foster asked. "You know, the one Americans call soccer?"

"I mean the one with helmets and shoulder pads. Those guys are always playing hurt."

"It's a worthy contender," Foster answered. "But my vote would be gymnastics or ice hockey." He heard the kitchen door open and saw Amanda enter the room.

"There's no hitting in gymnastics," Sams pointed out. "I gotta deduct a point for that. Plus, everybody in the sport is like five feet tall."

"Not everyone," Foster countered. "Besides, it takes a ton of strength and agility to do all of their maneuvers safely."

"What are you two talking about?" Amanda asked.

"Toughest physical sport," Sams said. "What's your vote?"

Amanda stood quietly for a moment. "Mixed martial arts," she said. "The training is really tough. And your opponent is trying to knock you out or break your arm."

"It's tough, but there's plenty of MMA fighters sporting a big old gut," Sams said. "But yeah, a bad day at the office for them has a completely different meaning than it does for most people."

"Malcolm, do you have a minute?" Amanda asked.

"Sure. But Sams and I are leaving to go on another scavenging trip soon."

"That's fine," Amanda said. "I just need a few minutes. Somewhere private." Sams' eyebrows immediately shot up, and she quickly added, "To just talk."

"Uh-huh," Sams said. "Well, don't keep the lady waiting, Malcolm. I'm just going to stay here and enjoy the fresh cup of coffee."

"After you," Foster said, gesturing for Amanda to lead the way. The two of them left the kitchen and walked through the house. Foster found an unoccupied bedroom, motioned for Amanda to go in, and followed her. He closed the door and turned toward her. The room was small to begin with, and with the two of them standing near the doorway, it was even more so.

"Is everything all right?" Malcolm asked.

"I'm not sure," Amanda began, "With everything going on right now, I want you to know where I'm coming from."

"Okay," Foster said, drawing out the word.

"It's just we're in danger again," Amanda said. "Only this time we're trying to stay alive with Reapers and some crazy cult chasing after us. I just don't feel like it's fair to the rest of the group to distract you when all of us need you to keep us safe."

"I have every intention of keeping all of us safe."

"I know that, Malcolm," Amanda said as she reached out and grabbed his hand and gave it a quick, reassuring squeeze. "I feel like we don't know really know much about each other."

"That's true," Foster said. "But in all fairness, it's not like we've had much opportunity to talk, let alone have something resembling a date."

Amanda laughed bitterly. "And that's my point. I mean, right now with everything going on, we can't even have a normal conversation. There are more important things for us to talk about. Like where to find food. Or medicine. Or where we can find more bullets because we can't risk running out of those."

Foster looked down, saying nothing.

"I know Sams is waiting for you, so let me just say one more thing. Please be patient with me, Malcolm. Let's get away from this current situation with Guardians and Reapers. Find someplace safe."

"Like Hope Island?"

"Yes. Then we can take the time to get to know each other. We can start spending time together like people used to be able to do."

"That's fair," Foster said. "Don't worry, Doc. I plan on holding you to that commitment." He flashed a quick boyish grin.

"And I look forward to you holding me to that commitment," Amanda said. She leaned over, give him a quick kiss on the cheek, and then made a shooing motion. "Now, go on. Sams is probably leaning against the door right now, trying to listen."

"Really? You think he'd be that childish and immature?"

Amanda gave him a knowing look. "Well, we can't rule it out either, can we?"

Foster sighed. "Fine. I'm going. Talk to you soon, Amanda."

"You, too, Malcolm."

———

Foster stepped out of the room and began heading toward the kitchen where he had left Sams. He had managed to take a few steps before he heard someone else calling his name.

"Hold up for a minute," Walker said. "If you don't mind." From the look on the former Ranger's face, it was obvious he wasn't making a request.

Foster took a slow, deep breath before asking, "What's on your mind, Nick?"

"Derrick tells me you and Amanda are getting close."

"And?"

"She's a great gal," Walker said. "Treat her right, and we won't have any problems."

"What the hell does that mean?"

"She's my wife's best friend. Don't make me have to choose sides."

"Then stay the hell out of my business, and you won't need to pick a side at all."

"It's not that easy." Walker growled. "You're talking about my wife's best friend."

"You think I don't know that?"

"I'm serious."

"So am I," Foster countered. "Not that it's any of your business, but Amanda already suggested we put anything that might be developing between us on hold."

"She did? Good," Walker said. His shoulders visibly relaxed. "Because you know, we got plenty of other shit to worry about right now."

"Yeah. So if you don't mind, I'm going to grab Sams and go on one last scavenging run."

"Sounds good. And Foster?"

"Yeah?"

"Sorry if I was getting a little heated."

"I get it, man. Amanda is a great gal."

"Yeah." Walker sighed. "Hey, be safe. I'll see you guys when you get back."

————

President Vickers stared across her desk at Rasheed Weindahl. The military man looked visibly uncomfortable, and she decided to proceed anyway with this last-minute meeting.

"General, I called you here to get an update on Operation Poison Arrow," she began. "Preferably something more than 'we're working on it.'"

"Of course," General Weindahl replied. "We're still moving assets into position, ma'am. We expect to be ready to launch in approximately eight hours."

"Do you have some way of guaranteeing that you're hitting a nest of Reapers?"

"We've actually come up with an idea in terms of that."

"Go on."

"Well, it appears the creatures are highly susceptible to noise," Weindahl said. "We're going to drop a public announcement system in the center of the town square."

"We're going to kill them with an announcement? By what? Boring the hell out of them?"

Weindahl chuckled. "Not exactly. We'll remotely use the system to broadcast a taped conversation of people talking. The noise should draw the monsters to us at that location."

"And once they're there, you can hit them with the attack."

"Yes, that's right."

"Great. I like it," Vickers said. "Do we need to worry about any of them figuring out that it's not actually real people?"

"We don't anticipate them knowing what's being said. But we're thinking we could broadcast a message that if you're human, you need to vacate the area."

"You didn't answer my question," Vickers pointed out. "What if they do understand it?"

The general fidgeted uncomfortably in place. "Based on the Reaper behavior we've seen so far," he said, "I believe it's highly unlikely they'll know what the recording is saying."

"Any chance that actual humans go and investigate the noise?"

"I suppose there's also a chance of civilians having an overwhelming sense of curiosity."

"Which might get them killed."

"I'm afraid so, Weindahl said. "With all respect, we've run through several different scenarios. In each one, there is still a risk of loss of human life. This plan is the one with the lowest chances of collateral damage."

"Let's hope any people in the area hear the recording and head for someplace safer. Zero civilian casualties would be ideal."

"I couldn't agree more, Madam President."

"Okay, what about the rest of the plan?"

"Of course, Madam President. Operation Poison Arrow involves the use of a M55 Missile System," Weindahl answered. "It's a land-based system for short to medium range targets."

"And the ordinance used?"

"VX."

Vickers felt her breath catch in her chest. "You're talking about using a chemical biological weapon. One which, if my memory serves me right, was previously outlawed."

"That is correct, Madam President. Since that Chemical Weapons Convention treaty was signed, we have slowly been disposing of our stockpile."

"Because it's hard to dispose of? Or because it's expensive to do so?"

"Both, actually," Weindahl admitted. "We've incurred multiple cost overruns and time delays as well. We're fortunate that this particular base in Kentucky is nearly two years behind schedule."

"In other words, the government running behind on something actually works in our favor." Vickers chuckled. "I'll count that as a lucky break."

"Indeed."

"Where's the target?"

"With all due respect, I've already mentioned we're luring the Reapers in with a recorded message being broadcasted."

"Let me rephrase the question. What town are we luring the hostiles into?"

"Richmond, Kentucky, Madam President. It was chosen based on the VX's current location. The town is just over five miles from the base."

"Wait. Five miles? Isn't that kind of short for a missile strike?"

"It is," Weindahl answered. He nervously shifted the papers in front of him.

Vickers studied the man in front of her, who was no longer making eye contact. "What aren't you telling me?"

"Well, the thing is, these missiles have never been fired in a combat situation."

"Wait, what?"

"Just in test cases and experimental simulations. There's never been a need for the U.S. military to launch these missiles at an actual enemy combatant."

"So there's a chance these missiles could blow up in the middle of the operation?"

"A low probability one," Weindahl admitted. "We're sending a Blackhawk to drop off an Army squad and a bioweapons specialist at the base. The soldiers will provide protective detail while the specialist inspects, primes, and fires the missile system. Once the weapon is fired, the soldiers will call for an immediate exfil."

"Couldn't you just land the copter so they don't have to wait for extraction?"

"We considered that, but we're worried about the noise."

"Because it might draw the Reapers to the base?"

"Correct, Madam President," Weindahl answered. "We're thinking if we can fast rope the soldiers and the specialist down, the chopper will only be in the area for a minute or two before heading off. The pilot could also take their flight path away from the base to act as a decoy."

"Hmm, okay. What are the odds of success?"

"We believe the mission has a very high probability."

"I'm looking for a number, General, not a pep talk."

"Close to 100 percent. But, there's no one there monitoring and maintaining these weapon systems," Weindahl said. "If there's a problem with the missile guidance system or with the missiles themselves, then we may have to scrap the mission."

"In which case you've got to get your boys out of there in a hurry?"

"Indeed."

"Well, fingers crossed that they don't run into anything they can't handle. Thanks for the update, General."

"It's my pleasure, Madam President."

The General began to rise from his chair and head for the door.

"Rasheed? Just one more thing."

Weindahl froze in place and turned slowly toward the Commander in Chief.

"Yes, Madam President?"

"What did the doctor say about your leg?"

"He gave me some ibuprofen."

"That's not what I asked you."

"He was busy with other patients, and I didn't want to interrupt him. So I asked the nurse for some medicine."

Vickers threw her hands up in frustration. "You're unbelievable. What am I going to do with you? You disobeyed a direct order."

"I think *delayed acting on it* would be more accurate," Weindahl countered. "I will still make an appointment with the doctor about my leg. But it needs to wait until after Operation Poison Arrow has been completed."

"I'm going to hold you to that, Rasheed," Vickers warned. "In case you hadn't noticed, I'm concerned about you."

"I've noticed, ma'am." Weindahl smiled. "And I promise I'll go the doctor. But not until after this mission."

Vickers shook her head. "Are all men this pig-headed stubborn?"

"I prefer persistent, ma'am. It better represents the fighting spirit of our military."

"I can't argue that," Vickers said softly. "Let's hope this operation makes the battle much easier for everyone. Meeting's adjourned."

Weindahl saluted sharply and left.

Vickers watched the door close behind the general. She hoped he wasn't in a lot of pain with his leg. If this mission was successful, then she could justify Rasheed taking a long break to get it treated properly. But in the meantime, their country needed Weindahl to gut it out and keep leading what was left of their armed forces.

CHAPTER THIRTY-THREE

Back at Guardian headquarters, Silas was furious. Worse, he felt completely humiliated. How the hell could a bunch of women have won a gunfight against his Guardians? He looked at the men surrounding him. Pathetic. These men were a sorry excuse for a group of so-called fighters.

"Does anybody have anything to say for themselves?" Silas said aloud. "Anyone?"

One of the men shifted nervously from one foot the other. "I'm not sure what you want us to say," he said carefully. "Sir."

"What's that? Cat got your tongue?" Silas said. He drew the Bowie knife on his hip and brought it up.

"That's not going to help," somebody behind him muttered.

Silas spun around, looking for the person. "Who said that?" His eyes fell on Carl, and he immediately recognized him as the mystery speaker. "You got something to say, best say it to my face."

"This isn't helping," Carl said. "We didn't know how many of them were up there."

"It was a bunch of women and kids," Silas said. "And somehow they kicked your asses!"

"That's what you told us," Carl challenged. "But what if you're wrong? What if they had a bunch of trained shooters at the top of those stairs just waiting to unload on us? I think we should tell Ezekiel—"

"Oh, so now you're thinking, huh?" Silas interrupted. He drew his knife and began gesturing with it. "Are you an educated man, Carl?"

"What the hell are you talking about, man?"

"Are you one of those hoity-toity college boys?" Silas demanded. "One of those limp-dicked pussies who left home and got all educated and smart-like?"

"You got no right to call anyone names. It's your fault that—"

Silas slammed the Bowie into the man's arm in mid-sentence, and Carl immediately howled in pain. The wounded Guardian instinctively reached for the knife. But before his fingers could enclose it, Silas ripped the weapon away from his grasp. There was an immediate arterial spray, and Carl screamed as he clutched his mangled arm.

"Boy, I asked you a question," Silas scolded. "You better answer me." He shifted his grip on the Bowie and stabbed it into the back of the man's exposed hamstring. Carl screamed and crumpled to the floor. The man instinctively reached for the knife embedded in his injured leg with his damaged arm, but froze in mid-movement. The man curled into a protective ball, continuing to whimper in pain.

"Any other smart boys here?" Silas demanded. "Any of you wanna tell me how to run this crew?" He glared at each remaining man, daring them to challenge his authority. Every single one looked away uncomfortably.

Silas turned his attention back to the downed Guardian.

He bent down, grabbed the Bowie still embedded in Carl's leg, and gave the knife a sharp twist.

Carl shrieked in pain again.

"I can't hear you," Silas cooed. "Carl, I need you to remind everyone who's in charge." He twisted the knife a bit more in the opposite direction.

"You!" the man shrieked.

"Anybody else got a problem with that?" Silas challenged. "No? Then it's settled." He yanked the knife out, and Carl let out a whimper before mercifully losing consciousness.

"This boy is a bleeder," Silas announced. "Get him out of here, before he makes a mess of this place."

One of the men stepped forward. He tried to lift Carl by himself, lost his grip, and accidentally dropped the injured man. Carl landed hard and yelped in pain.

Silas pointed toward one of the men standing and watching the exchange. "You there," he said. "What's your name?"

"It's Will," the man stammered. "You're in charge, boss."

"Glad to hear you didn't forget that," Silas answered. "Help him get that piece of shit out of here. I want both of you to come back then and join us."

Will nodded eagerly and hustled over to the Guardian standing by Carl's body. The two of them silently grabbed the unconscious man and began carrying him out of the room.

Silas scanned the faces of the remaining men. They looked spooked, scared. None of them would make eye contact with him. *Good. They know who's still in charge.*

They were his to lead. Unquestioned. And unopposed.

CHAPTER THIRTY-FOUR

Angel bounded easily alongside her pack mates, weaving in and around the tall structures. A small voice in the back of her head told her they were called buildings. She silently thanked it for helping her remember the difficult word. Her mind was frequently a jumble of voices and thoughts, which confused her even more. The small voice in the back of her head told her it hadn't always been that way. And if the voice was right, it would help explain why now, more than ever, she felt so confused. She had this creature who answered to the name Beeks that kept insisting she was family. But that little voice in her head kept telling her he was lying.

So far the only thing Beeks had said that seemed to make any sense was her name.

Angel.

A small voice in her head had told her it really was her name. If she was being honest, it was why she had embraced being called that name.

She'd resisted their efforts to eat what they had been offered. That small voice in her head had warned her there was something wrong with the meat. But then a louder voice had gone off in her head like a firing cannon. It insisted the meat was fine, and it wouldn't make her sick.

The voices had taken to arguing with each other in her head, and it was jarring to say the least. When Angel was alone, she'd find herself pleading with the voices to stop fighting.

Was she going crazy? She wasn't sure. It would help if she had someone else that she could talk to. But she couldn't shake the feeling that she couldn't completely trust those around her. And that lack of trust made it feel right to refuse whatever food they offered. Maybe finding her own food would help her feel better.

The front of the pack had begun to slow down, and Angel followed suit. She looked around, saw they were stopped in front of one of the structures. There were pieces of wood at seemingly random places. The wood didn't cover what was behind it completely, and Angel could see some type of clear material behind it. The substance didn't do a thing to stop her from seeing inside. Angel couldn't help but wonder why someone had tried to cover it up with pieces of wood.

Suddenly, there was a series of nearby loud noises and explosions. Angel instinctively stopped and started looking for a place to hide as small pieces of metal began flying through the air. One of them struck her in the leg and she howled in pain, her voice sounding like a wounded animal. Angel staggered backward and leaned against a tree. She risked a look at her lower leg and saw blood rushing out of a fresh wound. *Her blood.*

You've been shot by a bullet. Don't worry, a loud voice said in her mind.

Angel shook her head in disbelief. Why shouldn't she worry? There was something wrong with her leg.

She looked back at her injured limb, and as she did, something weird began to happen. The piece of metal was slowly being pushed out of her body. A moment later, the foreign object exited her skin and fell harmlessly onto the ground. Angel felt her lower leg muscles begin to reknit themselves. A moment later, her leg felt as good as new.

It didn't make any sense to her. Was this something only she could do? Angel turned her attention back to her surroundings. As she panned her vision from her left to right, she saw a number of her pack mates getting struck by flying metal, too. Most of them seemed to immediately heal from the wound. But as she watched, one of her pack mates was struck in the head by a piece of flying metal. The male dropped to the ground, seemingly lifeless. Angel watched his body for any signs of recovery, but there was none.

Your ability to heal doesn't work if you get shot in the head, the loud voice in her head lectured.

A low growl sounded near her. Angel turned her attention toward the sound and saw it was the pack leader. She didn't know his name. Beeks hadn't told her, either. And if she were being honest, she wasn't sure she wanted to know. He was somebody she didn't want to spend any more time with than she absolutely had to.

"Charge!" the pack leader snarled. He signaled for them to rush toward the one part of the structure. The pack moved as one and rushed forward.

Angel dropped to all fours and bounded after the rest of her pack. She was the last one to enter the building. As she entered to the structure, she saw humans fighting with her pack mates. Angel felt a low growl exit her throat. There was a person with a metal object in his hands. He pointed it at one of her pack mates and pulled a trigger. The object made a loud noise, and Angel saw her pack mate get hit by a bullet. Angel felt her teeth bare. This human was dangerous, and she needed to be careful.

It didn't make sense. Beeks told her they were just going

to talk to the humans, but that's not what was happening. Angel shrank back, hugging a nearby shadowed wall.

As she waffled in indecision, she saw the pack leader slam into the armed human from behind. The man hit the ground hard. He managed to roll onto his back a split second before the pack leader grabbed his throat with its teeth. The man tried to scream, but his voice was cut short as Reaper teeth punctured his throat. Angel heard a loud crunch and saw an immediate gush of blood spray out.

Angel felt a wave of horror wash over her. This wasn't talking. This was killing. As she looked around the room, she saw that the rest of her pack mates were killing the humans, too. Worse, a few of them had already begun to feed on the dead.

Angel stood up. She felt her body shaking uncontrollably. This wasn't what Beeks told her they were supposed to do.

"Stop," Angel whimpered. "This isn't right."

"Quiet, pup," the pack leader growled before diving back onto the dead human. A man. His lifeless body was lying in a growing pool of blood. And yet her pack leader was feeding on the remains.

This wasn't right. This isn't what Beeks had told her that her family would be doing. Angel backed out of the building. She had to get away. Angel dropped to all fours and began to run away as fast as she could.

CHAPTER THIRTY-FIVE

"Hey, you got the reverend's ear, don't you?"

Joseph stopped and turned slowly toward the voice's source. He looked the man up and down once before answering. "I'm sorry?"

"You're Ezekiel's assistant, right?"

"Joseph," he corrected. "And yes, I've been known to help the reverend. Is there something that you need?"

"I'm not sure who to talk to about this," the man stammered.

"Well, what is it?"

"More like a who. Silas."

"Lower your voice," Joseph hissed.

"Sorry," the man mumbled.

Joseph looked in both directions of the hallway. There didn't appear to be anyone else in sight. He lowered his voice and asked, "What about him?"

"I'm not sure he's all there."

"Meaning?"

"Well, he was going after that group we're supposed to find, led by that former cop."

"Ah, yes, I know who you're talking about," Joseph said. "I'm sorry I didn't catch your name."

"Right. Sorry," the man said. He offered a handshake. "Name's Will."

Joseph looked it at quizzically and decided it was better to accept it than risk alienating the man. He grasped the man's hand, which was cold and clammy. He flashed a quick smile. "Nice to meet you. You were saying?"

"Right," Will stammered. "Well, we tried to take them above a store."

"Them?"

"The cop and his friends."

"I see. Please continue."

"So we tried to get them. Except they were holed up real good, and we couldn't reach them. They shot a couple of our men, and Silas didn't take it too well. One guy tried to leave, but Silas just shot him down."

"What?" Joseph said. He felt the blood leave his face.

"He shot him like he was nothing but a broken-down old dog. Made us all leave him there to die. It was cold-blooded, man. And that's not all."

"There's more?" Joseph stammered. "Oh, dear." He looked around for an open chair. He found one and moved to sit down. He flopped into it. The chair groaned loudly but held his weight.

"We headed back to HQ and Silas just started reading all of us the riot act, Carl tried to talk to him. But Silas just snapped," Will said. "Stabbed him in the arm and then a leg. Started to torture the guy until Carl told him what he wanted to hear."

"I-I don't know what to say," Joseph stammered. "This isn't the type of behavior we condone."

"Well, in case you hadn't noticed, the guy is fucking nuts,"

Will said. "Look, I don't know how much longer I can keep working for this guy."

"I understand. You did the right thing by telling me."

"I-I don't want to die, man," Will pleaded. "I only signed up to be a Guardian because it meant better lodging and status in the church."

"Don't worry," Joseph answered. "I'll talk to Ezekiel about it."

"Thank you. I really appreciate it, man."

"You're welcome. And I'm terribly sorry, but I completely spaced your name again."

"It's okay. You've probably got a lot on your mind and meet lots of congregation members every day. Especially since you're helping Ezekiel with so many things," the man said. "My name is Will."

"Will, I promise you I'll get to the bottom of this. I'll have Ezekiel talk to Silas about it, right away."

"Thank you, Joseph. Thank you."

———

It had taken every ounce of self-restraint Silas had to remain out of sight and not spring immediately into action. Especially after he heard his name being mentioned. Silas had followed Will on nothing but a gut feeling. But now he knew the truth. The man was nothing but a little tattletale. And tattletales couldn't be trusted. Silas carefully retreated back the way he had come. He'd find a way to make him pay for his transgression. But only when Silas was ready to collect.

———

Foster walked up to the door and knocked twice. He heard Walker's voice tell him to enter. Foster opened the door, and as it swung open, he saw Sams sitting there at one end of a table. There was a pile of bullets and other material in front of him. "Emily said you wanted to see me?" he said carefully.

"Mandatory class," Walker said. "Grab a seat and get comfortable."

"Any chance of seeing a syllabus?"

"None," Walker answered. "You don't need one. You two are going to learn how to make Reaper bullets."

"Any particular reason why?"

"Yeah," Sams said. "He's fucking tired of making all of them by himself."

"I can't say I blame him," Foster said. "It's a lot of work for one person to have to do. Especially with the number of bullets we've been using lately."

"Redundancy," Walker said. "Right now, if something happens to me, you lose your only Reaper bullet maker."

"Nah, ain't no Reaper going to kill you," Sams said with a boyish grin. "You're too tough for that."

"Tough, not immortal," Walker said. "Keep in mind, we've been lucky so far that we haven't been separated from each other for any lengthy period of time. What happens if we are? What happens if I take another shot to the head, but I don't come to right away?"

"In other words," Foster said, "plan for the worst and hope for the best."

"Exactly. Redundancy."

"All right," Foster said. "Let's get to it, professor."

———

"Where is she?" Beeks asked.

"I do not know, my Lord," the Reaper pack leader answered. He kept his eyes glued to the floor in front of him.

"You were in charge of keeping an eye on her," Beeks snarled. "What part of your job wasn't clear?"

"I don't know what happened. We were feeding. I was preparing food for her. And when I turned, she was gone."

"Really?" Beeks said. "Is that what really happened?"

"Yes, my Lord."

"Don't move," Beeks ordered. He slid off his throne and moved toward the still kneeling soldier.

"What? I don't understand—"

"Hold still." Beeks reached out and seized the Reaper pack leader's mind. He began looking through its memories, stopping on the ones of Angel. He quickly replayed their exchange, using the minion's memories like a prerecorded video. After a few minutes of review, he let go of the mental images and turned his attention to the creature now shaking in front of him.

"You lied to me," Beeks snarled. "You were busy stuffing your own face. And then you yelled at her when she complained."

"My Lord, I can—"

"Shut up," Beeks said. "You failed me."

"I'm sorry, Master. I'll make it up to you."

"Too late," Beeks said. He reached out strongly, seized the pack leader's mind, and mentally began to squeeze. The creature stiffened and screamed out in pain. Beeks continued to squeeze until the soldier collapsed lifeless on the ground.

Beeks slowly checked the rest of the throne room. As he visually scanned the room, each one looked away. Except for one soldier. The minion stood firmly in place and didn't break eye contact.

"You," Beeks said softly.

"Yes, my Lord."

"You are now in charge of his pack. Your predecessor failed me. Do not fail me like he did."

"I understand. I honor and obey your word."

"The one who answers to the name Angel did not feed with the others," Beeks answered. "I want you to find her and bring her back. Alive."

"Of course, my Lord."

"Go," Beeks ordered. "Take as many of your pack as you need with you. Bring my Angel back to me."

CHAPTER THIRTY-SIX

There was a knock on the door, and Ezekiel shouted for the person to enter. He didn't have to look up to see who it was. He knew from the distinctive knock and footsteps that his trusted assistant had entered his office.

"Sir?" the man said carefully.

"Yes, what is it, Joseph?"

"We need to talk."

"About what?" Ezekiel asked as he slowly closed the book he had been reading and placed it on the corner of his desk.

"The new leadership of the Guardians."

"Close the door, please," Ezekiel commanded. He waited till the door closed. He set the book he had been reading down on his desk, walked over to the liquor cabinet, and poured a drink, keeping Joseph waiting the entire time. "Do you have a problem with Silas?" Ezekiel asked carefully.

"I wouldn't say that I personally do, but..."

"But what?" Ezekiel demanded. He could feel his impatience rising and tamped it back down. Joseph didn't deserve to be treated that way, even if he had interrupted Ezekiel getting to an exciting part of the thriller novel he was reading.

"Some members of the congregation have come to me in confidence. They're worried about some of his methods. It appears Silas has been using the Disciples' beliefs as an excuse to torture people."

"Tough times call for tough leadership, Joseph. I am fully confident Silas will do what needs to be done."

"I-I don't understand," Joseph stammered.

Ezekiel studied the man. He looked like he was ready to faint. "Do you think this man Foster will follow Canterbury rules?"

"Sir?"

"Do you think Foster or any of his group of trained killers will hesitate for one moment to come in here and treat us fairly?"

"Well, I don't know," Joseph said, "I haven't met any of them."

"Be glad that you haven't."

"They're human."

"And humans have a long history of doing a multiple of sins," Ezekiel said. "Do you think they will have any remorse in their hearts that will keep them from slaughtering every man, woman, and child in that chapel? I must remind you that every single one of them is relying on us to keep them safe."

"They're afraid of us. We have allied with the Reapers. We far outnumber Foster's group."

"Oh, they're not afraid. Not at all. If they were, then why didn't they flee when the Guardians confronted them at the marina?"

"But what about the congregation? Don't you believe they'll come together to keep each other safe if we're attacked?"

"I hope so. But let's look at the facts. The flock say they believe in us. They believe in the Guardians, too," Ezekiel said. "But what are they really believing in? I'll tell you what it is. That we will keep them safe from all harm outside. And that harm includes Foster and his group. The minute that safety disappears, the flock will scatter to the four winds."

"I-I think I understand."

"Good. Anybody else has a problem with Silas, please tell them to come talk to me directly themselves."

"As you wish, sir," Joseph said. "If there's nothing else, then I guess I'll be leaving."

"That's fine," Ezekiel said. He reached for the book sitting on the corner of his desk. "Please see yourself out."

CHAPTER THIRTY-SEVEN

It was almost eight o'clock as Will hurried through the cathedral's rows of pews. One of the other Guardians had told him Silas was looking for him. From the tone of his friend's voice, Silas wasn't looking for casual conversation. Will had gotten the hint. It was time to get out while the getting was good. Will made his way out the back side door of the church, walking as quickly as he dared, fighting the urge to run every step of the way. Running would only draw attention to himself, and right now he was trying to be as inconspicuous as possible.

He made his way to the street and picked up his pace. What the hell had he been thinking by ratting out his boss? He knew if Silas found out, there would be repercussions. He needed to get out of town. Sure, he'd had a good run with the Guardians. Safety in numbers, steady food that he didn't have to hunt for himself. Walter, the previous leader of the Guardians, didn't mind looking the other way if one of his men wanted to enjoy the company of a woman on a given night.

Will could have taken advantage of that unadvertised perk

a few times himself. Especially after his wife decided to leave him. He'd lied to the rest of the cult when he told them that Megan had gone to stay with her sick mother in Ohio. But the truth was his mother-in-law was in perfect health, and his wife had hit him with divorce papers two days before the Reapers showed up.

Ironically, they had joined the Disciples of the Divine because Megan insisted they become members. Something about a spiritual connection and how it would bring them closer as a couple. Except six months later, they were no longer together. Hell, they were living in two different parts of the country now.

At least she had gotten out in time. There was part of him that was glad she had left when she did. At least she wasn't in deep shit like he currently was.

Maybe if Silas had some kind of accident, then I wouldn't have to leave town, he silently thought. He dismissed the idea right away. Nobody was going to arrange for Silas to die unexpectedly. Will wasn't the type of man that would bushwhack someone, either. Especially when that somebody was the guy Ezekiel had chosen to lead the Guardians.

He really missed Walter. The man had always been fair to him. At times made him feel like an adopted son. Will heard a truck engine in the distance and veered in between two yards to get off the street. It had to be one of the Guardian patrols driving. None of the residents under Guardian protection had been allowed to keep their own working vehicles. He stopped in place and strained to hear. The engine sounded like it was heading away from his position. Will let out the breath he hadn't realized he'd been holding. He needed to keep moving. He didn't want to get spotted. Especially if Silas had sent the other Guardians to track him down. Will hopped over a small garden fence, cutting through and carefully opening a privacy fence door.

There was a low growl near him, and he quickly froze. A pair of yellow eyes shone through the darkness, and Will said, "Easy, boy." He slowly pointed toward the armband on his arm. "Friendly, see?"

The Reaper growled once more and turned its attention back to feeding on something on the ground.

Will carefully went around the Reaper. He didn't know what that damn thing was eating, and quite frankly he didn't want to know either.

He asked Walter once how Ezekiel managed to control these animals. Walter was probably the smartest man he had ever known. But even he didn't have a clue on how their esteemed leader kept the Reapers in check.

Will hurried down the street, cutting across again. He heard a truck engine getting closer. Suddenly, a pair of headlights swung onto the roadway, catching him in their light. Will took off running, and he heard the truck begin racing after him. He hopped over a short gardening fence, running past another homeowner's residence and into their backyard. Suddenly something struck him in the chest, and Will tumbled onto the ground. As he looked up, his eyes made out a metal pole to his left. He looked to his right and saw another one standing there. There was a lingering burning sensation across his chest from where he'd been struck. *Rope burn. You idiot. You just ran through somebody's damn clothesline in the dark.*

Will picked up himself and continued walking swiftly, trying to keep the noise to a minimum. He cut through some trees on another property. Just a few more blocks, and he'd be home. He'd pack his shit and get the hell out while he could. He wasn't supposed to have a vehicle of his own, even as a Guardian. But Will had somehow managed to keep the one in his garage a secret. If anybody had ever asked, he would have claimed ignorance. Or that he owned it before became he ever became a Guardian. But nobody had ever asked him, and it wasn't the type of information he thought was worth volunteering, either.

He could see his house up ahead. It was dark. Well, most of the houses on his street were lights out, too. He heard an engine approaching and he threw caution to the wind, racing for the safety of his own home. Suddenly, the engine was nearly on top of him, and he saw a pickup truck screech to a halt in front of him.

As Will looked at the vehicle in front of him, he saw Silas was sitting in the passenger seat. Several other Guardians were riding in the back of the truck. None of them were smiling.

"Jesus, guys," he gasped. "You scared the hell out of me."

"Get in the truck," Silas ordered.

"Did you need something?" Will stammered. "I'm off duty and was just getting ready to go home and get some—"

"I'm not going to repeat myself again," Silas said. He slowly pulled back his coat, revealing a gun in a holster. "Get in the fucking back of the truck."

"Right," Will said. He carefully climbed into the cargo bed, squeezing between two of the squatting Guardians.

The truck backed out of his driveway and took off down the street. Will felt his heart pounding, racing. He was unsure of what was going to happen. He felt the truck pick up speed. Will thought about jumping out, but quickly vetoed the idea. He was surrounded by several Guardians. He'd be lucky to get out of the speeding truck without any of them stopping him. The vehicle was moving pretty fast right now. Even if he could jump out of it safely, there was no guarantee he wouldn't land on something that could injure him even worse.

They pulled to a stop in a driveway in front of another house. A garage door was open, and the lights were on. Will heard both doors open and slam shut on the truck. There was a gun in Silas's hand. "Get out. Slowly."

"Silas, man, you're freaking me the hell out," Will said, "What are you doing?" Suddenly Will felt something strike him in the back of his head. The blow dropped him to his knees, and he instinctively grabbed his head. As he pulled his hand back, it came back wet. He looked at his hand and saw blood.

"Pick him up," Silas said, "Take him to the garage."

Several hands roughly grabbed Will and yanked him up onto his feet.

"I don't understand," Will pleaded. "What are you doing?"

"String him up," Silas ordered.

Will began to fight back, but it was no use. He was completely overwhelmed by an unknown number of Guardians. He felt some type of metal band slapped onto his left wrist, then his right. A moment later, each of his ankles were similarly secured.

He looked at each of his limbs. There were manacles attached to his wrists and ankles. He saw there were chains running from each one. He watched as the slack in the chain slowly began to disappear a moment before a stretching sensation in his limbs began. But as the chains were pulled up, the stretch quickly turned into pain, and Will let out a scream of agony.

"Let me go," Will pleaded. "For the love of God, I don't know what I did wrong. Just let me go. Please." His eyes darted around. There were four Guardians there, and none of them would make eye contact with him.

"You boys can go take a break," Silas said very calmly. "There's some cold sodas in the fridge in the kitchen. Might even be a few beers. Help yourself."

The quartet of Guardians nodded quietly and exited as one into the rest of the house. Will watched as Silas walked over and pushed a button on the garage door opener. The garage door began to close.

"Didn't your mama ever tell you that nobody likes a tattle-tale," Silas said slowly. He picked up a knife and slowly turned it side to side, letting the light shine off of it.

"What are you talking about?" Will said. "Come on, man, you're scaring me."

"I'm talking about how you decided it was a good idea to go blabbing about me."

"I didn't. I swear."

He saw Silas's fist come racing toward his face and braced himself for the impact. It was a decent hit. Will had been hit harder before in his life, but the blow was enough that he felt his lip split.

"Damn, boy, you got a hard head," Silas said, shaking his hand. "I have to remember not to do that again." Silas picked up a knife. "Not when I got this."

"I don't know what I said that got you so mad, but I apologize," Will pleaded. "All right? You need me to tell somebody that I lied?"

"So you admit you did talk."

"That's not what I—" Will suddenly screamed in agony. As he looked toward the source of the pain, he saw there was a fresh cut across his abdomen. He looked over, and the knife that Silas was holding was covered with blood. His blood.

"Please, Silas, I'm begging you. Just stop, man."

"Stop? No, I don't think so. We've only begun. You've got a lot more begging to do. I'm going to make an example out of you. People need to know what happens to tattletales."

"No, please, pl—" Will screamed in agony again. This time, a new searing pain in the back of his calf.

"Squeal all you want," Silas taunted. "Nobody is coming to save you."

Silas slowly walked around him, taunting him and continuing to periodically slice new cuts on Will's body.

At some point, Will passed out from the pain, only to be woken up when a bucket of ice-cold water was thrown on him.

Four hours and several dozens of cuts later, Will's body finally gave out and he mercifully died.

CHAPTER THIRTY-EIGHT

It was nearly eight a.m., and Foster felt the best he had in days. He'd finally managed to grab some solid sleep in their new base, even if it had been broken up with a few shifts of guard duty.

Foster was fixing himself a cup of coffee when his satellite phone began to ring.

"Is that who I think it is?" Amanda asked.

"It should be," Foster replied. "I don't know who else would have the phone number." He hit a button on the phone to accept the incoming call.

"Foster speaking."

"Today must be your lucky day," Black said. "Abrahams has agreed to send the chopper."

"Is it him?" Amanda whispered.

Foster nodded his head.

Amanda motioned that she was going to leave the room.

Foster waited until the door closed behind her before turning his attention back to the sat phone. "Will we be able to fit everybody on it?"

"Should be," Black answered. "Unless you guys have a shit ton of luggage."

"Yeah, that won't be a problem," Foster said. "How long until the chopper gets to the airfield?"

"Fly boys say they can be there to pick you up this afternoon. You call once you get there and make sure the landing area is secure. And then you get on the copter. Before you know it, you'll be on your way here. Can't get much more straightforward and easier than that."

"From your lips to God's ears," Foster said. "I'm hoping it goes as easy as you said."

"Humph. If I was you, I wouldn't count on Mr. Murphy not making an appearance."

"Yeah, Murphy and his damn law. He always seems to find a way to throw a wrench in things," Foster said. "Let's hope he's on vacation this week."

Black chuckled. "Yeah, let's hope so. All right, I gotta run. Give me a call once you're secure at the airfield."

"You got it. Talk soon," Foster said before disconnecting the call. He slowly stowed the sat phone back in his vest.

There was a light knock at the closed door, and then it opened almost immediately.

Charles stepped into the room. "Hope I'm not interrupting anything, but we have a bit of a situation."

"Good timing," Foster answered. "I just got off a call. What's up?"

"Nick and Derrick got back an hour ago from doing another recon. They said there's even more Guardians and Reapers patrolling the exit points for town. There's also a Reaper outside."

"What?"

"Relax. I think it's a messenger. Actually, I know it is."

"Care to elaborate?"

"It arrived about five minutes ago. Walker and Sams

approached it. Almost shot it immediately, to be honest. But the creature was kneeling with its hands up in the air."

"Like the one outside the farmhouse did."

"Yes, that's right," Charles said. "It's asking for you. Nicholas thinks it might be a trap."

"And Sams?"

"He's leaning toward messenger."

"Sounds like it came in peace," Foster said. "But it can't hurt to be cautious."

He stepped into the living room. The air felt charged with electricity. Foster glanced at Walker and Sams. Both men had their body armor and game faces on.

"Charles told you?" Walker asked.

"Yeah. There's no harm in erring on the side of caution."

"Derrick and I talked it over," Walker continued. "We think it's best if you approach it alone. We'll be on over-watch. The two of us will be ground level, and Lizzy will be covering long-range from the second-floor window. All of us will be on the lookout for any additional hostiles."

"I'm surprised you're not taking the sniper position personally. Aren't you a better long-range shot?"

"I suggested it," Sams answered. "But there's no fucking way he's putting his wife out in the open with potential hostiles if he can help it."

"Makes sense," Foster replied. "I don't blame him. Listen, Black came through for us. They're sending a chopper to pick us up this afternoon."

"That's great," Sams said. "You go find out what this Reaper wants, and then send it away. We make some more silver bullets and then get out of here with plenty of time to catch our ride."

"Sounds like a solid plan," Foster said. "Okay, let's do this."

"Lizzy!" Walker shouted. "We're going out front. We need you on second-floor overwatch."

"I'm on it!" she yelled back. "Be careful, guys."

The three men moved in tandem to the front door. Sams moved to one side. He motioned for Foster to stack behind him.

Foster moved into position. He watched as Walker shifted to the opposite side of the doorway. The former Ranger held up three fingers and slowly lowered one finger at a time. When his hand had transformed into a fist, Sams opened the front door, stepped out, and moved to the right. Foster stepped out the front, keeping his gun hand close to his holstered Glock. Using his peripheral vision, he saw Walker move to his left behind him. He turned his eyes onto the still kneeling Reaper about twenty yards ahead of him. Keeping his head still, Foster scanned from his left to his right, looking for any signs of a potential trap.

"Message for Fos-ter," the creature said softly. "Message for Fos-ter."

"You got him," Foster answered. "Who sent you?"

"My master," the Reaper answered. "Message is, I need your answer."

"The answer is yes," Foster replied. "But we have a problem. I need to meet."

The monster's head went down for a long, uncomfortable minute.

Foster watched as the creature slowly lifted its head and spoke robotically. "Same meeting place as before. Midnight tonight. Come alone."

"I'll be there," Foster said.

CHAPTER THIRTY-NINE

After a very long and stressful day, Joseph was feeling a bit more tired than usual. He had been stuck at the church all day long and was finally able to head home much later than usual. The worst part was he didn't see things improving in the near future. Not with Ezekiel making a bigger push to recruit new members. Silas and the Guardians were busy hunting Foster, which had created a whole new set of unexpected problems Joseph hadn't counted on.

Silas.

Joseph shook his head. He didn't know what he was thinking to suggest a guy like that. And thanks to what Will had told him, Joseph was even more convinced that the new leader of the Guardians was a sociopath. He had tried to warn Ezekiel, but their esteemed leader had just blown him off. Maybe Silas was the right person to do their dirty work. He could see why Ezekiel wanted the psycho to catch Foster and his other rebels. Especially after they had killed so many of the Guardians. Even so, Ezekiel needed to be kept up to date on Silas's actions. And that uncomfortable task was yet another one that only Joseph seemed capable of doing.

Joseph reached his door to his apartment. It wasn't anything to brag about. Sure, Ezekiel had given him a wide range of options for his personal dwelling. Joseph had picked a basic one-bedroom apartment in a less popular part of the clan's complex. Some men in Joseph's position might consider the apartment to be below their own level of status. But he didn't care. It was a place where he wouldn't be bothered when he retired for the evening. And just as importantly, it was a place where he could indulge his own vices without interruption.

One of the other Disciples had turned up some grade-A marijuana in their scavenging efforts. Joseph, recognizing an opportunity when it showed up, had confiscated the drugs. Joseph had told the man he was taking them for the good of the congregation. The naive man seemed to accept the bull-shit story. Of course, there was a chance he'd simply caved because of Joseph's status in the church.

Joseph didn't care. After a very long and stressful day, Joseph couldn't wait to smoke a joint and try to forget about everything that had happened.

Joseph put his hand on the doorknob, and as he started to turn it, the door swung inward easily.

"That's weird," he muttered. "I didn't think I left it unlocked."

But he couldn't rule it out, either. His life was insanely hectic lately. He'd even slept through his alarm this morning, which was something he would have never done before. He had been forced to throw on clothes and rush out the door. He barely made it to the chapel on time. All to avoid Ezekiel's ire.

Of course, his boss was a complete hypocrite. The leader of their cult was almost never on time for anything. But he was quick to find fault if anyone else was late and made him wait for them. Especially Joseph.

It was dark in the apartment, and as Joseph stepped in, he reached for the light switch just inside the entranceway.

Suddenly, Joseph felt a blow to the back of his head, and he yelped in pain. A second and third blow came down on his neck and upper back, driving him to the floor. Joseph felt his body falling down, but he was powerless to stop it. His head cracked the floor hard, and then everything went black.

———

Joseph came to with a start. He wasn't sure how long he had been unconscious, but he immediately noticed one of the interior lights was now on in his apartment. As he strained to look from his left to right, his eyes stopped on a man sitting across from him. Joseph's eyes began to regain focus, and he immediately recognized the uninvited visitor.

"You," Joseph demanded. "What are you doing here?"

"We need to have a little talk," Silas said. There was a large knife in his hands, which he appeared to be toying with. "I've been waiting all day to catch up with you. I hear you've been saying some things about me."

If he was trying to scare Joseph, it was working.

"I don't know what you're talking about, but you need to leave," Joseph blurted out. "Right now."

Silas began to softly laugh.

Joseph went to move out of the chair, and something stopped the movement. As he looked down at his right arm, he saw it had been zip-tied to the chair. He looked to his left arm and saw it was similarly bound. Joseph began to push against his bonds, struggling to try and get free.

"Oh, settle down. No need to get your derriere bent out of shape," Silas said. "I wanted to make sure that you weren't going to try and rush right out of here and go tattle to the boss."

"You need to let me go," Joseph said. "If you leave right now, I won't tell Ezekiel a thing about this."

Silas laughed as if he had heard the funniest joke in the world. "Do you expect me to believe you? I don't know what other shit you've already told Ezekiel. Real fucked-up name that is. Is that really his name?"

"I-I couldn't say," Joseph said. "It's what he's always told all of us to call him."

"Huh. Well, it's not like I can brag with a name like Silas," the man muttered. "But Ezekiel isn't here right now. So it's time for you and me to have a little chat."

"So what do you want to talk about?" Joseph answered with a calmness that he didn't feel.

"Let's start with what you've been saying about me. I can't have you spreading lies and other stories."

"But I haven't. Everything—"

"So you admit you've been talking about me."

Joseph clammed up immediately and looked away.

"Uh-huh. That's what I thought."

"What you did to that man by the gun shop was unacceptable," Joseph countered. "That's not how we do things around here."

"That's not how we do things around here," Silas mocked. "See, that's why you need someone like me. Somebody who isn't afraid to get his hands dirty. A man who is not afraid to do things differently the way they need to be handled. So while you hide behind these walls here and drink tea with your pinky extended—"

"I never—"

"Shut up, lightweight," Silas said, "I'm talking. Dammit, I lost my train of thought."

"Drinking tea, boss," a male voice said somewhere behind Joseph.

The confined man looked around wildly, trying to find the

source. But he couldn't see them in the darkened corners of his home and quickly gave up trying.

"Thank you," Silas answered. "While you're busy hiding, I'm the one out there taking all the risks."

"Let me go, Silas," Joseph pleaded. "For the love of—"

"Let me go, Silas," the man imitated. "You're boring me, boy." He stood up slowly.

Joseph saw his captor begin to walk over. As Silas approached, Joseph saw the man shift the knife in his hand. The knife went up, paused in mid-air, and suddenly came flashing down. Joseph felt a sharp pain in his left thigh as the knife struck. He howled uncontrollably.

"You're quite the screamer now, aren't you?" Silas mocked. "No, we can't have that." He reached over and grabbed Joseph's foot.

Joseph felt his shoe being yanked off. A moment later, the other shoe followed suit. "W-what are you doing to me?"

"I told you to be quiet," Silas warned. "But you're not listening."

Joseph felt first one sock and then the other being pulled off. Silas stood up, and Joseph saw the man was holding up a pair of black socks. *His socks.*

"Hold his mouth open," Silas ordered.

Several unseen hands grabbed his head roughly. Joseph tried to keep his mouth shut but was quickly overpowered. A wave of fear swept over him. He saw Silas's hand come rushing forward and felt the woolen socks being shoved roughly into his mouth. The fabric hit his gag reflex, and he immediately started to retch. Joseph felt hands grab the sides of his head again a split second before his head was slammed against the back of the chair. He felt an immediate shot of pain as the previously injured lump on the back of his head slammed into the unforgiving wood chair back.

"Gimme the tape," Silas ordered.

Joseph saw someone hand the Guardian leader a roll of duct tape. The man held the roll up where Joseph couldn't help but see it and began to slowly pull a strip off it. Silas tore the tape off of the roll with a flourish and slapped it over Joseph's mouth.

"Give me the cleaver," Silas ordered.

A wave of terror rushed over Joseph, and he blacked out.

———

A wave of cold water woke Joseph with a start. As the water ran down his face and away from his eyes, he spotted one of the Guardians holding an empty bucket.

"Help me," Joseph tried to plead, but the makeshift gag in his mouth turned the sound into a strangled mumble.

"Wakey, wakey," Silas taunted. "We're going to have some fun now." He held a meat cleaver up and turned it slowly, letting the overhead light reflect off the blade.

Joseph screamed and began fighting against his bindings.

"Well, I'm going to have some fun. You're not going to like this," Silas admitted. The man bent down in front of Joseph's right foot. "This little piggy went to market. This little piggy went home. This little piggy... Oh, the hell with it." Silas swung the cleaver down.

The blade slammed into Joseph's foot, and he immediately screamed in agony. He bucked against his restraints, but none of them offered any give. As the wave of pain started to ebb, Joseph looked bleary-eyed at the floor. There was something lying by the side of his bleeding foot. He blinked his eyes and tried to focus his eyes once more. His foot was missing a digit and a wave of shock came over him. Lying next to his foot was his now-separated little toe.

"Like I said, I'm going to have some fun," Silas continued.

"You need to learn there are certain people in this world that a pissant like you doesn't ever fuck with."

Joseph saw the meat cleaver rise up in the air and then come rushing downward again. He felt an impact on his foot, a split second before a new shot of pain rushed up his leg. Joseph screamed uncontrollably against the gag in his mouth. He had to get away from this madman. He fought vainly against his bindings, harder than he had ever battled anything in his life. But the restraints were stronger than his body could manage to overpower. He saw the cleaver rise up in the air again, and this time Joseph fainted before the weapon struck home.

———

Silas looked over at the dead man still strapped into the chair. He was tired but pleasantly sated. He had been working over Joseph for several hours now. He had to have his men revive the little shit a few times, because he kept passing out. But eventually there was no reviving left to do.

Silas looked around the room. It wouldn't do for Ezekiel to automatically think someone in the congregation had tortured and murdered his beloved Joseph.

Silas needed a scapegoat. Should he pin it on one of his men? He glanced at the men who had watched the entire situation play out. Two of them looked like they were ready to pass out. Another one refused to make eye contact with him at all. No, blaming them for his actions might create more problems than it solved. If he framed one of his men, then he'd have to worry about the remaining ones running to Ezekiel. As he thought it through, a new plan began to form in his mind. When he was ready, he cleared his throat for dramatic effect.

"Toss the place," Silas ordered.

"Like somebody robbed him?" a male voice asked.

Silas didn't bother to look at who had spoken. "Yeah."

"You think he had something worth killing for?" the same foot soldier asked.

"Probably. Look for anything he wasn't supposed to have. Or valuables," Silas answered. He pointed to a nearby dining room table. "Put them there."

The men moved slowly, pulling out drawers and staging a home robbery.

A few minutes later, Silas was looking at a pretty pitiful pile of potential loot. Three hundred dollars and two bags of marijuana. He didn't smoke the stuff, but maybe he could trade it with somebody else. He stuffed the drugs in his pocket. He took the cash and distributed it equally between his men. Several of them looked uncomfortable taking the money, but Silas didn't give a damn. By taking the money, they were even more involved in Joseph's murder. Now it was time to fully commit them to the story he was about to concoct.

Silas reached into his jacket, searching for one specific item. His fingers quickly found it, and he slowly pulled it out of his pocket. He glanced at the police badge in hands. A few days ago, he'd found it on the body of a dead Reaper. He didn't know why he pocketed it then. But it was exactly what he needed right now. He took the badge and dropped it on Joseph's mutilated body.

"Well, that's just terrible," he said in a mocking tone. "Boys, it looks like we were too late to save ol' Joseph from being tortured. Any one of you have any doubts that Foster wasn't responsible for this man's untimely demise?" He stared at the remaining Guardians, defying any of them to oppose him.

A series of no's quickly blurted out.

"Good. I'm glad we are all in agreement," Silas said. "We

need to tidy up here a little before we head back. Once we get back to home base, I'll report our findings to Ezekiel personally."

The men quietly set about removing any self-incriminating evidence and withdrew from the apartment. Silas was pleased that each one of his men avoided eye contact with him and did not say a word about what had happened. A few minutes later, they were ready to leave and head back to the Guardian headquarters.

As the men rode back in silence, Silas quietly thought about what he'd managed to pull off. Now more than ever, Ezekiel would need him. He would need him to avenge the death of his beloved assistant. With the evidence that Silas had left behind, it wouldn't be much of a stretch to suggest Foster had been the one who had killed Joseph.

CHAPTER FORTY

Foster slowly approached the veterinary clinic. The neighborhood was quiet, but that was how he expected it to be. Most people would be at home sleeping. Haas and his army of Reapers were expecting him. And if the Disciples showed up, then he'd call for help. He wasn't expecting trouble, but then it was never a good idea to walk into a meeting with a potentially hostile contact unprepared. Today's version of a Quick Response Force was Sams and Lizzy waiting in the Chevy Suburban two blocks away. Foster had brought his Glock, along with two extra magazines topped off with Reaper bullets. Worst case, if he ran out of ammo, he'd use his silver dagger to fight his way out. He was feeling a bit more anxious than normal. He blamed it on his recent call to Black. The SWAT Sergeant was not happy at all to hear that they had to delay the pickup by twenty-four hours and that the only explanation Foster could offer was he was still working on something important. He hadn't liked leaving his ally in the dark. But right now, it was better for Foster if Black didn't have the full story.

Foster worked his way around the building and entered from the rear.

"Foster," a voice called out. "You came alone. That's good."

"Of course."

"You did leave a few friends nearby," Haas answered.

"Backup," Foster answered. "In case the Disciples show up."

Haas chuckled. "I understand. But they won't be a problem. You called this meeting. What do you want?"

"Remember your whole big speech?" Foster said. "The one about enemy of my enemy?"

"Of course." Haas sneered. "Don't you?"

"Sure, but here's the thing. In order for me to get to our mutual problem, we still need a way out of town," Foster said. "Between the Guardian Disciples and your soldiers, this town is pretty much locked down," Foster said.

"The Guardians asked for more help with patrols," Haas answered. "As you humans might say, my hands are tied. I can't refuse to help them if I'm going to keep up appearances. Why can't you shoot your way past the Guardians?"

"We can get in a shootout. But the odds are probably not in our favor."

"Are you scared, human?" Haas chuckled. "How pitiful."

"Not at all. Smart. Gunfire is loud. The Guardians will be shooting back and can call for reinforcements. If we start out fighting a handful of enemies, then in a matter of minutes, hundreds more are drawn by the noise. Including more of your Reapers."

"So what do you want? A personal escort out of town?"

"That's not practical," Foster said. "Like you said, it's probably not a good idea for the two of us to be seen together."

"Get to the point, human. You're making my head hurt."

"We need a way out. Can you arrange for one of the guard posts to be unmanned?"

Haas absently stroked his chin. After a long, uncomfortable moment, he said, "Probably not. It would raise too many questions. But perhaps one location could only have a few guards. Would that work?"

"It depends. If your soldiers are blocking the road, then we'll have no choice but to engage them. It could mean we have to kill those soldiers in order to escape. Are you okay if that happens?"

Haas let out a low grumble. "It would be an acceptable loss under the circumstances."

"We'll do our best to avoid bloodshed, if possible."

"I said it would be an acceptable loss." Haas grumbled. "Don't make me repeat myself."

"Great. You'll forgive me if I don't want to shake hands."

"Feeling's the same, human."

"Right," Foster answered. "When will you have things in place for us?"

Haas rumbled. "Whenever you want. You pick a location, and I give the command to my warriors. They will obey without hesitation."

Foster proceeded to describe where they wanted to leave town.

"I'm familiar with that area," Haas rumbled. "I'll arrange for things to be easy to leave town from there."

"That works. Thank you."

"Of course. Now, I must go. It's risky if we are seen together."

"I understand," Foster answered. "I'll wait two minutes and leave in a different direction." He watched as Haas retreated into the shadows and then was gone. Foster let out the breath he didn't realize he had been holding. The meeting had gone better than he expected. It was risky to count on a new ally that he barely knew to be able to help them escape. But the only way he'd consider helping Haas overthrow his Reaper King was for the former human to lend some help to Foster's group first.

CHAPTER FORTY-ONE

The truck pulled to a stop in front of the chapel. Silas climbed out and headed inside, not bothering to check if the rest of his men were following his lead. He spotted a pair of Guardians just inside. The sentries immediately snapped to attention.

"I need to talk Ezekiel right now," Silas ordered. "Call him and tell him that I'm on my way."

"But it's the middle of the night," one of them protested. "He's not going to be happy about being woken up."

"I don't care. Tell him it's an emergency," Silas replied. "I'll be there in ten minutes." He strode off without waiting for their reply.

———

Silas only needed a few minutes to actually reach Ezekiel's private chambers. But he figured their esteemed leader would need the extra time to get somewhat presentable.

In precisely ten minutes, he arrived in front of the cult leader's quarters. Silas knocked twice and waited until he heard Ezekiel give him permission before entering the domicile. His eyes fell on a young blonde who looked like she had just woken up.

"Leave us," Ezekiel ordered. The woman scurried out of the chambers. He waited until the door closed before blurting, "This better be good."

"I have bad news," Silas said calmly. He added what he hoped sounded like a somber tone to his voice. "I think you might want to sit down."

"That bad?"

Silas nodded silently.

"Oh, boy," Ezekiel muttered. He made a beeline toward a home bar. He paused and said, "Do you want a drink?"

"Thanks, but I'm on duty."

"Of course you are," Ezekiel said. He grabbed the bottle of Angel's Envy bourbon and poured himself a double. He walked back to his desk and sat down heavily.

"Okay, what's so important that you had to wake me up in the middle of the night?"

"Joseph is dead," Silas blurted out.

"What?"

Silas put a troubled look on his face. He continued speaking in what he hoped was a convincing performance. "We got a tip from a confidential informant that Joseph might be in danger. Time was of the essence, so I pulled together a small team and rushed to his apartment. But we were too late. From what we found, it appeared he had been tortured before he was killed."

"Why? The man wouldn't have hurt a fly," Ezekiel mumbled. He slammed back his drink and headed back to the bar for a refill.

Silas waited for him to return back to his seat. "There was a police badge lying on his body. Like a fucking calling card."

"Wait, a badge?" Ezekiel stammered. "Foster was a cop."

"Really? Then he would know how to break into places. They're trained on how to pick locks and do all kinds of things," Silas answered. He decided to add a bit more gusto to his growing lie. "Lots of sneaky shit. I've heard that's how they catch criminals a lot of times."

"Uh-huh," Ezekiel mumbled. He took another long sip of his bourbon.

"I'm close to getting that son of a bitch," Silas said. "But I need help."

"What kind of help?"

"More men. Get them for me, and I promise you I'll drag Foster's sorry ass in here so he can pay for what he has done."

"You'll have it. Whatever you need."

"Thank you, sir," Silas said.

Ezekiel's words were beginning to slur. "Was there anything else?"

"No, I don't think so," Silas said. He could feel his mouth watering over the bourbon's wonderful smell. But he fought the urge to pour himself a healthy share. He needed to maintain a strong front in front of Ezekiel. "I've got a couple of leads on where that son of a bitch might be. If you don't mind, sir, I'd like to go pursue them."

"Go ahead," Ezekiel said. "Oh, and Silas?"

"Yes?"

"If you can bring him back alive, that would be nice," Ezekiel said. His voice began to climb steadily in volume. "But if he fights you or gives you no other recourse, then you can bring that bastard's body to me instead."

"I understand, sir."

"I don't care how you do it," Ezekiel said. His voice was growing louder. "Dead or alive. I don't care. Bring me Malcolm Foster."

"With pleasure, sir," Silas said.

CHAPTER FORTY-TWO

The sun wouldn't be rising for another hour, but President Vickers was already up and working at her desk. There was far too much that needed her attention right now. And that growing list of worries was enough to keep her from sleeping soundly. Vickers had tossed and turned for hours before finally giving up and started her work day earlier than she would have liked. There was a soft knock on her cabin door, and she called out for the person to enter.

The door swung open slowly, and Vickers saw Special Agent Malory Nash in the doorway.

"President Vickers, it's time," Nash said. The Secret Service agent and personal bodyguard stood rigidly by the open door, watching her surroundings for any potential threat to the Commander in Chief.

"Thank you, Agent Nash," Vickers answered. She stood up from behind her desk and quietly followed her personal protector out of the room. The two of them moved quietly, working their way to the command center, located deep in the ship. As she walked into the room, the rest of the people in the room stood and saluted in attention.

"At ease. Where are we at?"

"Approximately ninety minutes from launching our attack," General Weindahl said. "Operation Poison Arrow is still a go."

"Well, I hope everybody brought their own beverage and a big bucket of popcorn," Vickers quipped. "If this works as well as we hope, then we can start taking the fight back to these things."

Vickers headed to an executive chair at the top of the table. It was larger and more prominent than the other ones in the room. Someone had added it to the room, and she hated it. She didn't like feeling like she was being put on a pedestal compared to everybody else in the room. That's not who she was. It wasn't how she thought of herself, either. With this battle against the Reapers, it took each and every one of them working together to come up with a way to beat these bastards once and for all. Nobody was above the rest of the group, and she wanted to emphasize that.

But it wasn't the right time to raise her personal objection. They were minutes away from launching a critical mission. A proverbial test strike against the Reapers, that if it worked could shift the balance of the fight in their favor. They really could use a win after everything they'd been through. So for now, she'd check her personal feelings and focus on what was best for the country.

"Hurry up and wait." Vickers sighed. "My favorite thing to do."

"Madam President, we've got an incoming call from Hawaii."

"Put it on screen," the President ordered. The image flickered, and then a harried-looking Doctor Compton appeared on one camera.

"Doctor, we're a few minutes away from launching the

mission," Vickers said. "If you have something to report, please make it quick."

"Well, that's why I'm calling, Madam President," Compton said. "I'm not sure this attack is a good idea."

"Care to elaborate?" Vickers said.

"We don't know if it will kill the Reapers or not," Compton argued. "We don't have enough information to say either way for sure."

"Doctor Compton, I appreciate your concern," Weindahl said. "But this mission is a small test."

"Yeah, I know," Compton argued. "Nothing ventured, nothing gained."

"Indeed," Weindahl said. "If it works as well as we hope, then the military gains a new way to kill the Reapers without putting our troops in immediate danger."

"Well, what if it doesn't?" Compton argued. "Then where the hell are we?"

"Then we'll know what not to do," President Vickers said. "I appreciate your concern, Amelia, I really do. Do you have anything else for us this point?"

"No. I'll let you know when I do." Compton sighed. She disconnected the call with a flourish of her hands.

"We really need to have someone talk to her about her people skills," Vickers quipped. "She frequently forgets who she's talking to."

"I can't say I disagree, Madam President," Weindahl said. "I will try to find someone to discuss it with our esteemed doctor."

"And the odds that they will be successful?"

"Probably pretty low," Weindahl admitted. "But keep in mind, our options are pretty limited at this time."

"No, I understand," Vickers said. "I'd rather not replace her if we don't have to."

"We have a bit of time before the mission goes live," Weindahl said. "Let me make some calls and see if I can arrange for the good doctor to get some additional coaching."

"That's fine," Vickers quipped. "I'll just sit here and try to look presidential."

CHAPTER FORTY-THREE

The congregation was gathered and seated in the chapel for the emergency meeting. Ezekiel stood carefully behind a speaker's lectern. Not because he needed it to remember what he wanted to say. And not because he'd called this meeting at far too early in the morning. He really needed the lectern to help keep him steady on his feet because he had drunk a bit too much bourbon.

But he couldn't help it. Joseph was the one person he counted on the most. The proverbial wizard behind the curtain who knew nearly all of Ezekiel's secrets. He knew Ezekiel wasn't really a religious man. But Joseph kept his mouth shut every step of the way and never wavered in his support. Now, things were completely different. He had to continue to act like a cult leader handpicked by God to lead his flock. And the one person he trusted the most to help him do it was gone forever.

"Ladies and gentlemen," Ezekiel began. "I come before you with some very disturbing news and a very heavy heart. While most of us were quietly sleeping in our own beds, our beloved Joseph was murdered in his home."

A loud murmur began to grow. Several people began to openly sob.

"I know you're hurting," Ezekiel said softly. "I'm hurting, too. We have compelling evidence that a former police officer, Malcolm Foster, is responsible."

The mood of the crowd began to shift, and Ezekiel could feel their anger beginning to grow.

"The Guardians need your help," Ezekiel continued. "I need your help. Right now. That's why we're meeting so early this morning. We need able-bodied men to help track down this man and bring him in to face justice."

"Can the Guardians do it?"

"Of course. But they need help. This man, Foster? I believe he's been touched by the Devil."

The room went immediately silent, and Ezekiel went for the proverbial kill.

"If more brave men were to step up and assist, then the process of capturing this evil man would become far easier. I shouldn't have to remind you that Malcolm Foster has killed members of our flock before. And now with striking down Joseph, he's targeting the very hearts of our congregation."

"What about women?" a female voice called out. "Can we join the Guardians?"

Ezekiel did a double-take. It wasn't something that Walter had ever suggested. The previous role of the Guardians was to act as his own group of protectors and enforcers of his word. But that role had begun to change. And Silas hadn't told him that he wouldn't accept women in his ranks, either. He glanced at Silas, who was standing near the exit. The man's arms were crossed, and he was slowly shaking his head side to side. Ezekiel looked away before the leader of the Guardians noticed he was looking at him.

"Our world has become increasingly dangerous," Ezekiel said as he carefully chose his words. "I think we've reached the point where any able-bodied person who is willing to join the Guardians and help protect all of us should be able to do so."

"Even if they got young children?" a man's voice shouted out.

"Being a Guardian does come with a certain amount of risk," Ezekiel answered. "I'll admit it, I'm a bit old-fashioned. I would be far more comfortable if mothers with young ones didn't become a Guardian. After all, none of us can guarantee any Guardian's safety at all times. And any mother who might be killed in the line of duty would be leaving children behind. But that shouldn't prevent anyone from fulfilling their calling."

"Yeah, and what if they're pregnant?" the same man demanded.

"Well, I suppose they could be moved into a job role which was less physically demanding or dangerous. I would need to defer to the leader of the Guardians on what types of jobs those might be. Silas, would you care to explain this for everyone?"

The man looked visibly uncomfortable as he walked slowly toward the lectern. Ezekiel stepped to his right, making room for the Guardian leader, and motioned for him to speak.

"Yeah, uh, the thing is, I don't have an exact plan for people like that," Silas stammered. "But there's different roles in the Guardians that don't put someone in the line of fire. It's kind of like our own military. Somebody has to handle communications, inventory, and lots of other stuff besides pointing a gun and shooting bad folks."

Ezekiel took over. "Thank you, Brother Silas. It may not be the most exciting work, but there's a place for everyone who wants to be a Guardian to be able to help. Isn't that right?"

"Yeah," Silas grumbled.

"Excellent," Ezekiel said with a well-practiced flourish. "That's all I have for now. If you are interested in joining the Guardians, then please see Brother Silas at your earliest opportunity."

Ezekiel stepped away from the lectern and saw there were already a dozen people in line to talk to Silas. He made a strategic retreat toward his office. There was a bottle of bourbon waiting for him that he couldn't wait to use to drown his grief.

CHAPTER FORTY-FOUR

It was nearly sunrise, and Foster was waiting patiently for Sams to return and report what he'd discovered. He watched as the former Ranger seemed to emerge quietly out of the shadows and move slowly toward him.

"Anything?" Foster whispered.

"Four Reapers stationed at the next intersection," Sams said softly. "I thought it was supposed to be unmanned?"

"I didn't say that," Foster answered. "I said we were promised an easy way out."

"It's four freaking Reapers," Sams pointed out. "We've got to sneak past them or kill them without drawing any extra attention. How's that easy?"

"Some of the other locations had two dozen," Foster pointed out. "I'd say four is a big improvement. Wouldn't you agree?"

"I guess."

"How do you want to handle this?"

"You take two. I'll take two," Foster said. "Charles and Gregory pull rear guard. Walker and Lizzy act as our quick reaction force. Kids stay in the vehicles until we confirm the coast is clear."

"Simple. I like it," Sams said. "Ready when you are."

"What's a quick reaction force?" Lizzy asked.

"Simple explanation," Walker said with a big grin. "If our resident tough guys get in deep shit, then you and I swoop in and pull our asses out of the fire."

"Oooh, I like that," Lizzy said. "I can't wait to rescue them."

"Maybe next time," Sams answered. "As long as flatfoot can shoot straight, this should be easy-peasy."

"Don't worry about me, Army," Foster said. "I'm a better shot than you."

"We'll see about that," Sams grumbled. "Try to keep up, man."

Foster watched as Sams moved quietly back into the shadows. He counted silently to two and followed his friend.

As the two men approached the intersection, Foster saw Sams motion he wanted him to take the two enemies on the left. The former Ranger moved to get into position and would handle the remaining two enemies.

Foster set up behind a parked Camry and sighted on the Reaper facing closest to them. He adjusted his aim until the Reaper's face was appearing in the middle of his rifle's scope. Foster exhaled slowly and pulled the trigger once. The suppressed rifle let out a small sound. He didn't wait to see until the monster completely dropped before he shifted his aim to the next closest target. The remaining Reaper realized something was wrong. The creature managed to get three quarters of the way turned around before Foster's shot nailed it in the ear. The monster's head collapsed inward, and it was dead before its body hit the ground. He glassed the area with his rifle scope and saw the other two monsters were also down.

"Looks clear," Sams said. "Proceeding. Cover me."

"Copy that," Foster said. He watched Sams slowly move forward. And kept looking, ever vigilant for any ambush surprises. It still appeared to be clear.

"Clear," Sams said. He cued his comms and added, "Walker, bring the rest of the group up. We have a clear exfil path."

"Copy that," Walker answered. "Rolling out."

Moments later, the two vehicles pulled up. Foster climbed in the passenger seat of one and saw Sams climb in the other.

"Looks like it was easy-peasy after all," Amanda said. "Next stop, airport."

"Looking forward to it, Doc," Foster said. "We got a flight to catch."

―――――――

There was a noise near the throne room entrance, and Beeks instinctively looked toward the disturbance. A pair of his soldiers were trying to stop another minion from getting access into the room.

"Let him in," Beeks commanded. He watched as his guards stepped aside just enough to let the unannounced visitor step through. As soon as he did, they moved to close the gap once more.

"What is it?" Beeks asked.

"Good news, my Lord," the soldier said. "We have found the one who had gone missing."

"Excellent. I want her brought here."

"Master, I thought you might. She fought against coming back home."

"Is that so?" Beeks said. "Interesting."

There was a loud noise in the hallway, and a moment later, three more soldiers dragged a visibly battered Angel into the room. They deposited her in front of Beeks. The female snarled, jumped to her feet, and headed toward the door, only to be met by further resistance. The minions grabbed her once more, and this time they threw her even harder in front of Beeks.

"Seal the throne room," Beeks commanded. "No one in or out."

The soldiers scurried about, quickly blocking access to the room's only doorway.

Beeks turned his attention to the glaring female in front of him. "Angel," he said in as soothing a voice as he could fake. "Why did you run away?"

"Leave me alone. I'm not like you."

"Sure you are," Beeks said. "Look around you. All of us look the same."

"No."

"Angel, look at your own arms and your legs. Your body fur. Heck, look at your hands." Beeks said, showing his razor-sharp claws. "You are like us. We are family."

"I don't wanna be. Why can't you just leave me alone?"

"That's not an option," Beeks said. "And I'm growing quite tired of your disrespect. Kneel."

"No."

"What?" Beeks snarled. "Kneel. Now."

Angel shook her head vigorously side to side.

"I think your sister has forgotten her manners," Beeks said. "Show her what she needs to do."

Four Reapers stepped forward, each grabbing part of Angel's limbs. She started to fight, but it was futile. The quartet of warriors simply overpowered her and forced her down onto one knee.

"Now, bow your head," Beeks said. "Show me the respect I deserve."

Angel glared at him with fierce eyes. A low growl began to grow in her throat.

Beeks lost his cool. He mentally reached out and lashed at her mind as if he were slapping a petulant child.

Angel let out a yelp of pain, then dropped her chin toward the floor.

"I warned you." Beeks growled. "We are your family, and I am your master."

"I don't think—"

"I didn't ask you what you think," Beeks said. He reached out telepathically once more and squeezed her mind. He gradually increased the pressure until she stopped fighting. "You will learn your place in the pack," he continued. "You will learn to obey. You will learn to eat what your pack mates provide for you. Do you understand me?"

"I don't— Ahhh!" Angel shrieked in pain. "Okay." Tears began to roll down her face.

Beeks was pleased. "I mean it. I will not warn you again."

"I... I understand." Angel whimpered.

"Do you swear to obey?"

"I... will."

Beeks felt his heart swell with pride. Maybe this former military woman wasn't so tough after all. He looked forward to continuing to groom her in her place in his pack. Perhaps one day he would choose her to carry his offspring. But it wasn't time to consider breeding. There was too much for him still to do. There were too many remaining pockets of resistance in the United States and Canada. He hadn't even begun to spread his family into the rest of the world.

"Sir," Angel said carefully.

"Not *sir*," Beeks corrected. "Master or Lord."

"Master, I'm... I'm feeling very tired. Is it okay if I go back to my room to sleep?"

"Yes. Go rest up. We have very exciting plans and things to do together, Angel."

"Okay," she muttered, never breaking eye contact with the ground.

"You are dismissed," Beeks said. He turned his attention to the guards still standing at attention. "One of you can escort her to her room. See that she gets there, or you'll answer to me."

"Yes, my Lord," the group answered together.

Several of them stepped forward together and began to argue amongst themselves. After a few muttered snarls, one came forward while the rest returned to their posts. The lone minion moved quickly to escort Angel out of the room.

CHAPTER FORTY-FIVE

The walkie-talkie blasted unexpectedly, and Silas startled in mid-step. He rushed to lower the volume to a more appropriate level. They were in the middle of a patrol. The last thing they needed to do was announce their presence to the neighborhood.

"Guardian One, this is Guardian Central."

"Yeah," Silas answered. "Go ahead, Guardian Central."

"We've got a report from a civilian about a disturbance outside of town."

"Yeah, we'll check on that in a little while," Silas says. "We're kind of in the middle of something right now."

Being on patrol was definitely not his usual routine. But his men were acting a little skittish lately, so Silas decided to mix things up a bit. He'd doubled the size of his usual personal patrol. There were nine other Guardians surrounding him that should be able to capable of handling Foster's group if they found them. Silas wanted his men to be on their toes, so he had insisted they park a few blocks away and check each guard position in person. Maybe they'd find Foster while on patrol. Or maybe he'd find some dumb schmuck sleeping on guard duty. Either way, he could work his frustrations out on someone else.

Silas felt like there was no one that he needed to answer to. He was Ezekiel's chosen leader of the Guardians. And that meant he could go anywhere in the town that he wanted and do anything he saw fit to do.

Which is why Ezekiel's public proclamation to let anyone join the Guardians was so infuriating. It was his militia, not Ezekiel's. The preacher man needed to stick to what he did best, which was convince the sheep to follow his so-called gospel advice. He'd heard somebody once say that it took a con artist to spot a con being worked. And if Silas were being honest, Ezekiel was pulling a doozy on his unsuspecting congregation. He wasn't sure why the Reapers didn't attack anyone wearing the designated armbands. But right now, he didn't give a shit. He was just glad he didn't have to worry about being personally attacked by those damn things.

As Silas proceeded along the street, he looked around and saw what looked to be a mess.

"Got bodies," the foot soldier said.

"Check it out," Silas said. He gestured with his head toward a group of Guardians standing nearby. "And take him with you."

"Who? Jones?" the soldier asked.

"Yeah, sure," Silas said. "Take him with you."

Silas watched as his two foot soldiers moved forward cautiously. They approached the dead bodies, and he watched as Jones cautiously kicked one of them, and then another.

"Dead Reapers," Jones said. "Four of them."

"Any idea who might have done it?" the other guy said.

"Doesn't matter," Silas said. "I say we need to investigate."

"But aren't we supposed to stay on patrol?"

"We go where I say," Silas answered. "Anyone got a problem with that?"

Jones shook his head vigorously, as did the other man. "Good."

"Guardian Central, this is Guardian One."

"Go, Guardian One."

"Yeah, we've got four dead Reapers here. I'm going to take my boys and check it out. We need to rule out a possible security breach here."

"It might be related to that disturbance."

"Yeah, okay," Silas said. "Any idea who reported it?"

"One of the congregation. Artie Wilkerson."

Silas grimaced. Wilkerson was not one of his favorite people in the world. For starters, the guy was a retired deputy sheriff. And being around cops always made Silas a little nervous.

Wilkerson was a member in good standing. He had offered to join the Guardians, but Silas had declined. Told the guy there weren't any openings right now. But if he was being honest, it was because Wilkerson was in his sixties and extremely obese. Silas wasn't sure the guy could touch his toes, let alone find them.

Of course, with one big plea in the chapel, Ezekiel unknowingly nuked Silas's excuse. It was only a matter of time until Wilkerson hit him up again to join the Guardians. And this time, Silas would be hard-pressed to refuse him.

But give the fat guy his due. Silas couldn't deny that as a former law enforcement officer, Wilkerson should be able to spot someone trying to flee a scene.

Silas mentally groaned. He might as well suck it up and get this over with. "Guardian Central, any chance you can raise Wilkerson for me? I have a few questions."

"Yeah, hold on, Guardian One. I'll try reaching him."

There was a short lull, and then Silas heard a man's voice. "This is Artie Wilkerson. Someone wanted to talk to me?"

"Yes," Silas answered. "This is Silas. Time is of the essence. Artie, I need you tell me what you just saw."

"Sure. Two SUVs, heading north out of Rehoboth at a high rate of speed."

"How long ago?"

"Maybe five minutes. Why?"

"Where are you?"

"Route 1. Northbound. I'm in my Prius."

Silas grimaced. As far as he was concerned, a Prius hardly qualified as a real vehicle. It was another ding against Artie ever becoming a Guardian. Silas took the thought and shoved it to the back of his mind. He took a quick breath to help him feel a little bit more focused before speaking. "Okay, Artie, I need you to listen to me very carefully," Silas warned. "I need you to follow them, but without being spotted."

"Excuse me?"

"Follow them. Don't engage. They're extremely dangerous."

"Okay," Wilkerson said.

"Does he know how to tail somebody?" Jones asked.

Silas released the transmit button and turned toward his underling. "He's a former sheriff's deputy," he answered. "Anyone who ever worked in law enforcement knows how to do a proper tail."

"Sorry, boss," Jones mumbled.

Silas flashed a quick smile at his foot soldier and turned his attention back to the walkie. "Artie, we're on our way there. But I need you to follow them until we can catch up to you."

"You want to know where they go?"

"Yes, that's right," Silas answered. "The people who you saw leaving are extremely dangerous. They killed a number of Guardians in a recent encounter. So I don't want you to be playing hero by yourself there. There's no point in making your wife a widow."

"I can handle myself. I was—"

"I'm sure you can," Silas interrupted. "But you have zero backup right now. You're not armed."

"I have a Beretta—"

"Just follow them from a distance and see where they go," Silas ordered. "I'm bringing nine other Guardians with me. All of us are heavily armed. Once we get to your location, we'll take it from there."

"All right. I'll call you back with an update."

"Thanks, Artie," Silas said. "Guardian Central, this is Guardian One."

"Go ahead."

"Classify Artie Wilkerson as a deputized Guardian and give him clearance to reach you or me directly. Show us moving to Artie's current location to intercept potential hostiles."

"Wait, we can deputize people?" Jones asked. "When did that happen?"

"No idea," Silas said. "But I did it." He made a shooing motion. The foot soldier immediately clammed up and quickly retreated.

"Understood," the dispatcher announced. "Safe hunting."

"Roger that. Silas out."

CHAPTER FORTY-SIX

Haas had returned to the animal hospital. It was close enough for him to reach most of the town if needed. Just as important, it offered a dry and isolated location for him and his warriors to spend the night. He had tasked a pair of his fighters to go find several animals that would provide a late meal for them. Preferably rabbits, which would challenge his warriors to catch them. Haas was resting comfortably on a padded surface when he felt four separate life forces sever from him. He flinched instinctively in discomfort. He reached out to one of the dying troops and confirmed it was Foster's group before he released the mental hold on the dying fighter. He wasn't happy about having to sacrifice any of his soldiers, but it was more important right now to ensure Foster and his group managed to escape the town safely. He silently hoped his loyal warriors hadn't suffered before they died. It would have been best if their deaths had come swiftly. He still had plenty of fighters. Worst case, he'd pressure Ezekiel to provide more humans to be transformed.

Meat for the grinder, he thought absently. *That's all they are.*

Another voice unexpectedly popped into his mind, and Haas immediately bolted to his feet.

"Haas, where are you?" Beeks said impatiently.

"The same place I was when you asked me last time," Haas answered impatiently. Beeks was the last person he wanted to deal with right now.

"Wait. You haven't left that town?"

"Of course not," Haas answered. *"You told me to stay here."*

"I want a report on Foster's whereabouts."

"It's not that simple."

"What do you mean? Don't you have soldiers keeping an eye on him, trying to track him down?"

"Of course."

"So why don't you have anything new to tell me?" Beeks scolded. *"What are you doing there? Do I have to do everything myself?"*

Haas deliberately kept his voice calm. *"A handful of our warriors unexpectedly turned up dead."*

"What? What happened?"

"It appears someone killed them near one of the roads out of town. I don't know who is responsible, but we'll find them."

"Foster."

"Maybe. Maybe not. It might be someone other than him."

"It has to be Foster," Beeks snarled. *"Dammit. I thought you had him cornered."*

"I thought so, too," Haas lied. *"But let's face it, the man has been slippery like an eel. And dangerous, too. Correct me if I'm wrong, but didn't he kill both Malice and Nails?"*

Haas heard Beeks growl in frustration. *"Don't remind me. This human has been a thorn in my side for far too long."*

"So let's say that you're right."

"Of course I'm right," Beeks declared. *"Why wouldn't I be? I'm the master of millions of soldiers. Including you."*

"I wasn't looking to start an argument with you," Haas said

carefully. If he could steer Beeks carefully, then he'd have his oppressor's blessing to pursue his plan. *"Suppose you are right and it was this human, Foster. Do you want me to track him down and see where he's gone?"*

"Hmm, you raise a good point. No, I want you to stay where you're at."

"But didn't you just complain about me still being here?"

There was an uncomfortable moment of silence, and then he heard Beeks say, *"I don't know why I'm telling you this, but I have someone else nearby."*

"Achilles?"

"Of course."

"With all due respect, sir, I'm not sure Achilles could find his way out of a cardboard box. I mean, he's not exactly the brightest—"

"Achilles will pursue this," Beeks interrupted. *"I want you and the soldiers you have remaining to continue to search that town for Foster. Maybe it's a decoy and he's still there."*

"You think someone else dared to kill some of our soldiers and then flee town?"

"It's possible."

Haas chuckled softly. *"If you say so."*

"You dare to question my judgment?"

"Of course not, Horatio."

"You need to be more respectful to me."

"Right. Sorry."

"And don't call me Horatio, dammit. You know I hate that name."

"I meant no disrespect," Haas said with a forced smile. *"I assumed since we were talking privately that no one else had to know how we talked to each other. Or have you forgotten our past history together?"*

"No, I haven't forgotten. I still remember you kneeling in front of me not that long ago. Don't you?"

Haas clenched his teeth and quietly seethed.

"I'm waiting for your answer."

"Yes. I remember."

"Good. I'd hate to have to remind you again so soon," Beeks gloated. *"Find me Foster or some clue of where he has gone. I don't care what you need to do. Tear that town apart, if you need to. I want Foster found."*

"As you wish, sir." Haas felt a connection break, and then Beeks was no longer in his mind. Haas began to pace the room nervously. Did he handle it correctly? Would Beeks ever suspect that he had helped Foster escape from town? He hoped not.

"Achilles," Haas said aloud. He didn't care for the other red-eyed Reaper. But Haas had to give him credit. He'd be a powerful foe for nearly any human opponent. There wasn't much he could do right now to help Foster. He'd have to hope the human could elude Achilles and whatever soldiers that Beeks had sent in pursuit.

CHAPTER FORTY-SEVEN

President Vickers could feel her heart racing. This was it. In less than one minute, their attack on the Reapers would begin. She turned her attention to the wall-mounted screens. There were hundreds of Reapers gathered around the sound system. Someone had managed to surround the speaker system in some type of secure metal caging to protect it prior to deploying it. Even so, she watched as different Reapers continued to attack the enclosure, trying to get to the source of the sound. A noise near her pulled her attention away from the live event.

"Five, four, three," a tech counted aloud. "Two, one, initiate. Operation Poison Arrow is now live."

Vickers frowned. She shouldn't have been so easily distracted. It was a not-so-subtle hint that she was running on fumes lately. If this military operation was a success, then it would turn the tide in their favor, and then she'd be able to sleep for as long as she wanted. Vickers turned her attention back to the display of wall-mounted monitors once more. There were two different overhead drones sending their own live footage. She saw a large streaking light come across one of the screens. There was a loud explosion, and she watched as the dust plumed up into the sky.

"Target has been hit," the tech called out.

A loud cheer sounded out through the room.

Vickers felt her spirits begin to soar. "Keep the cameras running," she shouted over the noise. "Let's see how well this works."

————

Beeks paced the throne room. He was feeling high-strung, but he didn't know why. Well, that wasn't quite true. He knew exactly why. He was completely bored out of his mind. In his position of absolute rule, there wasn't much for him to do. He'd give a command, and his minions did it without question until it was completed. Even now, his soldiers were pushing the offensive against the remaining pockets of resistance scattered through the United States and Canada. And there was absolutely nothing for him to do until one of the squad leaders reported any problems. Sighing, Beeks flopped down on his throne. His stomach gurgled, and Beeks realized he couldn't remember the last time he ate.

"You... there," he said.

"Master?" one of his guards said, dropping to a knee immediately and looking at the floor as expected.

"I'm hungry," Beeks said. "Find me something to eat."

"A-As you wish, my Lord," the guard bolted toward the door. He got partway through the door, stopped, and turned around.

"Yes? What is it?" Beak said impatiently.

"My Lord, I don't know what you want to eat."

"I don't care. Find me some type of livestock."

"Uh, Master, forgive me for asking. But what is livestock?"

Beeks felt his ire rising. "Find a live cow or a pig. Kill it and bring it to me."

"Yes, my Lord. Of course, my Lord. Right away, sir." The soldier stumbled backwards in his haste to leave the room.

Beeks waited until the minion left before groaning aloud. It had gotten to a point where even bullying his underlings was losing its appeal. His soldiers were still having trouble finding Foster. It was the same shit, different day in pretty much every facet of his life. He needed something new to happen. Something to distract his mind from the monotony.

Suddenly, Beeks felt a strange burning sensation traveling up his arms and into his neck. He clamped down his teeth.

What the hell was happening? Was he having some kind of heart attack? Wait, no, it wasn't his pain. It was some of his children. He focused his attention on trying to track down where the pain was coming from.

A lone voice sounded out in his head. *"It hurts, Master. Make it stop! Make it stop!"*

A split second later, a cascade of new voices joined the first one in his mind, each screaming in pain.

Beeks felt his body buck in agony.

"What is happening?" he growled.

Beeks reached out to one of the minions howling in pain. He seized control of their mind.

"Show me what you see," he commanded.

As the minion's eyes began to focus on its surroundings, Beeks saw there was a loud plume of dust and smoke around them. He saw his soldiers lying on the ground, writhing. A growing number of voices in his head were screaming at once in anguish and pain.

"Stay strong, my children," Beeks commanded instinctively.

"It burns. It burns so bad."

"Fight the burn. It will pass. I promise." Beeks felt the sensa-

tion begin to diminish from his minions. It began fading a little bit moment by moment, and then it was gone.

———

As the dust settled, Vickers could see nearly all the Reapers had fallen on the ground. Dozens were staggering away, trying to get away from the chemicals. She watched on camera as several dropped to one knee, or onto the ground, and she felt her spirits rise. It was actually working.

She felt them crash down a split second later. One of the Reapers that had fallen stood up. She watched on camera as its tattered shirt began to tear.

"There," she ordered. "Focus on that Reaper."

The camera zoomed in on the Reaper in question, and Vickers watched in horror as the Reaper's shoulders and chest seemed to grow bigger. Its bare arms became immense, and striations of muscle became visible. The Reaper pounded its chest and let out a roar. More Reapers began to stand up, and they too began to grow bigger. One roar led to a second, then a third. Soon, hundreds of visibly enhanced Reapers were roaring as one.

"Holy shit, those things are huge," someone in the room blurted.

"Cut the damn camera," Vickers said. "It's like you just hit them with a bunch of steroids."

"We had no idea, Madam President," General Weindahl said. The man looked visibly shaken. "That shouldn't have happened."

"Cease fire on the chemical weapons until we know what actually kills these bastards," Vickers ordered. "I want the next test done by our scientists in a controlled environment. We just created who knows how many jacked-up Reapers. That's completely unacceptable."

"I'm sorry, President Vickers," Weindahl offered. "There was nothing in our research to suggest something like this."

"Well, I think it's safe to say the research was wrong. This is unacceptable. We can't take a chance on something like that happening ever again." She stood up, and the rest of the room slowly stood on delayed reaction.

"Madam President," Weindahl muttered. "If you would like my resignation—"

"Not a chance in hell," Vickers interrupted. "Your country needs their best people in place and not retreating in shame."

"We'll do better."

"We have to," Vickers answered. "For the sake of our nation. And maybe the rest of the world."

Vickers looked around the room. No one else had moved. "Meeting's adjourned," she ordered. "Find me something that will actually kill these bastards, not turn them into even bigger brutes." She turned and left the room without waiting for an answer.

Vickers walked as quickly as she could back to her office. It was taking everything she had to not burst out in tears now. The last thing she needed was for her military advisors and the people on this ship to see her looking less than presidential. No, she was the Commander in Chief. And now, more than ever, her country needed her to be strong. Even if she was currently feeling like all hope was lost.

———

The burning had completely halted. Freed from his soldiers' pain, Beeks rose up from his throne and seized control of the recently affected minions. He forced every one of the creatures to look around him. Each of the surrounding soldiers appeared bigger, more muscular. He forced the soldier's eyes to look at its own limbs. They were massively muscular.

Another minion stumbled into the one he was in control of. "Watch where you're going!" Beeks blurted.

The creature turned, spun, and looked. It began to growl.

Beeks squinted. There was something different about this enhanced Reaper's eyes. They were orange.

Beeks began to laugh aloud. The United States government had tried to kill some of his children. But in their haste to eradicate his kind, they had created a new breed of warriors for him. These Betas were an unexpected gift. And Beeks fully intended to use this gift to his complete benefit.

"Hear me now, children," Beeks mentally ordered. "Those of you who felt the burn, find where it came from. Go now!"

"Yes, my Lord," Hundreds of voices called out as one. Beeks watched as hundreds of Betas charged off like an enraged pack of predators. He broke the mental connection with his minions. This obviously had been some kind of attack by the humans. An attack that had backfired. And like every other failed attack by the puny humans, there would be payback.

CHAPTER FORTY-EIGHT

The sound of the tires on the roadway was almost hypnotic, and Foster found himself fighting to stay awake. Last night's meeting with Haas, combined with the early-morning escape out of town, had left him running on minimal sleep. To be honest, it had been a hellacious couple of days between battling the Reapers and the Disciples. It seemed like danger had been coming at them from every which way. But that was about to change.

In a few hours, they'd be on a helicopter and heading to Hope Island. At the same time, he couldn't help but wonder if he truly should keep his word with Haas. If this creature was telling him the truth about one King Reaper controlling them all, then killing their top dog could prevent the human race from being wiped out.

He was on the fence as to what he wanted to do. On one hand, he wanted to go with his friends to the safety that Hope Island seemed to offer. On the other, there was a sense of duty and honor that came with being a police officer. Despite the recent events, Foster had spent too many years as a cop to forget his instincts. He couldn't forget the pledge that he had taken while becoming a police officer, either.

But then there was Amanda. Was there something there that would develop into a meaningful relationship? He wasn't opposed to the idea. In his mind, she was beautiful, smart, and funny. Conversation with her most of the time was pretty effortless. But would things change once they got to Hope Island and the threat of imminent danger was no longer hanging over their heads? He just didn't know. There were just too many unknowns and variables to quickly figure out. And that frustrated Foster nearly as much as the mountain of problems he felt he had to overcome.

Suddenly, there was a loud *thunk*, and something flew off the front vehicle. Foster felt his body lurch forward in his seat as Walker hit the brakes and the SUV came to an abrupt stop.

"The hell was that?" Foster asked.

"I don't know," Walker said. "Might have been a person. Or an animal."

"Could it have been a Reaper instead?"

"I don't know," Walker said.

"You need to check if they're okay," Lizzy said. "We can't just leave them there."

"We don't know what I hit," Walker answered.

"Nicholas, don't be an asshole," Lizzy scolded. "If you hit somebody, you need to find out. What if the Reapers find them and turn them into one of those monsters?"

"Dammit," Walker mumbled. He slowly pulled the vehicle over to the side, shifted the engine into park, and turned the vehicle off.

The walkie-talkie chirped. "Yo, buddy," Sams said. "Why are we stopping?"

"I got to check on something," Walker answered. "I might have hit a person."

"Copy that," Sams answered. "We'll set up a perimeter."

"Hon, stay inside," Nick ordered. "Foster, you're with me."

"I can help," Lizzy said.

"Yes, you can. By staying here. If it's a person, I'll come get you. But I'll feel better knowing that you're safe while we're searching for a possible body in the dark."

Walker and Foster slid out of the vehicle.

Foster could hear Lizzy complaining as he closed the doors.

"Let me check for the body," Foster offered. "You stay on overwatch for any potential trouble. If we got something, I'll call you."

"That works," Walker said.

Foster pulled his Glock and penlight out. He turned on the light, casting a narrow light in front of himself. He began scanning left to right, working his way to the side of the road. He didn't have to go far until he saw a pair of legs thrashing from side to side. Foster slowly worked the light along the person's body and toward their head.

But as the light revealed more, Foster saw it was no longer a medium-size man. The Reaper tried to lift its head up, and it flopped back awkwardly. The creature let out a weak growl. From the weird position of the monster's head, Foster guessed it had suffered a broken neck. Left on its own, the creature might regenerate enough to restore its normal abilities. But there wasn't any point in letting that happen. Not when it might go on to kill or turn another human.

Foster brought his Glock up, aimed carefully, and fired once, striking the wounded Reaper in the head. The creature's legs stopped moving immediately. He lowered his Glock and retraced his steps back to the SUV.

"Problem?" Walker asked.

"You hit a Reaper," Foster said. "It's dead now."

The two men climbed back in the car.

"I heard a gunshot," Lizzy said. There was a hint of nervousness in her voice.

"Nick hit a Reaper," Foster said. "I made sure it was dead."

"Oh," Lizzy said.

Walker activated his comms. "Hostile eliminated," he said. "Ready to roll out when you are."

"Copy that," Sams answered. "We'll be ready in one minute."

The vehicle grew uncomfortably silent.

Foster heard the SUV behind them start, and a moment later Walker did the same. Foster felt the vehicle shift into gear, and it began to pull back onto the highway. He turned his attention to the passenger-side window, watching the terrain slowly pass behind them. In about forty minutes, they should reach the airport museum. He couldn't wait to board the chopper.

———

Achilles felt alive as he loped along the roadway. It was liberating to be out and running. He looked to his left and then to his right. His nearly one hundred fighters were keeping up with the aggressive pace he was setting. Achilles felt his heart swell with pride. Each one of his warriors had been personally turned by him. Each one was an eager and willing fighter, ready to give their life at his command.

Lead from the front. He'd heard that phrase someplace else before, but he had never understood what it really meant. Until now. Now, he would lead his pack of fighters to wherever the lowly human Foster was hiding. And once they found him, then he'd make his master proud.

The miles were quickly passing as they worked their way along the roadways and through patches of open woods. Achilles wasn't sure where exactly they were heading. Right now, it was more of a gut feeling where he thought the fugitive might be heading.

"Achilles, where are you?" Beeks' voice blurted in his mind. The interruption immediately shattered the calmness of the moment.

"Everyone halt," Achilles ordered. He took a few steps away from the rest of his warriors before answering Beeks' mental message.

"I'm here, my Lord. What's wrong?"

"Nothing. Why does something have to be wrong?" Beeks said. *"I'm calling with information."*

"Yes, Master," Achilles said simply. *"What is it?"*

"Another family member crossed paths with Foster. Not far from where you're at now."

"Are they sure?"

"As sure as one can be before getting shot in the head. I've retrieved their memories. It looks like Foster. The human is wearing the same top with the distinctive word on it."

"Po-lice?" Achilles said carefully.

"Yes, that's right."

"Where is he?"

A visual image popped in Achilles' mind.

"Make your way there," Beeks ordered. *"There's a series of buildings nearby. They might be going there to hide."*

"We'll check it out, my Lord."

"Excellent. Oh, and Achilles?"

"Yes?"

"You didn't say thank you. I just made your job easier."

"Of course, Master," Achilles said with a forced smile. *"Thank you for your guidance and your help."*

"*My pleasure,*" Beeks answered before cutting the connection.

Achilles let out the breath that he had been holding. It wasn't considered good form to talk badly about his master. He certainly wouldn't do it in front of the soldiers that he commanded, but there were times where his master's antics grew quite tiresome.

"We have a possible location nearby," Achilles announced to his fighters. "Be on the lookout for Fos-ter or any of his friends."

Achilles dropped to all fours and began bounding in the direction. As he did, he noticed a brown sign. He didn't understand the words on it, but the red, white, and blue star captured his attention. Achilles lengthened his stride, and his soldiers followed suit. They were getting close. He could feel it in his gut. And once he confronted the pesky human, he'd end Foster's life, which would please his Master immensely.

———

Silas tapped nervously on the dashboard. He'd called Artie twice in the last ten minutes. The retired deputy had managed to tail the pair of SUVs without drawing any attention.

Silas glanced out the window as they zipped past a brown street sign announcing some kind of upcoming tourist trap. He quietly hoped Foster was in one of those vehicles. Because if he was, then Silas would be happy to put a bullet in the guy's head. Sure, Ezekiel might want Foster dead because he'd killed a bunch of Guardians near the marina. And now that the preacher man thought that Foster had killed his little pet Joseph, he wanted the cop even more.

But Silas had a bigger reason for wanting to eliminate the guy. Removing a loose end. A dead Foster couldn't expose his lie about Joseph's death. And once Foster was taken out of the picture, Silas could hunt down and kill the bitches who had humiliated him at the gun shop. The sooner it happened, the better. Then his men would have no choice but to completely respect Silas as their leader.

CHAPTER FORTY-NINE

The SUV was quickly approaching a large brown sign. Foster studied the display a bit closer. There was a prominent red, white, and blue National Star in the one corner. The sign had large white letters that announced they were approaching the Air Mobility Command Museum.

"What is this place?" Walker asked. "I've never heard of it before."

"Probably because you're an Army grunt," Lizzy teased. "My dad used to bring me here as a kid."

"Huh. So how come you haven't taken me here?"

"I thought about it," Lizzy said. "More than once. But I haven't been here since my father died. It was kind of our place we went together when we wanted to take a day trip away from the rest of the family."

"Lots of security fencing," Walker pointed out. "Is this part of Dover Air Force Base?"

"No," Lizzy answered. "The base is a few miles from here."

"Which means the Reapers might have completely

ignored it when they attacked Dover," Walker said. "Talk about a lucky break for us."

"We don't know that yet," Foster cautioned. "But I'd say the odds are good that this place is Reaper-free."

"Hon, what can you tell me about this place?" Walker asked.

"Lots. My dad and I visited this place so many times," Lizzy said. "During World War II, it was known as Dover Army Airfield. Lots of top-secret rocket development. From the 1950s to the 1970s, the military had a number of different fighter squadrons that called this place home. In the 1990s, it was restored and renamed the Air Mobility Command Museum."

"What kind of things are we going to find here?" Foster asked.

"A number of different bombers, cargo planes, tankers, and fighters. They should still have the A-26C and C-5A Galaxy. They even have an old Air Force Two."

"Really?" Walker blurted.

"Yes. A VC-9C."

"Damn, I wish we had come here before," Walker said. "You know, before all of this stuff happened."

"There's a good chance the museum was untouched," Foster pointed out. "The Reaper invasion started in the middle of the night. This place would have been closed then. If nobody was here, then the Reapers wouldn't have had any reason to attack it."

"Yeah, probably," Walker mumbled. "But I'll feel safer once we do a proper sweep." He turned the steering wheel, making a right turn onto Route 9.

The vehicle grew silent as everyone retreated into their own thoughts.

Foster watched as the long row of barbed wire topped metal fencing seemed to extend far into the distance. A few minutes later, they reached a new paved driveway which featured a pair of brick pillars embracing the path. To the right of the roadway, the fencing continued. Foster noticed two signs. A small sign listed a website address. A much larger one to its right proudly announced they had reached the Air Mobility Command Museum.

Foster watched as the SUV turned left onto the roadway and continued forward. The barbed wire topped metal fencing now surrounded each side of the road.

"This is good," Walker said. "No signs of Reaper activity. Definitely a defensible position."

"What do you mean?" Lizzy asked.

"The fencing," Walker answered. "Not easy for the Reapers to attack from multiple directions unless they breach the fencing. It's a well-designed fatal funnel. No signs of a recent battle. This place might actually be Reaper-free."

"I sure hope so," Lizzy said softly.

Artie Wilkerson had followed the SUVs for miles. As luck would have it, they didn't seem to notice his hybrid blue Prius tailing them from a block distance. In the past, there would have been far too many other vehicles on the roadways to hang back so far on a tail. But now, there were very few drivers on the roads anymore. He missed his old squad car. That Dodge Charger had some serious muscle under the hood. But he was retired now. He didn't need something that he could jam the pedal down and go balls out fast on demand. He needed something that got great gas mileage and was cheap to drive instead. Sure, he'd heard some of the other men snicker about his Prius. Artie chose to ignore them. Thanks to the Reapers, a lot of the supply chains had been disrupted. Some of them might be broken for good. Six months from now, gasoline was going to be pretty hard to find. Those naysayers would be complaining about how hard it was to find enough fuel to keep their gas guzzlers running. And Artie? Well, he'd just smile before heading off somewhere in his Prius.

Wilkerson drove past the entrance to the Air Mobility Command Museum and continued for another quarter mile. He came to a stop and checked his rearview mirror. Satisfied that no one was following him, he did a careful three-point turn. Once he managed to turn the Prius around, he pulled to the side of the road so he could watch the museum's entrance. Wilkerson pulled out his cell phone and hit redial. The phone rang twice, and then he heard someone answer.

"Silas," the Guardian leader said.

"They turned off," Wilkerson replied. "I'm outside the entrance of the Air Mobility Command Museum."

"You're not following them anymore?"

"Relax," Wilkerson answered. "There's only one way in or out of that place."

"Good," Silas answered. "We're a few minutes out. Call me if anything changes."

"Okay, will do. Listen, if you need my help, then—"

There was a loud beeping sound. Wilkerson stopped talking and looked at his phone. The display was showing the call had ended. Wilkerson frowned. Silas had hung up on him while he was still talking. Maybe his wife was right when she had said the guy was a bona-fide prick. But Artie had dealt with plenty of people who were jerks when he worked in law enforcement. And if dealing with one like Silas kept him and his wife safe from the Reapers, then he was willing to smile politely and eat whatever shit sandwich Silas handed him for now.

CHAPTER FIFTY

The SUV pulled into a parking lot and came to a stop. An Air Force T-33 plane was parked on top of a sign that announced they had reached the Air Mobility Command Museum.

"How far from the turnoff?" Foster asked.

Lizzy snorted. "What makes you think Nick measured the distance—"

"Unless the odometer is off," Walker reported, "about seven tenths of a mile."

"Are you serious?" Lizzy stammered.

"Completely," Foster answered. "I saw Nick look at the dashboard gauges when we turned off the road. It would be better if it was a couple miles of distance from the turnoff. But nearly a mile is still respectable."

"I'm not following," Lizzy said. "Why does the distance matter?"

"Noise," Walker answered. "The farther away from a main road, the less likely any Reapers passing by might see or hear us." He turned the ignition off, and the engine immediately cut out. Walker removed the key and tucked it behind the driver's side visor before opening the door.

Foster followed his friend's lead and climbed out of the passenger side of the SUV. He carefully stood and stretched, working out a few of the physical kinks he'd gained while they were stuck in the vehicle. He saw Sams and the rest of them disembark from their SUV and work their way toward him.

"Interesting looking place," Sams said as he approached. "Your idea?"

"Lizzy's," Foster volunteered. "She used to visit this place as a kid."

"Nice," Sams answered. "This might work well to bring in a helicopter."

"Let's clear this place first," Walker said. "Then we'll worry about landing our next ride."

"Head that way," Lizzy pointed. "It's the Museum's Hall of Fame. They have a souvenir shop there."

"Good idea," Sams said. "We'll probably find some beverages and food that we can grab and take with us to Hope Island."

"Or we can work from there to clear the area," Walker countered. "The sooner we know the place is clear, the quicker we can call for our ride."

"Let's get it done, then," Sams said. "I'm ready to blow this pop stand."

———

They caught a major break when they discovered that most of the buildings were locked up tight. A quick discussion with the group was had on whether they should break into each building and do a complete top-to-bottom search. A consensus was quickly reached. They only needed to ensure the area was secure enough for the Hope Island copter to land and then take off again. If there were Reapers sleeping in one of the other locked-up buildings, then they'd worry about dealing with them if they figured out how to break out of the building and made an uninvited appearance.

As a result of their decision, it had only taken them a few minutes to clear the immediate area. The group then divided into smaller teams and set up overwatch positions at the primary entranceways of the Hall of Fame building. In the interest of keeping potential noise to a minimum, Foster moved into the souvenir shop to make one last call. The store was located deep in the larger building. Just as important, it was positioned where there was no chance of anyone outside of the room hearing him talking.

The sat phone had already rung four times before he heard someone answer the call.

"Your timing sucks," Black grumbled.

"In the bathroom?" Foster asked.

"Doesn't matter where I was," Black answered. "Your timing is still lousy."

"This was the first chance I had to call you with an update."

"Uh-huh. Where are you now?"

"A place called Air Mobility Command Museum," Foster said. "We've done a sweep, and the place is secure."

"Are you sure?"

"Positive. The museum is a few miles from Dover Air Force. The place is surrounded by metal fencing. There's barbed wire on the top of it to keep anyone from climbing over."

"Anyone or anything," Black said. "All right, it took some serious arm wrenching, but I got Abrahams on board. He'll send the chopper to your location for a fast extraction. But it's a one-shot deal. If your group isn't ready or the extraction zone is overrun with Reapers, then the deal is off."

"We're ready. The area is secure right now. We've set up lookouts to spot any potential hostiles."

"Excellent. I'll see you in about thirty minutes."

"Wait, what? You're coming for the extraction?"

"Uh-huh. Lead from the front, Malcolm," Black said. "Lost half of my boys on a recent mission. Gimble has a broken arm, and Keane is pretty banged up."

"But you're in charge of your SWAT unit. Couldn't you send Spagonelli?"

"Abrahams would have a complete shit fit if I did. He's on security detail here. The Rangers might not want to admit it, but Spags might be the best sniper on the island. So I'm the logical choice for a last-minute Uber service."

"Makes sense," Foster said. "I'll see you when you get here."

"Uh-huh," Black answered. "Stay frosty until then."

Foster disconnected the call and began to carefully put the sat phone away. He heard a series of hurried footsteps coming his way and instinctively reached for his rifle.

"Malcolm?" a voice called out.

Foster dropped his hands from his weapon. "I'm in here, Lizzy," he answered. He felt his heart pounding in his chest. He fought to bring his emotions back under control. The rush of footsteps had almost triggered him into opening fire at whatever might have appeared in the doorway.

Lizzy hustled into the room with Sams and Charles in tow.

"Our ride is on its way," Foster said simply. "Should be here within the next thirty minutes."

"That might be a problem," Sams answered. "We have incoming. We're not sure they've spotted us yet."

"So if we lay low, they might pass us by?" Foster asked.

"Maybe," Sams answered. "If the Reapers get too close for comfort, Gregory, Walker, and Amanda are set up to repel."

"Call Black back," Lizzy said. "Tell him we need more time."

"Not an option," Foster said. "The Army told him it's a one-shot deal. If they can't land safely, then they're not coming back for us."

"Fuck a duck," Sams muttered. He reached for the wireless comms and activated them. "Nick, come in."

Walker answered immediately. "Yeah, what's up?"

"Ride is en route," Sams said. "ETA is thirty mikes. They're making one pass. If we're not ready, then they're leaving without us."

"Understood. Hostiles aren't within range of our location yet."

"Where are they?"

"Wandering around."

"Any chance they could be led away?" Sams asked.

"Derrick," Foster warned. "If you're thinking of doing something reckless—"

"Not reckless," Sams answered. "Just a little Pied Piper action. If I can get them to chase one of our vehicles, I can lead them away from the airfield. I just need to be back in time to catch our ride."

"Affirmative on the distraction," Walker answered. "But it needs to be pretty noticeable to get their attention."

"I'm on it," Sams said. "If there's one thing I'm great at, it's getting attention." He turned towards Foster and said, "Keep your comms on. If I can't get back here in time, I'll call you."

"Be careful," Foster warned.

"Careful is my middle name," Sams said. He flashed a quick, boyish grin before darting out the door. A moment later, Foster heard his footsteps echoing away.

CHAPTER FIFTY-ONE

Derrick Sams ran like more than his own life was on the line. If he couldn't lead the Reapers away in time, then the rest of his group might not live long enough to catch their ride to Hope Island.

He came to a halt at the entranceway doors and opened them. A quick scan from left to right confirmed there wasn't anything waiting to eat his face. He stepped out in the open. As he did, he heard the sound of several vehicles entering the parking lot and rushed to duck behind cover. Sams peeked out and saw a Hummer screech to a halt. Several men disembarked immediately, and Sams felt his heart drop. Each one was wearing a very distinctive armband.

"Houston, we have a problem," Sams whispered into the comms. He brought his rifle up and shifted into a secure shooting position. "The Guardians just showed up to crash the party. I can't get to our vehicles."

———

The Hummer pulled to a screeching stop in front of the museum. Silas scanned the area in front of him left to right. As he did, his eyes fell on a pair of vehicles parked haphazardly.

"Wait," his driver said. "Aren't those the—"

"Yes," Silas interrupted. "Looks like old Artie was right. Foster and his thugs are here."

"Why the hell would he stop here? I don't think—"

"I didn't ask you to think," Silas said. "I asked you to follow orders."

"Sorry," the driver stammered.

"Tell the boys it's hunting time," Silas announced. "The first man that brings me Foster's head gets an extra week of dinner rations."

A series of affirmatives sounded out.

Silas climbed out of the Hummer, feeling more than seeing the rest of his men exit their vehicles and join him. This time, they had the advantage. They'd find whatever dark corner Foster was hiding in and drag his sorry butt out. He didn't care what Ezekiel said. Silas wanted Foster dead, no matter what. He'd just concoct a story to explain why the ex-cop wasn't brought back alive.

"Hey, boss," one of his men said. "We got Reapers."

"Make sure they can see your armband," Silas ordered. He checked to make sure his own was visible. Satisfied that his identification was soundly in place, he motioned his men to go on ahead of him. Silas watched as two of them took the lead and slowed his pace until the rest of his men were in front of him.

Silas cleared his throat and announced, "Hey. We need your help finding some humans."

Several of the Reapers turned toward the sound of his voice. One of them stood upright, let out an ear-shattering roar, and charged toward them.

"Whoa, friendly here," Silas shouted. He watched in horror as one of his men panicked, fumbling his rifle to bring it about. A split second later, the Reaper slammed into his man, driving him hard into the paved parking surface. The monster immediately latched onto the man's exposed neck. There was a loud crunch and arterial spray as the man screamed for a moment before the sound was cut off.

"Son of a bitch," Silas swore. He brought his rifle about and fired once, striking the Reaper in the ear, dropping it in place.

A series of growls sounded out around them, and the Reapers began moving as one toward the Guardians.

"I thought they were with us?" one of his men shouted.

"Not anymore!" Silas yelled back. "Kill every one of them freaks."

———

Achilles felt a jolt of pain. He quickly scanned his body and realized he wasn't the one who had been hurt. He felt several other jabs of pain and instinctively realized the pain was coming from his own soldiers.

Achilles mentally reached out and connected with his warriors who were being attacked. Finding one that was uninjured, he reached out and took control of the soldier's eyes.

There were a number of cars and trucks in front them. He forced his soldier to look around. Humans. And none of them looked familiar to him. He saw one of the humans bring up a metal rod and point it as his soldier. There were several flashes, and then his warrior's body spasmed in pain.

There was a noise near him, and Achilles broke the connection and looked toward the disruption. A different soldier had dared to approach without invitation, and Achilles readied himself for the unexpected attack.

But the soldier didn't attack. It stopped short of him and began to speak.

"Sir, Fos-ter and his humans are near," the warrior reported. "One of our scouts spotted them. They don't believe Fos-ter has seen them. We can move more warriors closer before we begin our attack."

Two packs of humans. One of them had started hurting his soldiers. The other contained Fos-ter. But the dreaded pack mate killer wasn't attacking. Why was he waiting? It didn't make sense unless Achilles was overlooking something.

A wave of sudden, uncontrollable fear rushed over him. He immediately reached out to Beeks.

"*Yes. What is it now?*" Beeks snarled.

"*Master? We're in trouble.*"

"*What?*"

"*I believe I have stumbled into a trap. We were following Fos-ter,*" Achilles stammered. "*There's another group of humans here who started attacking us. Fos-ter is waiting for some reason to begin fighting. We're in trouble.*"

"*Where are you?*"

"*Here,*" Achilles answered. He sent out a feeling of where he was and his memories of the buildings around him. "*I need help. Send whoever you have nearby. My soldiers and I are trapped between Foster and these other humans.*"

"*You are not allowed to die,*" Beeks ordered. "*I will send help. I'm ordering you to stay alive.*"

"*Y-Yes, Master. I shall do my best.*"

"*See that you do,*" Beeks snarled before cutting the mental transmission.

CHAPTER FIFTY-TWO

Haas had pushed the pace. He needed to catch up with Foster before the human managed to disappear for good. Haas had arranged for Foster and his group of humans to get out of town in the cover of darkness. But now it looked like the human might be trying to renege on his end of the deal. And that was unacceptable. Haas didn't want to risk his own neck to eliminate Beeks for good. Not when he could force this human to do his dirty work for him.

"Haas—"

The sound of his master's voice slamming into his head was totally unexpected, and Haas blurted out, *"What the hell do you want now?"*

"Excuse me?" Beeks demanded. *"I don't believe you should speak to your leader with that tone of voice."*

"Stop here," Haas ordered. *"Take a rest while I talk with our master."*

He began to walk away from his soldiers to someplace where he could talk to his annoying boss without interruption. *"I'm in the middle of something,"* Haas mentally growled. *"What do you need, oh mighty Master?"*

"It's not what I need. It's what Achilles needs."

"Uh-huh."

"He's surrounded by two groups of humans. One of them includes Foster."

Haas felt a wave of images pop into his head. Buildings surrounded by old planes and helicopters. A long row of metal fencing as far as could be seen in a single moment.

"All right. What do you want me to do?"

"Go help him," Beeks snarled. "Do I have to spell everything out for you, too?"

"I don't want to assume I know my master's biddings," Haas said. A low growl sounded in his head, and Haas was silently pleased his answer had gotten under Beeks' skin. "All right. I'm not far away. I'll bring the troops I have with me. But it won't be a lot."

"Why the hell not?"

"A number of them are on patrol on the other side of town. I brought a few fighters with me to check on a tip," Haas lied. "I can go now to help Achilles. Unless you want me to delay my departure until the rest of my warriors reach my current location?"

"No, I don't want you to drag your feet. Achilles is under attack. He needs your help right now."

"That's what I thought."

"Stop stalling," Beeks ordered. "Take what soldiers you have with you and go help Achilles."

A moment later, Haas felt the connection break, and then Beeks was gone. He walked back to where he had left his warriors. Haas looked around. He had maybe three dozen soldiers with him. Each one seemed poised and calm, which pleased him. He was proud of his fighters. He hoped they would be enough for what Beeks was asking him to do next.

"Come with me," Haas ordered. "We have a rescue mission to achieve." He wasn't sure what they could be running into. The location that had popped in his head seemed far enough away that Achilles could be dead by the time he got there. It would certainly make things easier for Haas. It would be one less fellow Alpha to kill when Haas was ready to make his move against Beeks. But maybe these other humans would still be there. And if they were, then maybe Foster would need his help after all. Because the human couldn't eliminate Beeks if he got himself killed first.

CHAPTER FIFTY-THREE

"The Guardians just showed up to crash the party."

As soon as he heard those words, Foster skidded to a halt.

"Derrick," Foster answered. "How many?"

"Two vehicles," Sams said. "Ten Guardians."

"Can you fall back to the exfil location?"

"Not likely. They'll probably see me move from my current position. Oh, shit."

"What's wrong?"

"Reapers just showed up. They're attacking the Guardians."

"Hang tight," Foster said. "I'm on my way."

"Malcolm!" Charles yelled. "What do you want us to do?"

Foster glanced at the ex-priest and then Lizzy. Both looked like they were scared, but ready to jump in if asked.

"Help Nick, Gregory, and Amanda," Foster said. "We need the landing area for the helicopter kept secure or none of us are getting out of here."

"I'm not sure how much I can help," Charles said. He gestured with the Benelli shotgun. "I'm almost out of ammunition."

Foster squatted down and retrieved the weapon from his ankle holster. He offered the "Baby Glock" to Charles. "Glock 26. There's ten bullets in the magazine. Uses 9mm ammo like everyone else's handguns," he said. "Tell Walker you're really low on ammo. He'll know what to do."

"Thank you, Malcolm," Charles said. "Go help Derrick, before it's too late."

"Don't worry. We'll be back soon," Foster promised. He took off in a full run toward the entranceway.

———

Walker glanced through his rifle's scope at the approaching Reaper herd. He started to do a head count and quickly gave up. It was too many for them to engage. He glanced to his left and saw Gregory fidgeting behind a pair of empty metal barrels. A quick look to his right showed Amanda was situated behind a tire of a Polaris MV800. He had been surprised to see the All-Terrain Vehicle here, but it would serve as a makeshift cover for his wife's best friend. He'd reminded both of them on how important it was to stay quiet. Fortunately, he didn't have to worry about the kids forgetting and making a bunch of noise. They were just inside the building behind him. As long as nothing snuck up behind them inside, they should be safe and secure. And if something did attack them, then being quiet probably wouldn't matter. Because the odds were, they would be seconds away from dying in an overwhelming avalanche of hostile Reapers.

But right now it was quiet, and Walker turned his attention back to the area in front of him. He was crouched behind a trio of barrels, doing his best to not have any part of his body visible behind the metal containers. The Reapers were spreading out and it was even more important to avoid detection.

Come on, Derrick, we need that distraction already.

He wasn't sure where Charles or Lizzy were at the moment. Hopefully with Foster.

Dammit, Nick, stay focused, he mentally scolded himself. Worrying about people who weren't there at the moment could get the rest of them killed. Worse, it could jeopardize getting the entire group out safely to Hope Island. He turned his attention back to the hostiles in front of him.

Several Reapers were getting close to Gregory's location. Walker shifted his position slowly, sighting on the closest monster. The Reaper looked like it was barely five feet tall, but that didn't matter. If the creature made one move toward them, Walker would pull the trigger and blow its damn head off.

Move along, little monster. No need to die today if you don't have to, Walker thought.

Suddenly there was a sharp noise to his left. Walker risked a glance and saw Gregory was sneezing uncontrollably into his elbow. A low growl sounded, and a pair of Reapers charged toward the still-distracted Gregory. Walker immediately open fire to protect his group mate.

———

Foster was hauling ass through the museum when two words stopped him in his tracks.

"Nick's down," Amanda shouted over the comms.

Foster felt his adrenaline immediately spike. What the hell should he do? Time was of the essence. On one hand, Amanda or Lizzy were quite capable of doing battlefield medicine. But on the other, it wasn't fair to expect a bunch of civilians to be able to hold the landing pad secure against an unknown number of Reapers until the chopper arrived. Especially with Charles already being low on ammo.

"Do you need me to come back?" Foster asked.

A new voice came over the comms. "No," Lizzy answered. "Reapers took some losses and then took off as soon as Charles and I arrived. We'll help Gregory and Amanda keep the area secure in case they come back."

"Is Nick okay?"

"Not really," Walker answered. "A huge Reaper landed on my leg. I never saw the damn thing coming. Amanda shot it before it could bite me, but my ankle is definitely busted. Go get Derrick. We'll be fine."

Should he go back to help with Walker? No, he needed to trust what he was being told. The rest of the group didn't need him right now. Foster needed to rescue Sams as soon as possible. And then the two of them needed to haul ass back to help the rest of the group before more hostiles might show up.

He ran hard until he could see the front entrance of the museum. He slowed down to half speed and cued the comms. "Derrick, I'm about two minutes out," he said quickly. "Coming up on your six."

"Don't come out the front entrance," Sams warned. There was a steady shot of gunfire in the background. "Reapers are keeping the Guardians busy, and none of them have seen me yet. If you come flying out the front, all of them will see us."

"Understood," Foster answered. "What do you want me to do?"

"See if you can flank them. Once you're in position, then we can take them out in a cross-fire."

"Copy that," Foster answered. "Finding an alternate route." He veered into another corridor. He wasn't sure it would take him where he wanted to go. But he had an idea where Sams was pinned and would work his way there.

CHAPTER FIFTY-FOUR

Somehow Silas had managed to extract himself from the battle and work his way in instead. He found himself in the museum area and leaned for support against several of the glass cases. He glanced at them and saw they were filled with military memorabilia. A sign on the wall said he was in the Medal of Honor hallway. He looked all around him. But he couldn't see any of his men except for his visibly scared driver.

He didn't know how long they had been here. He didn't know how many men he had lost or left behind, either, which wasn't good at all. He still hadn't found Foster, but one thing was becoming painfully clear. The Guardians were getting their asses kicked by the combined opposing forces.

"Take point," he ordered his driver.

"But boss, I can't," the man protested. "I'm almost out of ammo."

"I'm not," Silas answered as he brought his pistol up and pointed it at the man's head. "And I'm telling you to take point."

"Y-Yes, sir."

Silas watched as his man moved in front of him. The man looked like he wanted to be anywhere else. He began to move slowly along the corridor, looking in every direction for possible attackers.

They had reached the end of the hallway when there was a loud sudden roar. A Reaper appeared seemingly out of nowhere. The monster was wearing a red cape. The creature took two quick steps and grabbed his driver by the neck.

"You," the Reaper growled as it pointed a finger toward Silas.

Silas brought his pistol up, trying to get a target, but his driver kept squirming and blocking his aim. Silas frowned. He just needed his soldier to hold still long enough for Silas to get a clear shot at this damn showboat of a Reaper.

"You're one of the Disciple soldiers, aren't you?" the Reaper spoke.

"How the hell did you know that?" Silas demanded.

"The bands on your arms," the red-caped Reaper growled. "We are allies. There are enemies here. Enemies for both of us. It's not safe for you and your men."

Silas watched as the Reaper released its hold on his driver. The creature gently shoved the man back toward Silas. "You need to get out of here. My soldiers will keep the enemy occupied long enough for you to escape."

"Okay," Silas said. He lowered his weapon and began to backpedal. If this one was truly an ally, then maybe this thing could buy him the opportunity to get away.

"Wait. What do I call you?"

"I am Haas," the Reaper said.

"Right," Silas replied. "Listen, there's a really bad human here. Answers to the name Foster. He's killed a bunch of Disciples."

"Have you seen him?"

"No, but one of my men did," Silas lied. "We were hunting

him when those other Reapers showed up and attacked us. Foster is somewhere on this property."

"I will find him."

"Are you sure?" Silas asked with the best sincerity that he could fake. "I mean, we can help if you want."

"Get out now, while you can," Haas said. "Do not make me repeat myself."

"Boss, I think we should leave," the driver said, stammering. "You know, do what he says."

"Fine," Silas said. He reached for his walkie-talkie and pressed the transmit button. "All Guardians, fall back to the trucks and wait for me. We're getting out of here."

CHAPTER FIFTY-FIVE

Foster hadn't gotten very far before the shit hit the proverbial fan. As the corridor curved around a corner, he entered a bigger space and heard a loud roar. As he looked toward the sound, he saw a trio of Reapers bearing down on his location and unleashed a barrage of bullets. He saw one monster go down and then felt his weapon jam. He immediately dropped it, letting the shoulder harness catch its weight, and drew his Glock. He immediately fired twice at the closest Reaper. The creature's head snapped back, but Foster didn't have time to admire his marksmanship because the last standing Reaper was even closer to his position. Foster fired rapidly, stitching his shots upward from the monster's torso until several shots struck it in the throat and face. As the creature dropped, Foster noticed a new Reaper was standing back and watching the action. Foster looked it up and down. As he did, his eyes were drawn to the long red cape flowing down its back.

"You must be Fos-ter," the Reaper spoke. "I've heard of you."

"Yeah, sorry I can't say the same about you. You got a name?" Foster asked. "Or should I just call you Weasel Dick?"

The monster let out a low growl. "Achilles," he said as he emphasized each syllable.

"Uh-huh. You got something you want to say?"

"Surrender or die."

"Excuse me?"

"Surrender or die," Achilles repeated.

Foster didn't have time to tangle with this Reaper. Not when Sams might be moments from being overrun. If the Reapers didn't kill his friend, then the Guardians might. Maybe he could convince this red-caped asshole to avoid a fight. "You do realize I've killed a few of your buddies, right?" he said. "If you leave now, I promise I won't chase after you."

The low growl sounded out. The monster began moving toward him and inadvertently bumped into a nearby exhibit. The Reaper shoved the display, launching it airborne. Foster saw it crash to the floor about fifteen feet away.

"Impressive," Foster said. "Strong and furry."

"We fight. Now."

"I don't think so," Foster said. He brought his Glock up to a shooting position. As he did, the Reaper tucked its head and executed a forward roll. Foster felt his adrenaline spike as this Reaper surged toward him like a runaway boulder. He brought his Glock up and opened fire. But as he did, he saw several of the shots seemed to ricochet harmlessly off the back of the creature's shoulders and upper back. At the last possible moment, Foster spun like a matador out of the way and the monster rolled past him. Foster began backpedaling to create more space between his assailant and himself.

Damn, he's fast, Foster thought. *Too fast.*

Achilles popped up to its feet and turned toward Foster. The Reaper brought its hands up into a fighting posture. "Surrender or die."

"Not happening," Foster said. He began firing rapidly once more. The monster executed another rolling charge.

Foster watched in horror as his shots sailed past the attacking Reaper a split second before he felt something slam into his sternum. The blow knocked Foster clear off his feet.

Foster felt his body flying backwards and instinctively threw his arms out to try to break his fall. His reaction wasn't quick enough, and Foster landed hard on his back, a split second before the back of his head banged on the hard floor. He immediately felt a shot of pain. *Get up!* A voice in his head shouted, and Foster forced himself to stand up.

Foster felt a bit wobbly on his feet. His chest felt like he had been hit by a runaway truck. He tried to take a breath and immediately felt a jab of pain. *Bruised, nothing broken.*

He brought his rifle up, but the weapon didn't feel right in his hands. Foster stole a fast glance at the rifle. The weapon was visibly damaged from the bull rush. Even if he could clear the jam before the Reaper attacked again, he wasn't sure the weapon would even fire correctly.

Foster unslung the rifle and tossed it to the side. His upper body began to throb. Foster didn't know if he could take another one of those rolling attacks. He retreated and moved erratically to avoid Achilles' next attack and buy himself some more time.

Foster instinctively reached for the Glock he kept on his hip and came up empty-handed.

Where the hell was his gun?

A moment later, he realized what had happened. He had been using the weapon when Achilles knocked him over.

So where the hell was his Glock?

Foster risked a quick glance and saw his weapon lying on the floor, about halfway between the two of them. The Glock's slide was locked back.

His gun was empty.

There was no way in hell he'd be able to grab the weapon,

replace the spent magazine, and shoot Achilles before the Reaper reached him.

A low rumble emitted from Achilles. It gestured toward the gun once, as if it were mocking him.

"Fuck you, fur ball."

The Reaper began to growl even louder and brought its clawed hands up in what might resemble a fighting posture.

"You want a fight?" Foster answered. "Okay, you got one." He pulled out his dagger and shifted into a fighting stance.

The two combatants circled each other warily.

Foster jabbed quickly with the dagger, and Achilles easily danced out of harm's way.

Achilles swung a wide, arching side swipe with his right hand that Foster barely managed to dodge. He swung a wide left that came nowhere close to hitting Foster and clanged loudly off a metal display near the two combatants.

Foster quickly studied his opponent. Achilles was smaller and thinner than any other red-caped Alpha he'd seen to date. But the creature was fast as hell. There was no way Foster was going to underestimate him.

Okay, reality check. He's faster than you. He's a fucking Reaper, so he's probably stronger than you, too. You gotta find his weakness before he finishes you. And you gotta do it with nothing but a knife and your brains.

Achilles flexed his legs and launched into a nearly perfect spinning wheel kick. Foster barely managed to twist his head and torso out of the way in time before the Reaper's foot connected.

Foster bounced lightly on his feet, looking for an opening and not finding an easy one. He watched as the Reaper launched into another spinning kick. This time, the monster's foot passed close enough to Foster's face that he felt the movement near his ear.

Achilles landed lightly on his feet, took two steps toward

Foster, before launching another spinning kick that nearly connected.

Foster danced backwards, studying his opponent. He wasn't sure, but it looked like the monster telegraphed the kick with his shoulder. He watched the Reaper stalk toward him. Achilles let out a roar and then launched another spinning kick, which Foster darted away from a bit easier.

Yep, a definite tell. He dips his shoulder before he starts his big kick, Foster thought.

"You getting dizzy yet, fur ball?" Foster challenged. "A real man would have ditched the fucking cape already."

Achilles roared and slammed his chest twice before launching into a rolling attack.

Foster dove out of the way and came up onto his feet.

He tucks his head before he does that rolling charge. Another telegraph. I can use that, too, Foster thought to himself. He jabbed quickly with the dagger, and the creature easily moved out of harm's way.

Achilles dipped his shoulder and began to move into another spinning kick. As the monster's back began to turn, Foster fired a quick thrust kick. His foot connected with the Reaper's backside, and the creature stumbled awkwardly before regaining its balance a few steps later.

Foster motioned toward Achilles to come at him again. The Reaper roared in frustration, pounding its chest once more. As it ducked its head, Foster slid one long step to his left, clearing a path for the monster to harmlessly roll past him.

"Last chance to leave this room alive," Foster said between heaving breaths.

"Never," Achilles growled. He dropped his shoulder and began moving into another spinning kick.

As his foe's back began to turn, Foster swept its supporting foot out from underneath it. The Reaper crashed hard onto the floor, the hard fall leaving the creature momentarily stunned. Foster swung the dagger downward, burying it hilt-deep in the Reaper's leg.

Achilles went rigid and screamed in agony. He reached toward the silver-coated dagger and failed.

"You lose," Foster said. "Weasel Dick."

"I'm sorry, Master," Achilles whispered. "I—" He shuddered once more and then went still.

CHAPTER FIFTY-SIX

Foster wasn't sure how soon their ride was going to arrive, but he knew that Sams might still be in trouble. It was up to him to rescue Derrick. He was closest, and Amanda had confirmed that Walker's ankle was definitely broken. Like it or not, he was the best remaining option left to help Sams. Foster hustled through the museum, working his way toward flanking his friend's last-known location. There were dozens of dead Reapers seemingly everywhere without a visible wound to be found. It reassured him that he had killed their leader when he killed Achilles.

As he got closer to Sams' likely location, the mixture of bodies changed. There were pools of blood in random places, with both Guardians and Reapers among the dead. He heard several voices shouting and hurried to pick up his pace.

"I want to see Fos-ter," a voice growled. "Tell him that Haas commands him to show himself."

"I don't care what you want," Sams yelled back. "You'd already be dead if I hadn't seen you chase those Disciples away."

"You overestimate your abilities, human."

"Do you have any idea who you're talking to?" Sams demanded. "I'm a fucking Army Ranger. I will kick your ass from one end of this base to the other."

Foster came about the corner and saw Sams and Haas facing each other. A quick glance at both of their bodies told him it was quickly escalating to a likely physical confrontation.

"Stand down," Foster shouted. "Both of you."

"You sure?" Sams asked. "He claims he helped us."

"He's right," Foster said. "For now, consider him to be on our side."

"Of course I am," Haas answered. "Why wouldn't I be? Our goals are the same."

"Pipe down, Chewbacca," Sams interrupted. "Malcolm, what the hell is going on?"

Haas growled loudly. "Walk with me, Fos-ter," he said. He turned and walked toward an open hangar. "Leave the loud one here."

"Relax. Sams is with me," Foster said as he gestured toward Sams. "Whatever you want to tell me, you can say in front of him, too."

Haas grumbled. "Fine. But we need to go someplace less obvious."

"Follow me," Foster said. He retraced his steps back into the museum. He glanced back several times to make sure Sams and Haas were still following him. Neither one looked happy at all. They had gotten inside the building again when the red-caped Reaper spoke up.

"This is far enough," Haas announced. "We should be out of sight of anyone who could see us."

"What's on your mind?" Foster asked.

The walkie-talkie came alive.

"Malcolm, the helicopter is two minutes out," Amanda said. "Where are you?"

"Were you leaving? On the flying machine?" Haas asked. "You can't leave. You still owe me."

"Bullshit," Sams argued. "He doesn't owe you a thing."

"There's still something you need to do," Haas answered. "Otherwise, nothing will change."

"Are you serious?" Sams yelled. "You're actually thinking about doing a favor for this overgrown freak?"

Haas growled in response. "You need to learn to keep your mouth shut, human."

"His name is Haas," Foster interrupted. "His goals align with ours."

"And what exactly is that, huh?" Sams shouted. "Because all I'm hearing is this thing trying to boss both of us around."

"If someone kills the head," Foster answered, "the rest of the snake dies."

"What the hell are you talking about?" Sams asked.

"There is a one who rules all," Haas growled. "I tried to reason with him and failed. None of us are strong enough to stop him. But you could be."

"So, what, one guy against millions of Reapers?" Sams said. "That's fucking stupid, man."

"Not millions," Foster said. "Recon mission. We find this one top dog and then call Abrahams. He sends in the cavalry. They come in and kill the bastard. Then all of the Reapers keel over dead at once."

"And you're okay with this?" Sams said in an accusatory tone. "You'll die, too."

"I never asked for this," Haas said simply. "If I die, then I die."

"Foster, the chopper is incoming," Walker shouted over the comms. "We need Sams and you here now."

"Stall. We need another couple of minutes," Foster said. "It's important."

"Negative," Black interrupted over the comms. "We're

landing now. Your ride ain't waiting around forever. Shit or get off the pot, Malcolm."

"Give me a minute, Black," Foster said. He released the comms button and looked at Sams. "I'm staying. If I can find this King Reaper, then we can end this shitstorm forever. Otherwise, we're looking at years of battle to try and take back every piece of ground lost."

"Are you kidding me?" Sams said. "Do you have a fucking death wish?"

"Not at all," Foster answered. "You need to go before your ride leaves."

"And what? Leave you here?"

"Yes."

"Your plan sucks."

Foster said nothing.

"Oh, for chrissakes," Sams muttered. "Fine. I'm in. But only because somebody needs to make sure you actually complete this fucking mission."

Foster cued the comms. "Black, get the civilians out of there now. Sams and I are staying."

"Come again?"

"You got civvies and wounded. Get them to safety. Derrick and I have intel on a high-value target. We're going to recon and locate their position. Once we do, we'll let you know so you can send the Rangers in."

"Copy that. Watch your asses out there."

"Thanks, Black. Foster out."

―――――

The noise in the helicopter was ear-shattering. Black turned toward the pilot and made a gesture for the helicopter to take off.

Amanda crowded close enough to Black for him to hear.

"What are you doing?" she yelled. "Foster and Sams are still out there."

"I know," Black said. "He told me to take off."

Amanda did a double-take. "What?"

"Foster said something about going after a high-value target."

"I don't understand," Amanda yelled. "What the hell does that mean?"

"It means Foster must've found something that might shift things in our favor," Walker shouted. "Think about it. He wouldn't just stay behind if he didn't have a good reason."

Amanda moved back to her seat. She felt the tears start forming in the corner of her eyes and fought to bring her emotions back into check. She glanced out the window, watching as Foster and Sams grew smaller and smaller on the ground below as the copter moved away.

"Damn you, Malcolm," she said softly, "I thought we had a plan." She felt a hand on her arm and looked toward its owner.

Charles gave her a reassuring pat and withdrew his hand. "I'm sorry, Amanda," Charles said. "Sometimes plans change. Especially in the heat of battle."

"What are we going to do now?"

"We're going to Hope Island," Charles answered. "We'll give the military the edge they need to turn the tide against the Reapers."

"I meant about Malcolm and Derrick."

"We can pray," Charles suggested. "Pray that they stay safe and make it out unharmed."

CHAPTER FIFTY-SEVEN

Haas knelt on one knee as the self-proclaimed leader of the Reapers required everyone else to perform. The throne room floor was uncomfortable as hell, but right now it was best to keep his complaints to himself. He listened passively as Horatio Beeks continued his emotional tirade.

"We're supposed to be faster and stronger than humans," Beeks growled. "We're supposed to be better in every way. So how does one human continue to beat my warriors?"

"He is a police officer," Haas said carefully. "It's possible he has previously received training that would make him far more dangerous than the rest of the sheep."

Beeks paused and took a long drink from a metal cup. From the lingering smell, Haas guessed it was cow's blood.

"Like what?" Beeks asked carefully.

"I've heard he killed one Alpha with a long-range weapon."

"Pak," Beeks murmured. "Yes, our brother. Gone far too soon."

"I'm afraid I didn't know him."

"He was one of the scientists at Bergstrom. Somehow he got infected, too."

"Interesting," Haas rumbled. "You're suggesting that not all of us were forced to become what we are."

"And what's wrong with being better than we were before?"

Freedom, Haas thought silently. *Even inside prison, I was my own person. And now I bow to a power-hungry asshole.*

Haas continued to speak as his master paced. "Achilles was one of us. But he failed when he crossed paths with Foster."

"Achilles wasn't one of us."

"What?"

"Not an original. He was created after the fact."

"Well, that explains it," Haas answered. "Maybe he wasn't strong enough for the task."

"What are you talking about? I turned Achilles myself."

Haas laughed bitterly. "You sent a puppy to handle a grown dog's job," he answered. "Then you had to send me to rescue him after he got himself in trouble."

"You mock me."

"I mock no one. I speak the truth. If you had sent me in the first place, like I suggested, then the outcome would have been completely different."

"You lie."

"Not at all. The idiot attacked an armed group of my Disciples. Humans that I had tasked to track down Foster for me. Achilles gave them no choice but to protect themselves."

"Why didn't you tell me this sooner?"

"I didn't want to trouble my Lord with minor details," Haas lied. "But the facts are undeniable. By the time you asked me to assist, there was no chance for anyone to save your beloved pet. It was only through his gross incompetence that Foster managed to get away."

"Enough," Beeks roared. "I've grown tired of your antics. Perhaps it's time you retire to your quarters for the rest of the night."

Haas jumped up to his feet. "As you wish, my Lord," he said. He bowed quickly and headed for the exit.

Beeks growled softly. Haas had been far too quick to flee the throne room. But then it was his own fault. He had given the underling an out, and the soldier took it.

————

The guard motioned toward the open room. Angel stepped in, turned, and looked at him. She stared at him, and he failed to move. Angel let out a low growl and showed her teeth.

The guard raised both hands in front of him and stepped out of the room. He stopped just outside the doorway.

"Go away," she said. "Leave me alone."

"My Lord has commanded me to wait out here in the hallway."

"In case I try to flee?"

"I'm not sure. My Lord has commanded me to wait here in the hallway until he says otherwise."

"Stay out of my sight," Angel snarled. "Or you're going to have a problem you don't want."

The guard took moved sideways until he was no longer in view.

Angel shook her head in dismay. She really wanted the guard to leave for good, but the soldier wasn't willing to disobey the boss. Maybe out of sight would be good enough for her needs.

Angel moved deeper into her room. Her head was killing her. The headaches were becoming nearly unbearable. She wanted the pain to stop, but a voice in her head told her it was important that she keep fighting the transformation. She had to keep holding onto the few remaining pieces of her former life.

She didn't care what this Beeks creature told her. She was no monster, and this was not her family. The voice kept telling her that. She knew it, she just didn't know how to change things, not yet, at least. The voice said she needed to be patient and keep fighting. There were pictures of her former life that kept popping up in her head. One where she was in some type of flying machine. But it didn't make sense, because she didn't think people could fly. Her so-called family definitely couldn't, and all of them were capable of doing a lot of pretty amazing things like run for miles and heal wounds in a matter of seconds. Still, the memory seemed important to hold onto, so she kept trying to remember it.

Angel looked at the shirt she was wearing. It was the same clothing she'd worn for as long as she could remember. The lighting in the room wasn't great, but she could make out that there was some type of word on the front of it. She focused her attention on it and tried to say it aloud again.

"Vas... Quez," she said slowly. She wasn't sure what it was, but maybe it was important. There looked like there had been a spot on the side of the arm where something had once been, but it was missing now. A voice said it was part of her uniform, but she didn't understand what that meant. A shot of pain came across Angel's mind that nearly buckled her knees. She put her hand against the wall to catch herself.

The pain. She always felt it when she tried too hard to remember her past. She needed to be more careful and not push so hard to remember things.

Angel felt the pain slowly begin to subside. She began to walk to the other side of her room. It was nearly pitch black in this part of the room, but the dark didn't scare her. It was her secret place, one that none of her so-called family had discovered yet. And the little voice in her head told her if they did, it could mean the end of the life she kept trying to remember. She looked at the wall where she had used her claw to scratch out words as she remembered them. She looked at the wall once more. A voice told her to practice saying the words.

"An... Gel. Angel," she said carefully. She moved to the next line. It seemed to be missing a word, and then the word came to her. Using her claw, she carefully scratched the last three letters. She took a step back and looked at the phrase, at the words, and said carefully, "Aim high."

A small wave of dizziness came over her, and she slammed her hand against the wall to steady herself.

The small voice in her head came forward once more. It was the only voice she completely trusted.

"I don't understand," Angel whispered. "Help me."

The voice in her head gave her an answer.

"Air Force," she said softly. "Right. I can't forget."

Angel wasn't sure what it meant. It had to be important, but her only trusted friend had told her she couldn't forget it.

Angel took a slow, deep breath, let it out slowly, and read the entire motto once. "Aim high. Fly. Fight. Win."

She couldn't remember why it was important. But she had an overwhelming feeling that she couldn't ever forget it. As long as she could draw breath into her lungs, Angel would keep fighting to remember her old life. And once she remembered everything, she'd make whoever had stolen her memories pay for their actions.

CHAPTER FIFTY-EIGHT

Lieutenant Tom Abrahams walked carefully through the door. The civilians that had been evacuated were put in the quarantine area where they would stay for the next forty-eight hours. It was standard procedure for any new arrivals at Hope Island. He had every intention of leaving them there because he already had more shit on his to-do list than he could possibly handle in the near future. But all of that changed when he received an urgent call from one of the guards. Under normal circumstances, Abrahams wouldn't have bothered to be at some civilian's beck and call like this.

But still, his curiosity was getting the better of him. Especially when it came to why the hell Foster hadn't been on the helicopter, which landed a few hours ago. So he was breaking from his already busy schedule. Because maybe someone could give him some answers about where the hell the man was.

He walked up to the intercom system and pressed the button. "Name's Abrahams. Who am I speaking to?"

A man with a visible cast on his ankle hobbled over and pressed the intercom button. "Nick Walker, sir."

"Are you military, Walker?"

"Retired."

"I see."

"With all due respect, how soon are we getting out of this quarantine?"

"Forty-eight hours. We have to make sure none of you are infected," Abrahams said. "Wasn't that explained to you by one of my men?"

"Yeah, but I was hoping you were here to fast track us out of here."

"I can't do that. Base security protocol."

"You're wasting time," Walker said. "People turn a hell of a lot faster than two days."

"Well, if you are infected and do turn, then we'll now have our answer sooner than two days, won't we?"

"You've got to be fucking kidding me," Walker said. "Do you have any clue what's going on out there?"

"More than you might think, Mr. Walker," Abrahams answered. He paused for dramatic effect before continuing. "Care to tell me where Malcolm Foster is?"

"I'm not sure. One of the other members of the group said he was pursuing a new lead. Something that could end the Reaper threat once and for all. He took another one of our group with him to chase down the lead."

"Do you mean a wild goose chase?"

"Negative, sir. That's not how Foster operates. Every step of the way, he's had these people's safety in mind."

"Okay, let's say you're right and he's pursuing a lead. He's just one man. Hell, even if he's got somebody else with him who's former military like you, he's seriously outnumbered. Sorry, it must have slipped my memory. Which branch of the military did you say you were in?"

"I didn't," Walker replied simply.

"Right. Need to know, right?"

Walker said nothing.

"At some point, I fully expect you'll share those details with me. You hear me, Walker?"

"Loud and clear, sir."

"Thing is, all of your admission into this island was conditional. It was all based on information Foster was supposed to bring to me. Except he's not here now. Can you see my dilemma?"

"Sure. That's why he sent me. I have the information."

"Where is it?"

"Right here," Walker said as he tapped the side of his head. "I know how to kill these bastards faster and easier than ever."

"You mean in theory?"

"Nope, we proved it more than once. And it's not just shooting these things in the head. These things are deathly allergic to silver."

Abrahams did a double-take. "Silver?"

"Yep. And I know exactly how to deliver the payload that kills them every time," Walker said. "So the way I see it, you've got two choices, sir."

"I think you're forgetting who's in charge here."

"It's pretty clear-cut, sir. Option one, you let me sit here in this fucking room with everybody else for two more days. You can continue to shuffle paperwork while more people get killed. Or option two, you can let me the hell out. Then I can start showing you what kind of weapons you need to use to kill these things, pronto."

"What if you're infected? You could wind up killing somebody else in this island. Hell, you could wind up killing everybody here."

"Sometimes you need to take a risk in order to secure the win," Walker said. "I've got a busted ankle. It's not like I'm moving very fast."

"If you turn into one of those things, a broken bone isn't going to slow you down at all."

"Do you want to chain me to a desk someplace while I show you how to make these weapons? That's fine with me," Walker said. "The way I see it, we're getting our ass kicked out there. This is a way to level the playing field."

"That's easy for you to say. You don't have everyone's lives here to worry about."

"Maybe I don't. But maybe it's time to stop taking shit from these Reapers and start kicking their ass for a change."

Abrahams decided to try a different approach. "Talk to me about this way to kill these things," he said, "And get to the point quickly, please."

"It's a new kind of bullet," Walker answered. "Doesn't matter where you shoot a Reaper. It kills them instantly."

"Wait, what?"

"We call them Reaper Killers," Walker continued. "Get me a workbench, and I'll show you how to make them."

THE END

THE STORY CONTINUES

The Story Continues...

... in Wretched Uprising

AUTHOR NOTES AND ACKNOWLEDGMENTS

Author Notes:

Whew! This book was the most difficult one I've written to date. There were lots of personal life challenges, overwhelming amounts of work with my day job, and even a global pandemic being nearly constant distractions. I was deeply challenged to attempt to get my daily words written, and I wasn't always successful.

But "inch by inch," it's a cinch. And some days it felt like I was literally moving slower than a sloth's pace.

So this book may have taken me longer to write than usual. But I hope you enjoyed it as much as the previous books in this series.

On to the notes...

As of this writing, there is no Disciples of the Divine cult.

There is a Fieldcrest Drive in Rehoboth Beach. The house credited to Larry's brother is a fictional description by this author. Any resemblance to any existing home on Fieldcrest Drive is purely coincidental.

The Air Mobility Command Museum in Dover, Delaware,

is an absolutely wonderful place to take a day trip. I definitely recommend checking it out. There is lots of great military history contained inside and outside of its walls.

As of this writing, admission was free and no battles between humans and Reapers have occurred there.

The Blue Grass Chemical Agent-Destruction Pilot Plant is a chemical weapons destruction facility. It is located at the Blue Grass Army Depot (BGAD) near Richmond, Kentucky.

The plant is dedicated to the destruction of 523 short tons of sarin, VX, and mustard nerve agents.

Destruction of this stockpile is a requirement of international treaty and the Chemical Weapons Convention.

The United States Congress passed legislation mandating the destruction of the remaining U.S. national chemical stockpile by April 2012.

The deadline has been extended more than once. The most recent extension, the National Defense Authorization Act for Fiscal Year 2016, pushed the deadline to Dec. 31, 2023.

The M55 rocket was a chemical weapon developed by the United States in the 1950s. The United States Army produced both sarin and VX warheads for the M55.

The M55 was never used in combat, and in 1981 the Army declared it obsolete.

In 1985, Congress ordered the Department of Defense to destroy the complete U.S. stockpile of GB, VX, and HD weapons.

A deadline of December 31, 2004 was set.

Because of problems with the M55 rocket propellant, disposal has been extremely difficult.

Unlike other chemical warfare artillery rounds, it is not safe to just burn the whole rounds. A much more complicated process must be used.

As of this writing, there are still thousands of M55 rockets in storage. There are also plenty of VX warheads, too.

"What the hell do you think I'm doing? Ordering a pizza?" uttered by Sams is a riff off a line in the classic action movie "Die Hard".

"You're not Jack Bauer" is a tip of the hat to the old TV series "24" where Kiefer Sutherland would rush from scene to scene and all over town like a one-man army.

Mel Brooks' "History of the World, Part 1" might be one of my favorite movies of all time. Very funny... and very politically incorrect. Especially the part of the movie where Brooks himself plays the king. So I paid a bit of tribute when Beeks thought, *"It might not be a perfect life, but it was still damn good to be the king."*

Special thanks to:

To my wife, my two children, and my mom. Thank you for everything you do and who you are. I love you.

To my editors, Pat, Jen, and Wendy. Your efforts to whip my manuscript into even better shape is often overlooked, but always appreciated by me.

To Tom Abrahams, Sam Sisavath, Steve Konkoly, and Nicholas Sansbury Smith. Each of you are a great indie author. Each of you have offered up advice and help when I've needed it. I'm deeply appreciative.

Last, but not least, to my current and new readers. I hope you enjoyed *Wretched Aftermath*. If so, please take a few moments to leave a review where you purchased this novel. As a self-published author, every honest review helps other people know about my books and inspires me to keep writing them.

Thanks again for reading this book. You'll also want to sign up for my email newsletter at http://www.egmichaels.com, which will alert you when the next E.G. Michaels book is ready for your enjoyment. Periodically, I'll also share news, updates, and even other books I've read that I think you'll enjoy.